Prologue

THE INSTANT MAC GERARD touched her, he knew he'd made a big mistake. Awareness caught him fast and hard like a sucker punch, and he didn't want to walk away from their argument as much as he wanted to kiss her.

So, God help him, he did.

Her eyes widened a split second before his mouth came down on hers and he steeled himself for her reaction—knowing this woman, she'd likely draw her gun and shoot him.

But something happened, some *thing* he'd never felt before.

Not run-of-the-mill desire. Not even hot-under-the-collar passion. This was *need*. Sharp. Potent. Consuming. He wanted to absorb her, press their bodies close until they fused into one.

He didn't seem to be the only one experiencing the phenomenon, either, because she didn't go for her gun, she melted against him, all her curves catching him in exactly the right places. Her lips parted on a gasp and she slipped her arms around his neck to pull him harder into their kiss.

Mac caught the taste of her with his mouth, drank in her scent on a breath. He kissed her with an urgency that was closer to making him lose control than any argument they'd ever had at work. And that was saying a lot. He wanted to inhale her through his pores, feel her body unfold around him, underneath him, with an intensity that shocked him to the core.

This was *Harley Price*...the gun-toting, karate-kicking, too-competent private investigator who'd been making his life hell ever since he'd walked through the door of his new job.

Then it hit him, and Mac finally understood the real problem between them. It wasn't just a clash of personalities or a power struggle between two strong wills.

They were attracted to each other, big time.

And as the feel of her body imprinted itself on his, as the taste of her sweet mouth filtered through his senses, Mac knew he was in more trouble than he'd ever been in his life.

Because the only way he could fix the problem was to get this woman naked in bed.

"You're beautiful," he said in a throaty voice that sounded like sex

Harley braced herself for Mac's next move, expecting to feel his hard body against hers. But he stood, tugged her up and lifted her into his arms. She was forced to hang on, to bury her face against his shoulder, as much to avoid their reflection in the mirrors as to avoid that hungry, almost gentle expression on his face.

She could stand up to his challenges, but it had only taken a few orgasms to learn she couldn't bear up under his tenderness. At least not when she was feeling so raw herself.

"I'm no threat, Harley."

But he was a threat. A bigger threat than she was prepared to admit. She said nothing.

Mac carried her to the bed and lay her out before him wearing nothing but his bracelet and his wedding band. He stood above her, so terribly handsome with his hair gleaming in the candlelit darkness, his expression so intense.

"What happens now?" she asked, needing to hear a voice, even her own, to fill the silence.

He sank to the edge of the bed, all fluid muscle and grace.

"I find more ways to pleasure you."

service desk and asked, "Anthony in his office?"

Dear Reader,

All too often the path to love turns out to be a bumpy jaunt down a pothole-filled street rather than a smooth ride over new asphalt. But sometimes those bumps can help us learn things about others that teach us important things about ourselves.

Harley and Mac travel such a rocky road. She's a woman who faces life with her chin squared and her eyes fixed on the future. But it's learning about her past that helps Mac see how much *he* must grow to win this special woman's heart. And realizing he has the strength of character to take an honest look inward helps Harley find the courage to trust him, and herself.

Blaze is the place to explore red-hot romance, and I'm delighted to be among the ranks of the wonderful Harlequin authors who share their journeys to happily ever after. I hope *With This Fling* brings you to happily ever after, too. Let me know. Drop a line in care of Harlequin Books, 225 Duncan Mill Road, Don Mills, Ontario, Canada M3B 3K9, or visit my Web site at www.jeanielondon.com.

Very truly yours,

Jeanie London

Books by Jeanie London

HARLEQUIN BLAZE

WITH THIS FLING

Jeanie London

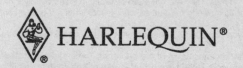

HARLEQUIN®

TORONTO • NEW YORK • LONDON
AMSTERDAM • PARIS • SYDNEY • HAMBURG
STOCKHOLM • ATHENS • TOKYO • MILAN • MADRID
PRAGUE • WARSAW • BUDAPEST • AUCKLAND

To my mom, Bonnie-Jean Hickman,
for always being a wonderful example and an inspiration…
a Cinderella story without the mice.

ISBN 0-373-79132-1

WITH THIS FLING

Copyright © 2004 by Jeanie LeGendre.

This edition published by arrangement with Harlequin Books S.A.

Visit us at www.eHarlequin.com

Printed in U.S.A.

1

"WITH THIS RING, I'd be dead," Harley Price whispered to no one in particular.

She'd once heard that the best reason to get married was the promise of around-the-clock orgasms. While she understood the appeal, an orgasm would have to register double digits on the Richter scale before she'd suffer *this* kind of torture.

This torture was the reception line at a wedding. As one of the very last guests to pass through, she greeted the new Mr. and Mrs. Christopher Sinclair, side by side in their first official performance as husband and wife.

They looked giddy. Every happy cliché she'd ever heard applied to them, from the way they seemed to be floating on air to the way they glowed. They smiled in unison and acted as though every guest at their wedding was a close friend.

The fact that the new Mr. and Mrs. Christopher Sinclair looked as though they'd stepped off the cover of a romance novel might have had something to do with the impression, too. They'd dressed in costumes reflecting the fashion of two centuries earlier. Admittedly, the costumes worked with the surroundings, as this wedding was taking place at an antebellum plantation.

"Best of luck," Harley said, wishing the newlyweds a lifetime of around-the-clock bliss. Technically she wouldn't have even come to this wedding if her boss hadn't insisted she make an appearance as a professional courtesy. But she'd come. She'd wished them well. Now she was out of here.

Moving beyond the reception line, Harley unscrewed her smile and fled for the nearest exit. Veering away from the tables, where gleaming china and exquisite floral arrangements beckoned guests, she slipped out of the ballroom.

She emerged in the hall, an octagonal rotunda that rose three stories above her, all curving staircases and high-luster balustrades. A crystal chandelier graciously illuminated her way to the exit and she measured her paces so her heels didn't tap loudly across the wooden floor.

She hadn't made the front exit when a female voice called out, "I told Josh you'd run for it if we took our eyes off you."

Harley groaned at the sight of the red-sequined bridesmaid emerging from the ballroom. Unfortunately, this wasn't just any bridesmaid—this was Lennon Eastman, her boss's wife.

And just her luck, her boss filed out the door right behind her. Josh was scowling and Harley scowled back, disliking his wife intensely at the moment—no easy feat considering Lennon was an absolute doll. Well-bred, confident and poised, she was also tall, blond and beautiful—as close to Harley's ideal of society perfection as any woman could possibly get.

And there was nothing like standing in the shadow of a socialite to make her feel underdressed, no matter how stylish her gown.

"You didn't drive all the way down here to sit through the wedding and miss the fun?" Josh asked.

"You told me to attend the *wedding*. I did."

Josh exchanged a glance with his wife and Harley knew trouble when she saw it. As a licensed private investigator, her observation skills were more developed than most, but she could have been blind in one eye and still recognized that these two meant business. The big question was *why?* What difference did it make if she showed up at the reception or not?

Better not to ask. She was already treading thin ice with her boss. A dark-haired man in his mid-thirties, Josh Eastman seemed more at home getting down and dirty with the bad guys than he did tuxed up in his Garden District persona. At least to her, anyway. Harley had known him for nearly seven years—long before she'd come to work for him.

The investigative agency she'd contracted with after college had been the one he'd used for additional manpower, and she'd been assigned to him while learning the ropes. Josh had impressed her with his do-whatever-it-takes investigation technique. He didn't mind getting his hands dirty and that had earned him her respect.

She'd apparently earned his, too, because he'd requested her services regularly and after he'd married Lennon and expanded his operation, he'd offered her full-time work. She'd accepted, thinking luck had been going her way...until he'd brought their newest investigator into the fold.

The thought of Mac Gerard reminded her that she'd pushed her luck enough for one day.

"All right, I'll rethink my plans," she said.

Josh only inclined his head, but Lennon grabbed her arm and led her back toward the ballroom. "You'll have fun. I had Ellen seat you at a table where you'll know some of the guests."

"Thanks." She tried to force some enthusiasm into her voice. "But shouldn't you be dancing with the wedding party?"

"We got out before the dancing started," Josh said. "Lucky thing Lennon saw you slip out when she did."

Lucky? That was a matter of interpretation. Especially when Lennon motioned to a table across the room.

"Your seat is over there," she said, looping her arm through her husband's and steering him onto the dance floor.

Harley took one look at the empty seat at her table and knew she'd been set up. Sitting right beside that empty space was the one man she didn't want to see again in this lifetime.

Mac Gerard.

She couldn't have missed him if she'd tried. Even among three hundred-plus guests, Gerard stood out. She wasn't sure what it was…perhaps the superior attitude that screamed, *Here I am!* or his deep-throated laughter that commanded the attention of everyone within earshot.

Maybe it was how the custom-cut suit sat on his broad shoulders. Or the masculine features that were so sculpted he almost didn't look real. Especially with the way his thick brown hair and tanned skin combined to make his quicksilver eyes look startling in his face.

This man was too damned attractive to be allowed, and that was his biggest flaw as far as Harley was concerned. Appearances could be so deceiving. Gerard looked as if he should be Mr. Wonderful—intelligent, sexy and charming. If he hadn't been so ridiculously gorgeous, it might not come as a shock that he was such an idiot.

And she got to sit beside him today. *Lucky* her.

Sweeping toward the table, she slipped into her chair before Gerard could clear his and do something civilized like stand. Mr. Blue Blood was nothing if not socially graceful and she wouldn't give him an edge when he already had a clear advantage—the world of upscale social events was his, not hers.

Along with Josh, Lennon and the groom, Gerard was one of "the Garden District Gang," a group of friends who'd been reared together in the exclusive neighborhood along New Orleans's Rue St. Charles. Though the Garden District wasn't far from where Harley had grown up, the city blocks had separated her upbringing from these blue bloods like a galaxy.

"Heard you couldn't get a date," she whispered.

His quicksilver gaze caught hers, eyes so clear beneath a thick fringe of black lashes that Harley felt his glance as a nearly physical pull straight to her toes.

"You're wearing a dress, Harley. And a tight one. Where'd you hide your gun?"

"No place you want to know about."

"Don't be so sure. I didn't bring a date because Lennon mentioned you weren't bringing one."

Now that wasn't what Harley had expected. But then, when did this man ever do what she expected? "What difference does it make whether or not I brought a date?"

"This is the first social event we've been at together since we attended the corporate training."

"So?"

He flashed her a smile that made her heart race on cue. This man's looks really were his greatest flaw. "I didn't want to miss an opportunity to socialize with you. I can handle you differently when we're not at work."

"You can't handle me at all."

"Wrong. I'm looking forward to handling you." He leaned in close and whispered for her ears alone, "We need to figure out how we're going to deal with being attracted to each other. Today's the perfect opportunity to discuss the problem."

Before she could respond to *that,* Gerard sat back, turned to the other guests and introduced her, cutting off any reply and making her feel stupid in the process. She supposed she should have acknowledged the others when she first sat down.

Several guests had attended the same corporate training session as they had, so she forced a smile. The others at the table were strangers, except one—Stuart, Gerard's grandfather.

At first Harley thought she was destined for an afternoon of torture—dealing with two generations of Gerard men couldn't possibly be a good thing. But the elder Mr. Gerard quickly proved that the boorish, arrogant genes had skipped at least one generation in the family.

A very distinguished looking man, he had a head full of wavy white hair and the same quicksilver eyes as his grandson. But there the similarities ended. The elder Mr. Gerard smiled easily and didn't raise her hackles with stupid remarks.

"So you're the skilled investigator I've been hearing so much about," he said. "It's a pleasure to meet you, young lady."

If he'd been hearing about her from his grandson, Harley would bet money *skilled* wasn't the only adjective used to describe her. "You, as well, sir. I know someone on the force who says you should have a square named after you for cutting back plea bargaining while you were district attorney."

"Nice to know I'm still remembered. It's been a few years since I retired."

"You dropped the percentage of plea-bargained cases from eighty percent to ten," Gerard said. "Impact like that lasts."

Stuart smiled graciously. "Fortunately the numbers are holding under the current administration."

No thanks to Stuart's grandson. Harley knew that Gerard had left his career with the district attorney's office and ditched his fiancée to indulge in an early midlife crisis. Rumor had it that his family and friends thought he'd lost his mind, and she sincerely wished that he'd continued in his grandfather's footsteps so he wouldn't have wound up working for Josh.

Keeping that thought to herself, she dodged the sudden silence by reaching for her water glass.

Gerard caught her hand. "Come on, let's dance."

"Excuse me?"

"Let's dance," he repeated. "You're wearing a dress."

Leave it to the whiz kid to notice the obvious. And he didn't look fazed in the least that half the table was hanging on his every word. Arrogance truly was an amazing thing.

"You don't want to dance with me any more than I want to dance with you," she whispered.

"Here's a classic example of how you think you have all the answers but don't."

"If Josh put you up to this, don't worry about it. I'll tell him to butt out. Making us come to the wedding was one thing, but he's out of his jurisdiction here. He can't assign us this much trash work."

A slow smile spread across Gerard's face, making Harley realize she spent so much time avoiding looking at this man that she'd never really noticed his mouth before. Wide, full lips. Straight white teeth. A hint of a dimple in his left cheek.

Then, in a move she was too distracted to see coming, he looped his fingers around her wrist and brought her hand to his mouth. He brushed those lips against her palm, a

With This Fling

warm press of skin against skin that sent a sizzle straight up her arm.

"Josh has nothing to do with this. I don't consider dancing with a beautiful woman trash work."

They were putting on a show for the whole table and Harley wished she had her gun. Unfortunately, it remained in the trunk of her car where she'd left it, but if she'd been armed, she'd have drawn and told him to let go. While she might not be as clean a shot left-handed, she was just as fast.

"Forget it, Gerard," she resorted to a verbal protest, which didn't have nearly the same impact. "This isn't my thing."

"What's not your thing?" With his mouth still brushing her palm, he leaned close and whispered, "The bartender will serve bottled beer if you ask nicely."

Now here was the Mac Gerard she knew and didn't love. Exhaling a breath that should have dispelled all those tingly feelings, Harley said more firmly, "I do not dance."

"You took me to the mat in defense training yesterday. Not an easy thing to do since I outweigh you by a hundred pounds. Trust me, you can dance." Then with that iron grip still clamped around her wrist, he dragged her out of her chair.

Short of causing a scene, there was nothing to do except be tugged onto the dance floor. With his broad shoulders and long strides, Gerard cleared a path through the couples. He moved effortlessly for such a big man, then drew her around to face him. Holding her hand in a death grip, he dropped his other to her waist, drawing her too close for comfort.

"It's easy. Just loosen up and trust me."

Trust him? Right. He was breaking rules here, forcing her to deal with him in a way they hadn't dealt with each other before. And it didn't help that the band played a slow song, which meant he tucked her so close she could feel each shift and flex of muscle as he led her through some slow steps.

"See, Harley, you move fine."

Moving just fine would have meant heading back to the table. Or better yet, New Orleans. Being forced to stand in his arms while her body reacted to their closeness—no matter how hard she willed it otherwise—was just plain torture.

She could deal with Gerard being an idiot, but she couldn't deal with being attracted to him. This chemistry sweeping through her, this rush of awareness so strong she half expected to feel wind whip around them, shouldn't be happening. Worse yet, she wasn't the only one feeling it. Gerard's gaze grew smoky, a look that hinted at moon-soaked nights and sex.

This was ridiculous. They really couldn't stand each other. The man went out of his way at work to challenge her. His ego had a rough time dealing with the fact that she—a woman who hadn't had the benefit of his privileged upbringing—had more experience on the job than he did. This blue-blooded man who was used to his pedigree paving his way.

"I don't like dancing with you," she said.

"I do. You feel nice."

To emphasize his point, he tightened his arm enough to tilt her off balance and press their thighs together. She had no choice but to arch against him and neither his slacks nor her gown did a damned thing to shield her from his hard muscles smothering her. Every nerve ending ignited with the contact, tempting her with an awareness so intense that she'd never felt the like, that she didn't want to feel.

"Knock it off," she muttered. "Or I'll drop you right here."

"You might have gotten me yesterday, but I wouldn't exactly call it a sure thing."

"The only thing saving you is that you're not worth losing my job over. Josh will have something to say if we cause a scene." She tried to put some distance between them, but he only tugged her closer. "You're holding me too close, Gerard. We look like we're doing something obscene."

"We're *dancing*. And I enjoy being close to you without having to block any punches."

Resting his cheek on the top of her head, he fell silent, leaving Harley to guess what he was trying to pull. "Why this sudden crush to hold me?"

"This is much more fun than you trying to kick my head off." His clear eyes flashed, a look that emphasized their closeness. "I want to explore our chemistry. It's become a fantasy of mine."

Harley's mouth popped open and it took Gerard's flashing dimple to bring her to her senses. "You're kidding?"

He shook his head.

"If you're trying to freak me out because you know I'm unarmed, you're doing a good job."

"A compliment. That's a first." He guided her away from a couple dancing within earshot. "And I don't trust that you're unarmed. Knowing you, there's a weapon hidden somewhere—"

"Which I couldn't reach without flashing the room."

He let his eyes flutter shut and inhaled deeply. "Now there's an image to keep me awake at night. I want to see you naked, Harley. That's another fantasy of mine."

"You're really pushing it—"

"Refreshing to see you two engaged in something other than combat for a change." Josh's voice filtered through the moment with the impact of a cooling rain on a summer day.

They swirled around to find him dancing with a smiling Lennon. Harley didn't smile back. She managed to squeeze a little breathing room between her and Gerard while letting Lennon know with a narrowed gaze that she disliked the seating arrangements.

"We promised to play nice for the day," Gerard said.

Harley didn't offer reassurances. Josh believed in actions over words and she wasn't someone who liked to waste her breath. She'd play nice as long as Gerard didn't do anything stupid—no guarantee with all his talk of fantasies.

"Getting away from the office is a good thing," Lennon said, daring Harley to disagree.

Harley didn't reply to that. Not with Josh peering down at his wife with one of *those* expressions, a look that wouldn't change even if Lennon turned blue and started gibbering in an incomprehensible alien tongue.

Harley had witnessed this phenomenon firsthand more than once, a phenomenon that never failed to take her by surprise. She'd watched Josh draw down on a gang, without blinking, to extract information on a missing kid, yet he softened around the edges whenever he gazed at his wife.

"Don't harass her, Mac," Josh said. "Or she won't make it through the reception without drawing her gun."

Gerard laughed as Josh danced Lennon away. "He thinks you're armed, too."

"Keep harassing me, and you'll find out."

With undisguised amusement, Gerard leaned into her, forcing her into a dip. She had no choice but to bend or fall on her butt in this tight dress.

"I'd rather be dancing and holding you close." Looking

She frowned. "Why won't you take no for an answer?"

down at her, eyes smoky with promise, he pressed his thigh between hers, so she had to hang on to keep her balance.

Heat pooled deep inside and she fought the impulse to ride against that hard muscle, feed the ache awakening inside her.

"Gerard," she growled.

He held her for another beat, two, just long enough to prove he had the control, a petty power play that convinced her he was very aware of how she reacted to him. And he made his point loud and clear when he lifted her out of the dip and brought her against him so hard she gasped.

His body enveloped her as he moved her around in the dance, his strong arms too solid, his hips anchored against her much too close for decency. They swayed together so erotically that she imagined they must look like two lovers who needed a room.

She knew he wanted to provoke her and she refused, absolutely refused, to give in to an almost overwhelming desire to fling him off her and knock him on his ass for good measure.

"The pulse jumping in your throat is very attractive," he said, and to her utter horror, he lowered his mouth to her skin.

Flames licked in the wake of his touch, making her insides tremble with excitement. Damn man. Damn dress. And she'd even questioned the low cut of the neckline.

"Just stop it," she said, and Gerard smiled.

"I'm not harassing you. I'm being honest."

It took a moment to manage her breathing and find her voice. "Honest? You expect me to believe this three-hundred-and-sixty-degree change of attitude isn't anything but harassment?"

"I would understand you feeling that way, except for the fact that we kissed."

"It wasn't a real kiss, Gerard. It was being here at the plantation. That ridiculous murder-mystery corporate training. All that rich food and stupidity about pirates falling in love. We got...*caught up.* Let me remind you we agreed to forget that inexplicable lapse of impulse control ever happened."

"You *suggested.* I never agreed. I liked kissing you."

He might have been smiling, but there was nothing amused about his expression. His jaw set in a hard line, his gaze as no-nonsense as she'd ever seen it. The man wasn't lying and that realization came at her sideways.

"What do you want from me?"

"I want *you,* Harley. You're haunting my dreams."

"Get over it."

"Come at this from a purely pragmatic standpoint." He ground against her, enough to share the growing erection he hid inside his expensive suit. "We're attracted to each other. Ignoring the way we feel isn't working. Our feelings are interfering with our jobs."

The instinct to deny his claim hit her hard, but Harley didn't do denial. No matter how much she might want to. She *was* attracted to him, and everyone within a twenty-mile radius of Eastman Investigations knew they didn't get along. Josh had even set up the teamwork training session exclusively to help them work together as a team.

"It was one stupid kiss!" she said.

"It was one awesome kiss."

"Did Lennon put you up to this?"

He lifted a silky dark brow as if daring her to think anyone could possibly make him do something he didn't want to do. Well, no argument there as she'd had daily proof.

"We need to work through these feelings, Harley, so we can get on with our lives. It's the only thing to do."

She would have disabused him of that notion, but he chose that exact moment to bend her back over his arm again when the music slowed to a bluesy tune. Her heart countered by mimicking the tempo with lazy, aching beats.

"We need to explore this attraction to get it out of our systems," he said. "We need to have a fling."

"Are you out of your mind?"

"No. I want you, me, in bed, naked." His smoky gaze raked over her face as intimately as a caress.

"Just because you want something doesn't mean it will become reality." She arched upward, desperate to get away.

He wouldn't let her go.

Short of throwing him off balance and causing a scene, she had no recourse but to wait until he decided to pull her out of the dip, which didn't look like it would happen anytime soon. "Forget the damn kiss, Gerard. End of discussion."

"Let me sweep you off your feet. You'll like it."

Unfortunately, she might, and Harley couldn't live with herself if she did. "Who do you think you are, Prince Charming?"

"You won't be able to resist me."

She could only marvel at the man's arrogance, and his luck. He was beyond lucky that she wasn't armed. She honestly didn't know if she could have controlled herself.

"I will resist, trust me. You aren't Prince Charming and I'm not Cinderella. If I were, you'd turn back into a mouse and this ball would be over."

"Hello, Ms. Price, Mackenzie," a deep male voice said. "Enjoying yourselves?"

They both glanced around to find Gerard's grandfather and his bright-eyed dance partner, Quinevere McDarby.

Gerard had the grace to pull her out of the dip and she sucked in an audible breath that made Miss Q, as she liked to be called, smile.

"Of course they're enjoying themselves, Stuart," she said. "If you could just see yourselves, my dears, you look as if you were made to be together."

As Lennon's great-aunt and Josh's great-aunt-in-law, Miss Q had diplomatic immunity from Harley's opinion. But Gerard, unfortunately, never knew when to keep his mouth shut.

"That's exactly what I've been telling Harley," he said. "She's a tough sell."

"What's to sell?" Miss Q raked those big baby blues over Gerard approvingly. "Look at him, Harley…he's perfect."

For what? To use as a practice target?

She kept her mouth shut. Not only were she and Miss Q clearly of two minds regarding the definition of perfect, but like her great-niece Lennon, Miss Q was one of those impossible-not-to-like types. Hands down, she was the most outrageous woman Harley had ever met, which said a lot since she'd met some real characters in her twenty-seven, almost twenty-eight years.

The way the talk on the street went, Miss Q had been responsible for matchmaking not only Lennon and Josh into their current marital state, but also the new Mr. and Mrs. Sinclair. Harley didn't know the details. She didn't want to know. But when she looked at Gerard and remembered that he was another of the Garden District gang…

She smiled at the elderly couple, a *real* smile. Lady Luck must have glanced down after all, because if Miss Q took an interest in Gerard's love life, she just might find a woman to distract him from wanting a fling with her. With Harley's lack of pedigree, she certainly wouldn't be on the short list of contenders for the job.

"Miss Q, would you mind if I cut in?" Harley asked, more than willing to suffer another dance to escape Gerard and give this little matchmaker a chance to pick his brain about his preferences. "I was hoping to talk with Mr. Gerard about his work as the district attorney."

"Of course not, my dear. I never turn down a dance with a handsome man."

"The verdict is still out on whether or not you're armed," Gerard said with a frown. "Should I be worried about my grandfather's safety?"

"Nothing to worry about, Mackenzie." Stuart motioned him off. "Your Ms. Price is charming."

Gerard had no choice but to let her go, but being the man he was, he couldn't resist a parting shot. His voice was low and silky when he whispered in her ear, "I'll get you in bed, Harley. Trust me."

She bit her tongue and made her escape. Stepping into Stuart's arms, she let him steer her into a dance, his grandson's threat still echoing in her head.

"So you wanted to talk about my work, young lady?"

Between the question in his voice and the dubiously arched brow, Harley got the impression he didn't believe her. She decided to be up-front. "To be honest, sir, I wanted to get away from your grandson. I see him all week at work. I need a break on the weekends."

"My good fortune then. After meeting you, I'd hoped we'd get the opportunity to chat."

"Really, sir? Why?"

"I've heard a great deal about you."

"I do hope you've heard more than your grandson's opinion. If not, I'm sunk."

Stuart might have been old, *really* old if she was to guess, but his strong features had weathered the time well. When he smiled, she recognized his grandson in his expression and suspected that one day Gerard would look a lot like this man.

"I have," he said. "In fact, that's why I wanted to talk. I like to form my own opinions and the only thing my grandson has said is that you're a very good investigator. He told me he's been learning a great deal."

"Really?"

"Really." He sounded decided, and Harley liked that he was playing as straight with her as she was with him. "But I suspect that you're not sure whether to believe me, Ms. Price."

"Call me Harley, please."

He inclined his head. "If you'll call me Stuart."

"Okay, Stuart. What makes you think I'm not sure?"

"I spent my entire adult life prosecuting criminals. That constitutes a *lot* of years. I pride myself on having become rather an expert at reading people."

"That's a handy skill in my line of work, too. And I don't question you at all," she assured him. "I'm reassessing the situation. If that's all your grandson has said and you still need to formulate an opinion, maybe it's everyone else's opinions I should be worried about."

"Not at all, young lady. Although I must tell you I'm fascinated by the stories. I've always found my grandson easy to get along with and, to my knowledge, he hasn't had problems on the job in the past."

"Oh, I'm sure he hasn't. He's the poster child of patience and ability. I'm the rogue element here."

"Touché." Stuart laughed. "I'm biased where Mackenzie is concerned. He's my late wife's namesake—Julia Mackenzie Gerard. As I'm so fond of him, I do hope you'll forgive me. But in order to correct my mistake, I'll need your take on the stories."

"They're nothing more than urban legends," she said dryly. "Your grandson and I get along fine. Not to worry."

Stuart shot a glance toward the grandson in question and his matchmaking dance partner. "I'm not worried at all. I believe my grandson may have finally met his match."

Gerard's threat echoed in her memory. *I'll get you in bed, Harley. Trust me.*

The man had met his match. She just hoped he was as smart as his grandfather to realize it.

2

Mac had no appointments scheduled this morning, but when he arrived at work shortly before nine, Melissa, Eastman Investigations's office manager, tipped the phone receiver fastened to her head and mouthed, "Your grandfather's here."

"In my office?" he asked, surprised.

She shook her head. "Josh's office, and Harley's with them. They told me to send you in when you got here."

Mac strode through the reception area and down the hallway. After knocking on his boss's door, he found Josh seated behind his desk, his grandfather in front and Harley half sitting on the side, contemplating him stoically.

She was back in black today, the narrow-legged slacks and blazer drawing his attention to the way her body stretched away from the desk, all graceful lines and sleek curves.

He nodded in greeting, then slipped a hand over his grandfather's shoulder. "What's going on?"

His grandfather glanced up with a somber expression. "Good morning, Mackenzie. I've been explaining to Josh and Harley that I seem to have a thief loose in my house."

Mac sat down beside his grandfather, frowning. The house in question was the house he'd been reared in, a Garden District mansion where both his grandfather and parents still lived.

"What's missing?"

"Your grandmother's wedding rings."

"No chance they were accidentally moved or misplaced?"

His grandfather shook his head. "You know I never move them. I suppose I should keep them in the safe, but…" He trailed off and shrugged.

Mac knew those rings stayed inside his grandmother's jewelry box on her dresser, where his grandfather could look at them whenever he wanted a reminder of the woman he'd loved for most of his life, and had so recently lost.

"Grandmother's jewelry should be safe in the house. What did you do after noticing the rings missing?"

"Took a thorough inventory of everything of value I don't lock up and asked your parents to do the same. All their things are accounted for, but I'm missing my father's pocket watch and your grandmother's pearls."

"You keep the pocket watch in your armoire?"

His grandfather nodded.

"So you're missing several items from various places. Narrows down the suspect list." He thought of the few employees who had access to his grandfather's private apartment. "Have you reported the thefts to the police yet?"

"Apparently there's a problem with that," Josh said, and Mac guessed by his tone that he wasn't happy with this problem, whatever it was. "That's what we were just discussing."

After so many years as a district attorney, his grandfather knew enough people in the police department that an investigation should have happened immediately. "What's up?"

"As I was telling Harley and Josh, once I discovered these pieces missing, I wrote a list of everyone with access to the house. Seemed to be a safe place to start." He gave a wan smile. "As I'm sure you're aware, Mackenzie, that list is small. James and Pearl have been with me for years and I trust them implicitly, which leaves me with the cleaning and lawn-maintenance services. As the lawn-maintenance people don't usually come inside..."

"You're left with the cleaning service."

"Right. But I've used the same service since your grand-mother hired them nearly sixty years ago. You can understand I'm wary about making accusations without proof."

Mac understood his grandfather's concern and agreed with his assessment of the house staff's trustworthiness. Pearl had been stuffing the family full of her Deep South specialties for as long as he could remember and James had spent nearly twenty years trying to direct Mac and his siblings' activities outside of the house, where the aftereffects were less noticeable.

"I know Mrs. Noralee's daughter is still running their business, Grandfather, but she has turnover with her staff. It's possible she's hired someone she can't trust."

"I agree, which is why I called some friends who use her cleaning service to see if they've had any problems."

"Good idea. What came of it?"

"Five other clients with similar losses." Harley reached for a document in front of Josh, handed Mac what turned out to be an inventory list. She was cool, professional, nothing in her expression letting on that they'd ever discussed a fling during the wedding. "They're all missing small, high-ticket items that usually aren't noticed immediately."

Mac scanned the list, recognized the names. He glanced up at Josh. "Miss Q's been hit, too."

Josh nodded. "Basically we've got Nice and Neat as the commonality, with a staff of twelve who regularly service the Garden District on rotating schedules."

Mac turned to his grandfather. "I don't see why the police can't investigate, so we can start attempting to recover the stolen items."

Unfortunately, the chance of recovery was slim, and one look at his grandfather's expression told Mac he knew it. Which left Mac to vainly question why, out of all the valuables in the family home, his grandmother's rings—irreplaceable for their sentimental value alone—had been taken.

"That's why I'm here, Mackenzie," his grandfather said. "We want to move quickly. We've all lost things that mean a great deal to us. We're pooling our efforts and hiring Eastman Investigations to investigate."

"I'm still missing something here." Mac cast a sidelong glance at Harley, found her watching him with an expression that revealed nothing.

"We can't go to the police because of Noralee," his grandfather said as if that explained everything. "She's a good friend. She started Noralee's Nice and Neat over *sixty years* ago. Those were different times, Mackenzie. Most women didn't run businesses back then, especially African-American women."

Leaning back in his chair, he steepled his hands before him, looked thoughtful. "Noralee was the Eastman's housekeeper until she approached Josh's grandfather about investing in her business. He backed her financially and Quinevere used their social contacts to help her find clients. She ran her business successfully until passing it along to her daughter when she retired. Evalee runs it now and has been training her daughter to take over. Nice and Neat has become a family operation with a sterling reputation that we don't want to damage."

"Someone is stealing."

"I agree but until we know if Noralee's daughter and granddaughter are involved, we'd prefer to handle it quietly. You've met Noralee, Mackenzie. She's older than I am and has worked so hard. We don't want to see her reputation harmed for no good reason. You need to find out what's going on. If her daughter and granddaughter aren't involved, the situation can be handled internally, *quietly*. If they are, well, at least we can warn Noralee before going to the authorities.''

''What are your thoughts on this?'' Mac asked Josh, who rocked back in his chair and shot him a narrowed glance.

''I've been backed into a neat corner,'' he said.

''Really?''

''Really. Your grandfather has been reminding me how instrumental my grandfather was in starting Nice and Neat. He believes that makes me invested in the outcome.''

''And…'' Harley leveled her gaze at him. ''Your grandfather threatened to sic Miss Q on him if he doesn't take the case.''

Mac glanced at his grandfather. ''I'm surprised you're playing the personal card here.''

''Why should you be? It's one of the few cards I have to play today and I want you to take our case.''

Harley chuckled and Mac looked back at her, even more surprised by her amusement than he was at his grandfather pulling rank. Laughter brightened her eyes and softened the edges of her beautiful face, an unexpected and welcome change from sarcasm.

His grandfather returned her smile. ''I want you all to give it some thought before you decide. We'll pay your professional fees and expenses and in addition, we're offering generous cash rewards for the recovery of any of the stolen items.''

''I appreciate cash bonuses as well as the next guy, Stuart,'' Harley said. ''But I see a problem.''

Josh leaned back in his chair, watching her as if he knew what was coming. All eyes fixed on her, waiting.

"We can run background checks on the Nice and Neat employees, but we can't conduct an investigation any more quietly than the police. If we don't explain ourselves when we ask questions, we won't get the answers we need. Now you're looking at inside surveillance."

"Which dramatically increases the time it'll take us to get information," Josh said.

"Which decreases our chances of recovering the stolen items," Mac added.

His grandfather waved a hand dismissively. "You'll work it out. I have total faith in your abilities. That's why I'm here."

"Give us twenty-four hours to do some research and discuss the case, Mr. Gerard." Josh rose, effectively bringing the conversation to an end. "I'll call you tomorrow to let you know what we come up with. Agreed?"

"Agreed," his grandfather said.

Mac stood. "I'll walk you out."

Leading his grandfather outside, he waited until they were in the parking lot of the upscale professional plaza that housed Eastman Investigations before saying, "I'm sorry they took Grandmother's rings. I know how much they mean to you. And me, too. I'll do whatever I can to get them back."

To Mac, his grandfather looked much the same as he always did. His hair was whiter, his face more lined, but he still stood tall, a proud man with an easy smile. And when he slid his hand over Mac's shoulder and squeezed, the gesture felt the way it always had—a vote of unfailing confidence.

"I know you will, Mackenzie. I'm counting on it."

Mac watched his grandfather drive from the parking lot

and disappear into traffic, while he considered the various ways to tackle this case. If he closed his eyes, he could still see the elegant diamond and platinum rings in his memory.

"My father used to say my engagement ring was as big as an ice-skating pond," his grandmother had once told him. *"So I'd ask him when he'd ever seen an ice-skating pond, since he was born and bred in New Orleans."*

"When had he?" Mac had asked.

"He hadn't. He was only teasing me, dear. He could never decide if your grandfather had bought such a big diamond to prove his worth or because he liked to show off."

This accounting was so different from the grandfather Mac knew that he'd asked curiously, *"Why did he?"*

She'd gazed lovingly at her rings with one of those expressions that usually warned Mac it was time to dodge a hug. *"Your grandfather wanted an engagement ring to always remind me of how much he loved me. He said this was the biggest he could find and it wasn't nearly big enough."*

Mac had been twelve at the time and remembered feeling uncomfortable with all the talk about love. But as an adult he remembered her words when he thought about his future—he, too, wanted to settle down with a woman he loved with the same devotion his grandfather had shown his grandmother.

And somehow his grandmother had known. After her funeral services, his grandfather had pulled Mac aside and pressed the rings into his hand. *"She wanted you to have these, Mackenzie. You were her namesake,"* he'd explained. *"She wanted to look down from heaven and know you loved someone as much as I loved her."*

Mac had been touched by his grandmother's regard, but he hadn't taken her rings that day. He'd known his grandfather would appreciate hanging on to them a while longer and, as Mac crossed the parking lot, he realized his reluctance to give his ex-fiancée those rings should have been his first clue that all hadn't been right in their relationship.

On some level he'd known his ex hadn't been his special woman. Fortunately for them both, he'd finally figured out what the problem was before getting himself and a very nice woman involved in a marriage destined to suffer from the same nagging discontent that he'd felt in so many other areas of his life.

He'd spent his whole life maintaining the status quo— thirty-three years of living up to the standards of old-moneyed New Orleans families. He had the education, the portfolio, the toys, the power and the social status to prove it…and a restlessness that had refused to go away.

Until Mac had decided he'd had enough.

Part of his decision to point his life in a new direction was a need to be challenged—by his work and by his pleasures—a part of life he'd ignored for way too long. He'd left his job with the District Attorney's office and washed his hands of the premeditated mating game he'd been playing since becoming marriage-marketable by society's standards. He wanted the thrill of the chase and long, hot nights with women who weren't focused on social standing, prenuptial agreements and gene pools.

What he'd gotten was a hard-on for Harley Price.

Yes, she was beautiful, intelligent and so accomplished as an investigator that his own inexperience had been hammering at his ego. But she was also cynical, impatient and so far removed from her emotions that she had to be the worst possible candidate as a companion to exploring life's pleasures.

Get over it, she'd told him.

He'd been trying. And while Harley might be willing to live in this state of edgy limbo, he wasn't. He needed to help his grandfather, not obsess about this woman. He wanted her out of his system, and all he had to do was convince Harley she wanted the same thing.

THE WEEKEND FROM HELL was barely over, and from where Harley sat—the driver's seat of a friend's car—the week was shaping up to be just as hellish. Not that there was anything wrong with the antique Firebird. It was a sweet ride—all showy red paint and polished chrome—despite the so-called power steering that was developing her biceps every time she turned the wheel.

The real problem with the Firebird was that she'd rather not have been driving it at all. Her own car had started acting up on her way home from the wedding, the transmission slipping while still on the plantation's oak-lined driveway. She'd pulled into a gas station to refill her fluids and—hopefully—resolve the problem. No such luck. This morning she hadn't been able to back out of her driveway.

Anthony had sent a tow truck.

Now she wheeled the Firebird into the busy parking lot of Anthony DiLeo Automotive. She parked in his reserved space and headed inside for the verdict, not looking forward to finding out how much worse the week could get.

A sixty-inch television broadcast a daytime talk show in the waiting area, where several customers sat, eyes fixed on the screen, waiting. The whole place had a still-new-around-the-edges feel to it that wouldn't hold up long under the daily traffic of grease-covered mechanics. Especially now that Anthony had more than doubled the size of his staff with the recent move into this larger facility.

Forcing a smile, she greeted the receptionist behind the service desk and asked, "Anthony in his office?"

"He's got your car on a lift."

Harley nodded and headed down the narrow hallway. Organized chaos was the only term to describe the garage. With twenty bays, and mechanics engaged in all manner of auto maintenance and repair from simple oil changes to major engine rebuilds, the place screamed thriving business. Harley had her fingers crossed these bays stayed filled, because Anthony had gambled everything on this move. He had some grand plans for his future and was accomplishing them one step at a time.

This move had been a big step.

She spotted her gray sedan and made her way back, waving at several of the mechanics who greeted her along the way.

"Hello, princess." Anthony DiLeo, the owner of Anthony DiLeo Automotive, stepped out from beneath the lift, where she got a bird's-eye view of her car's dismantled underbelly.

Harley had known Anthony since she'd been six years old, and her dad had rented the DiLeo family's garage apartment to live above the shop where he'd run his electronics business.

Anthony had been eight at the time, the middle son in a family of five boys and a girl. He hadn't known she'd existed—until his younger brother Damon had mistaken her for a target to practice his Bruce Lee moves on.

She'd convinced Damon of his error with a bloody nose.

Anthony had stepped in to break up the tussle and for some reason that Harley still couldn't explain, some twenty-plus years later, eight-year-old Anthony DiLeo had seemed everything the perfect boy should be. With his olive skin, tawny hair, golden brown eyes, he'd grown from perfect boy into perfect teen into perfect man, a man who—hopefully—had some good news for her.

"What's the verdict?"

He held out a grease-stained palm filled with metal shavings. "Your tranny's shot."

"Can you fix it?"

"I can replace it."

Oh, this was just getting better and better.

Grabbing a rag from a nearby tool caddy, he wiped his hands. "When did you say it first started slipping?"

"Saturday. And if you're going to tell me you could have fixed it if I'd brought it in sooner, don't."

He didn't miss the significance of that statement. "Didn't go well with the exterminator?"

Harley shook her head.

"Charlie," he called out. "Get the princess's wheels down and Iovocozzi's Navigator up. Put Sal on it and tell him I promised to have it done by five." He turned to her. "Come on."

She walked at his side, waited when he stopped at a sink to scrub his hands. Then he slipped his arm around her neck, felt for the outline of her holster and led her into his office.

"Sit," he said, then disappeared back out the door, returning a few minutes later with two cups of coffee. Pressing one into her hands, he half sat on the desk in front of her.

"Thanks." Harley felt her frayed edges begin to smooth out.

"What did the exterminator say?"

Lifting her gaze, she felt her throat tighten at the concern she saw in his. "I've got termites big time. No surprises there, since they've been falling on my head. But the damage, Anthony..." She swallowed hard to continue. "The exterminator said there's a lot. I met with him on my lunch hour and now he's coming back with a contractor this afternoon. They'll give me an estimate.''

"It might not be that bad.''

She nodded, sipped her coffee, her heart beating so fast she felt dizzy. Just her luck that she'd finally bought her own home, a *real* home like she'd wanted forever, and bugs were eating it from the inside out.

Anthony recognized how upset she was because he set his cup aside and leaned forward to press a kiss to the top of her head. She wasn't surprised by the intimacy. Technically they were in an off-again phase of their relationship—ever since she'd met Craig the cop and he'd met Rachel in retail.

Craig had taken a hike, but Rachel hadn't gotten her walking papers yet. As soon as she did, Anthony would be knocking on Harley's door again. As always, she'd welcome him. He'd taught her an orgasm was the best cure-all for whatever ailed her, and she could use a good one right now. She had termites, a shot transmission...and Mac Gerard in hot pursuit.

What a week!

Brushing hairs away from her forehead, Anthony smiled down at her. "Let's tackle one problem at a time here, princess.''

"Transmission.''

"Done deal.''

"I don't have the money for the parts.'' She barely had the money for her next meal, but she wouldn't tell him that. School loans had strapped her finances tight for too long, but once she'd bought the house... "I'm having heart palpitations about what the exterminator and contractor are going to say.''

"No problem. I'll cover the parts, but it's going to take me about a week to get them. My suppliers put me on

C.O.D. ever since the move. They want their cash up front until they're sure I won't crash and burn the business.''

He didn't have to say another word for Harley to know he was offended. He'd been doing business with his suppliers for nearly ten years. She also knew it was the first of the month, and since he'd only made his third mortgage payment on this high-square-footage property, his cash must be *really* tight.

''Is everything all right?'' She set her coffee cup on the desk. ''Are your mom and Damon doing okay?''

''I covered Damon's share of the mortgage again this month.''

She'd figured that would happen. Anthony DiLeo Automotive comprised one third—albeit the largest third—of what had become a DiLeo compound. Anthony had bought the huge property, then renovated the space into his new garage, his mother's new hair salon and his brother's new dojo.

Until Damon got his martial arts studio off the ground and built up his client base... ''I can put in a plug with Josh. Maybe he'll consider moving Eastman Investigations. The place we're training in now is a dive.''

Anthony smiled, one of those blinding, white-toothed grins that had been taking her breath away forever. ''That'd help. I'm going down to talk to the bank about modifying the mortgage now that the rates have dropped again. Until then, I'm screwed. Next to nobody pays cash and the credit card companies hold up my money for six weeks. But the banks cover the debit transactions every week, so I'll get your transmission then. Okay?''

She leaned back in her chair with a sigh. ''I honestly don't know what I'd do without you.''

Anthony reached for his coffee, looking satisfied. He always liked when she fed his ego—a full-time job even when he wasn't saving her ass.

"Well, that's one problem off my back, thank you very much," she said. "Now I have to figure out how I'm getting around. What's your loaner situation?"

"Not good. I'm taking on twice the business with only two spare vehicles."

"What are my chances of talking you out of the Firebird?"

"How about the chopper? I'm on Mama detail this week. We've got a doctor's appointment this afternoon, a casino cruise Friday night and a wedding on Saturday."

Harley was genuinely flattered that Anthony trusted her to drive his pride and joy. "Are you sure? Would you rather let Damon borrow the chopper? I'm sure he wouldn't mind lending me his car. He barely leaves the dojo anyway."

"Damon is not driving the chopper." He leaned across the desk to slide open a drawer. "I'll only trust you, princess."

"You'll kill me if I ding the paint."

He scooped the keys from a drawer and held them out to her, catching her gaze above his hand. "Then don't ding the paint."

She plucked the keys from his fingers and smiled.

Looked like her day had finally taken a turn for the better. Now if her luck just held through the afternoon...

3

Mac usually enjoyed an occasional night gambling at Harrah's. It was a new pastime in his repertoire, one that Josh had introduced him to. Josh had also been the one to insist they drop by the casino tonight, after returning to the office after-hours to find Mac still working.

While Mac appreciated the attempt to take his mind off the case, he finally left Josh in the Blue Dog Poker Room to walk off his restlessness in the fantasy world that made up Harrah's. His head was cluttered with questions about how best to recover the stolen items and he was struggling to think clearly while suffering a bad case of Harley on the brain.

So he wandered beneath the starry sky in the jazz court and tried to distract himself when the dueling pianos played music that reminded him of how good she'd felt in his arms when they'd danced at the wedding.

He finally made his way to the VIP lounge to get away from the music. Flashing his ID, he greeted the doorman, then stepped inside to savor the quiet…and find the very woman who'd been haunting his thoughts as if she'd materialized straight from his imagination.

Harley.

She sat alone, contemplating the drink she held with both hands. Gone was her requisite black—she'd dressed in cream leather, a formfitting pantsuit that molded her slim curves.

She presented him an unfamiliar opportunity to observe her without having to think on his feet or dodge physical blows. He simply admired the way the color emphasized her skin, how her delicate profile peeked through the tumble of red hair.

She seemed different tonight. Something more than the wardrobe change. Then he recognized what that difference was. Though Mac hadn't made the connection before, hadn't realized she functioned with shields up against the world, he suddenly understood now, when those shields were so noticeably absent.

Something about the slump of her shoulders. And the way she'd hooked her feet around the chair legs to lean forward, as if she needed the table to support her. She seemed somehow unguarded, all alone in the world.

This was Harley uncensored. The Harley he needed to seduce. They were making each other crazy with this unrequited lust and he didn't understand why she couldn't see that, why she fought him so hard. All they needed to do was satisfy their hunger and go their separate ways. It was simple. Inevitable.

Mac didn't hesitate. Covering the distance, he slid into the chair across from her. She snapped her head up and blinked those deep blue eyes.

"You're not seeing things, Harley. It's me."

She brought a shaky hand to her forehead. "I'm in hell."

"No, you're in Harrah's."

"No, you're here. I'm in hell." She dropped her face into her outspread hands and Mac thought he saw her shudder.

That was his second clue that all was not business as usual. The first had been her reaction to him—normally after she'd made the nasty comment, she would have taken off and left him to chase after her.

"Is everything all right?"

"Why are you here?" Her voice was muffled behind her hands

"I came with Josh."

That got her attention, and she lifted her head. "Josh is *here,* in the casino?"

Mac nodded but he didn't get a chance to gauge her reaction, because she slid the chair back and got to her feet, treating him to a head-to-toe view of slim curves enveloped in leather.

That sensation clenched low in his gut again as he took in those curves, so beautifully shaped and well toned for her obsession with the marital arts. Leather hugged her long legs like a second skin, outlining the length of her thighs and the sweep of her calves. Her shoes were stylish, but the heels low enough to run in. She was ever ready for trouble.

"I am so out of here," she said, staring down her nose. "Do me a favor and tell Josh you didn't see me."

Mac considered the logic of that statement and recognized his next clue that all was not right with Harley.

She was unsteady on her feet. Just the slightest waver, but enough to convince him that the nearly full drink she'd been nursing hadn't been her first.

"Allow me," he said, standing.

"I don't need your help."

She pulled away and there it was again. She wove a bit to the left like a ship listing in a breeze.

"I'm not offering my help." Slipping an arm around her shoulders, he steered her away from the table. "I'm trying to cop a feel. I have a hard time getting dates, so I haven't felt the real thing in a while."

Miracle of miracles, she didn't resist, just leaned into him so her shoulder fit neatly under his arm and her gun dug into his ribs. His next breath comprised of clean hair mingled with some spicy scent and Mac inhaled deeply, amazed and amused by the way the fragrance chased through his senses. He forced his legs into motion.

"You told me you didn't have problems getting dates," she said. "You said you went to the wedding alone because of me."

"I lied."

Tipping her head back, she lifted those big blue eyes to his. "Really? So you don't want to sleep with me?"

Steering her past the buffet, he angled his mouth close to her ear and whispered, "There's no want. I *intend* to sleep with you as soon as I can convince you to get naked."

Her eyes narrowed. "Oh, I get it now. You're desperate. You could have picked an easier mark, Gerard."

"True, but I don't want easy. I want you."

He couldn't have explained and didn't bother trying, not when bracing himself for her comeback. But to his surprise, she only gave an exasperated huff and kept walking.

Mac took advantage of the moment and buried his smile in her sweet-smelling hair. Alcohol might not outwardly impair her much but it certainly made her chatty.

Guiding her toward the door, he told the doorman, "Nigel, please get word to Josh Eastman that I was called away."

"I'll take care of it, Mr. Gerard."

He led Harley onto the floor where hundreds of slot machines flashed and beeped for attention. She blinked against the sudden glare.

"Sure you want to run off?" he asked. "It's still early."

Glancing at the slots, she said, "The night's over for me."

A cryptic remark from a woman who lived to be blunt? Mac suspected here was yet another clue that all was not well, although the fact she'd been drinking already confirmed it. The teamwork training session they'd attended had lasted a full five days, and during that time she'd declined even a sip of wine at dinner. He'd assumed her devotion to the martial arts meant she didn't drink alcohol— an assumption reinforced at the wedding when she'd toasted the bride and groom with lime-laced water.

He should have known not to assume.

A doorman swung the door wide in the front lobby and Mac led Harley to the valet. "Where's your ticket?"

She rummaged through her purse, bracing herself against him for support, before handing over her ticket.

The feel of her body pressed close did amazing things to his. He felt each smooth curve as a promise, the clothing separating them a reminder of the bare skin below. Pressing another smile into her hair, he treated himself to a breath filled with her faintly spicy scent, enjoyed a calm moment with a woman with whom calm didn't usually factor into the equation.

She finally tipped her head back, and those blue eyes searched his, the color of midnight in the glare of artificial lighting that threw the night-dark city into shadows beyond. She must not have liked what she saw because she pulled out of his arms and said, "Will you stop—"

The rapid-fire rumble of a motorcycle's engine drowned out her protest.

"Would you look at that," Mac said, admiring the Harley-Davidson chopper the valet pulled into the driveway. Sleek lines of highly polished chrome showcased a bright red body and a low-slung front wheel that was much sparser in design than any hog built today. A very well-maintained classic.

The valet left the bike to idle and slid off in front of them. He must have noticed Mac's interest because he shot him a smile and said, "It's awesome."

Mac watched in surprise as he handed the helmet to Harley. She accepted it, tipped the guy and turned to him.

"Harley on a Harley. That's just priceless, Price."

She ignored him, so he grabbed her hand. "I'll drive."

"It's a one-butt ride."

"It's a two-butt ride unless you've decided to spend the night in this casino." He brushed her aside, slid onto the smooth leather saddle and couldn't stop a low whistle. "I had no idea you were a closet biker. My opinion of you has just jumped several notches."

"Don't let it go to your head. I'm only baby-sitting it for a friend. He'll kill me if you ding his paint."

He'll kill me.

Well, here was unexpected info that fitted another piece of the puzzle into place. "I won't hurt the bike."

"You're not driving the chopper, Gerard."

"Neither are you, Harley."

The valet shifted his attention between them, understanding finally dawning. Mac had to give the kid a lot of credit when he faced down a scowling Harley and asked, "Miss, would you like me to call a cab?"

She exhaled sharply, obviously not alcohol-impaired enough to miss that she'd lost this battle.

"No, thanks. Looks like I've got a chauffeur."

The valet retreated and Mac kept his mouth shut as she tugged on the helmet and climbed behind him. His pulse kicked when she slipped her thighs against his and threaded her arms around his waist. He put the bike into gear, leaned into the throttle and steered onto the street.

Well, here was another perk to broadening his horizons. Mac hadn't ridden a bike since college. And never a ride as sweet as this or with a girl so tempting. He wiggled backward to make her spread her thighs wider.

Mmm-hmm. The heat of her body contrasted nicely with the cooling night air. The bike maneuvered silkily, tires chewing up the road beneath a steady rough-velvet roar of engine. Mac maneuvered through the streets toward the Garden District, enjoying the whip of the wind, the way it snapped his clothes against his skin.

The only negative tonight was learning there was someone who might interfere with his plans for Harley.

He'll kill me.

Who was *he?* Mac knew Harley wasn't married. They'd worked together closely for the past five months and he hadn't heard anything about a boyfriend or any sort of companion. He'd assumed Harley wasn't involved.

Another reminder never to assume with this woman. But he was finding out more about her tonight than he had since they'd first met and he wasn't about to retreat now. Not with a chance to find out what might be holding her back from a fling.

"Which house?" he yelled over the roar of the engine when he'd turned onto her street.

She directed him down several blocks then into the driveway of a mansion, only dimly lit in the glow of antique ironwork post lamps. Mac took in the pristine white facade, the huge classical pillars of the portico, tried to see if the mansion had been divided into apartments—the unfortunate fate of so many Garden District homes.

"Let me off," she said, and he brought the bike to a stop in the driveway. "I'll get the garage door."

She slipped off and headed up the drive unsteadily. He walked the bike behind her, prepared to catch her if she went down. He parked beside two high-ticket sedans, neither of which were Harley's cars. Plucking the helmet from her, he strapped it to the tail bar.

"Can you call someone to pick you up?" she asked.

He glanced at his watch, but couldn't make out the time in the dark. "Don't you want to invite me inside?"

"I'd rather you didn't even know where I live."

"Getting to know each other will help us get along."

"Or make us dislike each other more." Her bravado was slipping around the edges and he took the opportunity to wrap his arm around her shoulder and steer her out of the garage.

"That way." She motioned to a flagstone walkway leading away from the house.

Clouds separated, allowing moonlight to illuminate the neat lawn and a sizable cottage on the north corner of the property that had likely begun life as a guest house.

He helped her up the steps and waited while she fished through her purse for keys. After unlocking the door, she flipped on the porch light and he glimpsed the interior, an open floor plan, sparsely decorated and very neat. He recognized the lines of antebellum architecture and the gleam of wooden floors.

"Are you going to call a cab?" She swayed slightly before leaning against the doorjamb for support.

"Are you okay?"

A beat of silence passed before she admitted, "I don't usually drink."

Opportunity knocked again and Mac didn't hesitate. He scooped her into his arms and kicked the door shut.

"Gerard—"

"Hang on or I'll drop you. You're heavier than you look."

She made an unladylike grunt but did as he asked, wrapped her arms around his neck and rested her head on his shoulder. He navigated through the cottage easily in the darkness and found her bedroom off the living room. He reached for the light switch but she grabbed his hand.

"No light."

"You want the bathroom instead of the bed?" He'd already passed one but saw another doorway across the room that might lead to a private bath.

"No. My head is swimming. The bed."

He'd been fantasizing about hearing those words and it figured that when she finally said them she wouldn't mean them.

But he enjoyed the feel of her in his arms and took the opportunity to observe her inner sanctum. For a woman who made weapons and leather a fashion statement, her bedroom was surprisingly feminine. Tester bed with a lace canopy and a surplus of equally lacy pillows tossed over the matching comforter. Floral wallcovering. Filmy sheers on the windows.

So there was a real woman behind the shields. Wasn't Harley just full of surprises?

Depositing her gently on the bed, he watched her curl up and close her eyes.

"Come on. Off with the jacket." He lifted a boneless arm and tugged off the sleeve. She didn't resist until he tried to move her to get at the other.

"Leave me alone," she insisted. "Just let me sleep."

"After I get some of these clothes off you."

"You wish." She gave another of those unladylike snorts, her sarcasm firmly in place.

"No surprise there. Now come on, give me the gun. You can't sleep with it digging into your back."

"I can."

"No, you can't." Sinking to the edge of the bed, Mac lifted her into his arms to strip the jacket away. The instant he brought her up against him, awareness kicked in. She was a nice armful, much more appealing than when she was attacking him during training.

She helped him by shrugging off the jacket and each brush of her bare arms sharpened his awareness that they were sitting on her bed, at night, with the promise of skin between them.

He drew a deep breath. Another.

After dropping her jacket on the foot of the bed, he unfastened the holster. More contact with skin as he followed the leather straps down her back, around her waist. She shifted against him, her breathing growing shallower. He knew she must be aware of his hands hovering just through her clothes, because when he started on her one-piece pantsuit, she tried to brush him away and said, "Don't."

"Shh." He swept her hair away from the zipper. "I want to put you to bed so you can sleep comfortably."

Alcohol dropped her shields more than he'd realized, because she didn't resist. Or maybe she was just as paralyzed by awareness as he was, a sensation that had grown almost palpable.

Resting her face in the crook of his neck, she let him peel away her bodice. He eased the sleeves away one-handed, his blood heating dangerously when he realized she wasn't wearing a stitch below. Not a bra. Not a camisole. Not a thing to hide all that creamy skin.

She gave a shuddering sigh as he eased her back against the pillows, gifting him with a view of her full breasts and blush-colored nipples, delicate shoulders and the contour of her graceful neck up close and personal.

Just where Mac had longed to be. He couldn't ever remember being broadsided by the sight of a woman before, had *never* known the sort of anticipation that arced his body from zero to sixty in less than a heartbeat that throbbed so hard it hurt.

His hands actually shook when he maneuvered the leather over her hips and he revealed her sleek curves, her long, long legs with a reverence that was so entirely unfamiliar.

Her cream-colored thong came as a surprise for a woman who went braless and loved leather. Mac wasn't sure what he'd expected, but the sight of that lacy scrap of silk wasn't it. He had to force himself to keep dragging the pantsuit away because he so didn't want this show to end.

"Why are you fighting me so hard, Harley?" he asked, his voice raw in the late-night quiet. "You can't tell me you're not attracted to me. I know you're feeling what I do."

He shouldn't reveal so much. She'd only use his need against him, but with her stretched out before him, all gleaming skin and sleek curves, his need made him reckless.

"I don't want to feel anything for you."

"But you do." He couldn't resist the urge to prove it. Trailing a finger up her shapely leg, he touched her warm skin.

"Gerard…" Her voice trailed off, breathless.

"Why not, Harley? A fling makes sense."

He continued tracing a path up her thigh, a light touch that heightened the anticipation, a small defiance designed to entice the truth from her. Or maybe just entice her.

He wanted her to feel as reckless as he did right now.

Dragging his fingertip beneath her thong, he followed the lacy edge around her hip toward the juncture of her thighs.

She trembled.

He smiled.

She frowned. "Why won't you take no for an answer?"

"Because I want you. I want you to admit you want me."

Simple. Honest.

"What difference will it make if I admit it? I still won't sleep with you." Raising her arms above her head, she stretched, a languorous display of skin, a move meant to tempt him with the very thing he wanted.

Her move pressed her smooth abdomen into his fingertip, and he knew she was teasing him, inviting him, a boldness inspired by alcohol. But Mac couldn't resist the opportunity to touch her. Rounding the mound of her sex, he tested her heat through the scrap of sheer silk.

She was hot, moist, *definitely* aroused.

"You want me." He bent forward, pressed his mouth to that lacy triangle, breathed a hot breath through the silk.

Her muscles contracted sharply. "I do, but it doesn't make any difference."

Hearing her admission was such a bittersweet relief that he almost laughed at the irony. He wanted this beautiful woman sprawled before him more than he'd ever wanted before. His erection throbbed so hard he ached and he couldn't even test her claim, tempt her as much as she tempted him or try to change her mind.

Because Mac knew she meant what she said.

She might want him, but it didn't make a difference. She wouldn't let it. Not when she was sober. Not even now when those heavy-lidded eyes, so lazy with arousal, reminded him that she'd been drinking.

It was over. No matter how Mac came at this, he was pushing the limits of polite behavior. Harley might be arching that smooth body against him. She might be rubbing her sex against his hand and purring breathy little sighs, but her actions didn't change the fact that had she been clearheaded she'd probably be pointing her gun at his head.

Dragging his fingers from between her legs, he grazed them along her smooth stomach, a safe zone amid all that skin. Then with disappointment bitter in his mouth, he motioned her to roll over so he could pull the comforter out from under her.

She complied without argument, another reminder that she wasn't in her right mind, and burrowed her face in the pillow. Her red hair waved around her face like a vision from one of his fantasies and he covered her, feeling a sense of loss wildly out of balance with anything he'd ever known before.

"Another question, Harley, and then I'll leave you alone." When she nodded, he continued. "What upset you tonight?"

"What makes you think I'm upset?" Her eyes shuttered closed.

"You let me drive you home. If you hadn't been upset, you'd have drop-kicked me and told me to take a hike."

She gave a sleepy laugh. "I don't like you."

"I know. I don't like you, either." He paused. "Well?"

"Bad news. Now go away, Gerard." She gave an exasperated sigh. "And you were...*decent*."

He wondered if she realized just how decent he'd really been. Gazing down at her sleepy expression, he figured probably not, so he accepted her thanks and retreated from the bed. "Sweet dreams, Harley."

But Mac didn't go away. Walking from room to room, he searched for clues to help him understand this woman. He wondered what sort of bad news would drive her to drink.

He didn't have a clue. Companion problems? Ill health? Financial disaster? Death in the family? Now that he thought about it, he didn't recall ever hearing she had a family. Amazing how two people could work so closely together, butting heads at every turn… He'd have to find out a lot more about Harley's life if he intended to slip past her defenses.

And he did. Tonight had only fueled his resolve.

Flipping on a table lamp in the living room, he took in an elaborate computer system and a low-slung leather couch. Floor-to-ceiling windows overlooked an arbor that appeared to back up to the wall of the property. There was expensive music equipment housed in a unit on one wall, but no television.

Given the obvious age of the architecture, Mac suspected the walls had been recently refinished to their pristine condition and the wood beam floor had been brought back and polished to a gleaming luster.

The kitchen appeared to be a work in progress, with partially bald walls half stripped of dated wallpaper. And something about the way a wallpaper scraper and trowel sat side by side in the drainboard with coffee mugs and water glasses made him suspect Harley had been doing the work herself.

Another surprise—he wouldn't have pegged gun-toting, black-belt, chopper-riding Harley for the home-improvement type. Which went to show how much Mac needed to find out about her before he stood any chance of convincing her to let their attraction make a difference.

While checking out Harley's desk, Mac felt the first flutter against his cheek. He swatted away the offending critter and, as it was Louisiana in September, just assumed he'd left the door open too long when he'd carried her inside.

It wasn't until the third bug dive-bombed at him that he took a closer look. Grabbing the lamp from an end table, he noticed a spray of spider veins along the seam of one of her nicely refinished walls.

He hoped that whatever bad news she'd received today

hadn't pushed her too close to the edge, because she was facing even more if she hadn't already figured out that she had termites.

Making his way back into her bedroom, Mac sat down and considered his best course of action while he watched her sleep.

A headstrong woman with household pests. Well, he'd wanted a challenge.

4

HARLEY'S FIRST HINT that something was wrong came with the feeling someone had unloaded an assault rifle inside her head.

Her second came when the floorboard by her bed creaked.

She zoomed to awake in a second, but didn't open her eyes. Instead, she flexed her fingers under her pillow, touched the butt of the gun she kept there for emergencies. With a barely perceptible curl of her fingertips, she drew it into her hand. A perfect fit. She thumbed off the safety.

Her heart didn't pound with fear. Her pulse didn't rush on an adrenaline wave. Harley just felt...*quiet*. As if all distractions stopped to let her focus on the matter at hand.

She could hear the fine whoosh of breathing—a man's, she thought—could feel the air beside her bed stir as he leaned close.

Her muscles flexed in readiness, and in one blast of motion, she aimed the gun exactly where she heard the breathing, opened her eyes to find herself staring at...

"Anthony!"

He didn't look happy to be staring down the barrel of a gun. Arching a tawny brow, he used a scuffed finger to shift the muzzle away from his face. "Trigger-happy this morning, aren't we, princess? Must have been a rough night."

Her heart gave one hard throb and resumed beating. She

lowered the gun, flipped the safety back on and returned it under her pillow. "What are you doing here?"

"I heard you had to be carried out of Harrah's."

The fuzzy memory of Mac Gerard vied for attention in her pounding head, and she rolled onto her back and groaned when her head swam sickeningly. She closed her eyes. "Who narced on me?"

"The Gooch. He said he saw you playing faro and drinking. I had to come find out for myself."

"You came to check on the chopper."

"No, princess. I was worried."

"About your bike."

"About you." The mattress sank as he sat on the edge of the bed and she braced herself against the motion. "Look, I brought caffeine."

"Venti?" She wasn't offering reassurances or even sitting up for anything less.

"With five shots of leaded."

"The chopper is fine."

"I know. I checked the garage before I came in."

She exhaled a sound that made Anthony laugh. So much for being the number-one concern in this man's mind.

"Come on, princess. Sit up and drink. You'll feel better."

He gave her a shoulder to hang on to while she eased herself up and he stuffed pillows behind her to keep her upright. Then he handed her the cup.

Anthony was right, one sip of high-test brew slowed the rapid-fire pounding in her head. She sighed appreciatively.

"Went that bad with the exterminator yesterday?" he asked.

"The Gooch tell you that, too?"

"He didn't need to. This is the third time I've seen you

drink in twenty-two years. I don't need a P.I. license to know what that means.''

''Ten-thousand dollars worth of bad.''

The amusement fade from his face. ''Ouch.''

Ouch, indeed. Where the hell was she coming up with that kind of money? She'd had an idea last night and had taken her paycheck to Harrah's in a desperate attempt to change her fortune. The drinking hadn't started until she'd realized that Lady Luck had moved her to the *bad* luck list.

Now she was going to be behind on her mortgage, too.

She simply couldn't think about this right now or her head would explode. Closing her eyes, Harley leaned her head back against the pillows and staved off a renewed burst of pounding.

She felt Anthony's mouth brush against her forehead, a gesture of reassurance she appreciated, even if she didn't feel reassured. ''Don't worry. Something will break.''

Most likely *she'd* break before her financial troubles did, but she couldn't even manage sarcasm right now.

''Ah-hem.''

The deep-throated sound of a man wanting attention jarred the moment and she spun toward the sound to find…Gerard standing in her bathroom doorway.

Wrapped in a towel?

''Great bike,'' he said to Anthony in a voice as calm as a breeze off Lake Ponchartrain. ''You got a brother named Dominic with the police department?''

Obviously he'd decided not to leave last night. Harley supposed she shouldn't be surprised that he'd make himself at home without an invitation. Arrogant man. She also shouldn't be surprised that he'd pegged Anthony as Dominic DiLeo's brother. The man was a former assistant district attorney who would naturally be acquainted with the New Orleans Police Department where Dominic was a lieutenant. Given the strong family resemblance between all the DiLeo boys…

Swallowing hard, Harley dragged her gaze from the sight of all that bare tanned skin, the definition of a muscular chest, the rippled stomach and narrow waist, the toned legs arrowing down from beneath the hem of the towel.

Her hand shook, and Anthony must have noticed because he plucked the cup away and set it on the bedside table.

"Yeah, I do. Is this the knight in shining armor, princess?" He didn't wait for her reply, just got to his feet, his expression suddenly closed.

She knew he was gauging the situation and wondering what she'd done while under the influence last night. And whether or not he'd need to kick some ass this morning.

Harley hadn't done *too* much—thank goodness!—but she'd never appreciated how small her bedroom was until seeing two big men square off in the middle of it. Anthony was about an inch shy of Gerard, which put her co-worker at an easy six-two. He was as dark as Anthony was light, his near nakedness contrasting sharply with Anthony's fully dressed self. Gerard was attractive in a polished, sculpted sort of way, while Anthony was more rugged, earthy. That was where the differences ended—they were both virile men radiating testosterone.

To Gerard's credit though, he looked completely unfazed to be caught standing in a towel, facing what might have been an angry boyfriend or a protective older brother.

"Who are you?" Anthony asked.

"Mac Gerard."

Anthony knew that name. "So you're the co-worker from hell."

He made a dramatic show of dropping his gaze to Gerard's towel. He didn't extend his hand in greeting or introduce himself. He didn't need to. His work shirt had a name badge that read *Anthony* on the front with his company logo on the back.

"Do I thank this guy for getting you and the chopper home, princess, or do I start swinging?"

"Say thanks."

Anthony inclined his head and the tension dissolved, just like that. But the standoff wasn't quite over. Anthony waited for Gerard to back down and disappear into the bathroom.

Gerard didn't. He folded those strong arms across his chest, leaned casually against the doorjamb and said, "Don't let me disturb you."

Harley reached for the coffee, needing another sip to fortify her for what she sensed was coming next.

The Anthony DiLeo show.

True, they were in an off-again phase of their relationship and true, they'd dated other people through the years. But they didn't double-date. They didn't even bring dates to the DiLeo family home so they couldn't chance running into each other. Anthony didn't like any reminders that she wasn't sitting around waiting for him to come back to her. He was so Italian that way.

Unfortunately, Gerard had just reminded him.

Heading toward her, Anthony took the cup from her hand and helped himself—even though he didn't like what she drank. Black coffee, fine. Add five shots of espresso and you could walk on it. He tossed back a swallow as if he drank the stuff every day.

"Did you pick up my suit from the cleaners, princess? I've got an appointment at the bank at nine o'clock."

"The closet."

He returned the cup and stalked across the room to root through her clothing. Harley could feel Gerard's gaze on her but couldn't bring herself to return it. Not because she wouldn't have enjoyed seeing his reaction to what must look like a good reason why not to have a fling, but because she couldn't withstand another shot of Mr. Tanned, Muscular and Nearly Naked.

The coffee wasn't *that* strong.

Anthony found his suit and reemerged. "Can I leave you alone with this guy?"

He wasn't really worried about her safety or else he wouldn't have asked. But he liked to mark his territory to make it clear he'd only stepped out for a while.

"Harley will be fine," Gerard said before she could answer. "She can give me a ride back to my car."

"My pleasure," she said dryly.

Anthony nodded, kissed her on the head, flipped the dry-cleaning bag over his shoulder and didn't acknowledge Gerard as he walked out the door.

"Did you find everything you needed?" she asked Gerard, to bridge through her sudden awareness that they were alone.

He nodded. "Feeling better this morning?"

"Coffee's doing wonders."

He shoved his fingers through his damp hair, making his biceps pop enough to catch her attention. Forcing her attention upward, she met those penetrating eyes and more fuzz cleared from around her brain. Suddenly she remembered being cradled against his strong chest, the way his tight butt had felt between her thighs with the chopper growling beneath them. The way his touch had set her body on fire.

"I'll get dressed and, whenever you're ready, we can go," he said pleasantly. "Sound good?"

She nodded, and he disappeared into her bathroom in a flash of tanned motion. He didn't ask who Anthony was, didn't ask about their relationship. For a man who'd been gunning to get her into bed, he didn't seem interested in her personal life.

Unless meeting Anthony had convinced him to give up his stupid idea of a fling. Or maybe he was just like Anthony—willing to share so long as he got her undivided attention when his turn came around.

The thought alone made her scowl, and she couldn't decide why she felt so angry—at Anthony *and* Gerard.

Must be the hangover, because she certainly didn't care what Gerard wanted. But Anthony...well, okay, maybe she was a bit disappointed, but at least she knew what to expect from him.

ANTHONY DILEO AUTOMOTIVE wasn't a low-end auto-repair concern run out of the man's garage. This business rivaled the size of a service department at any car dealership and fitted a few puzzle pieces into place about Anthony DiLeo.

Ambitious. Business savvy. A hands-on owner, if Mac had read the work shirt right. But this character assessment didn't answer the all-important question—who was this guy to Harley?

Something about their relationship struck him wrong. If they'd been dating, would Anthony have left another man standing half-naked in her bedroom? Mac didn't think so, but he didn't have the whole picture—about Harley or her relationship with the auto mechanic. Yet.

Mac needed to clear his head so he could concentrate on his grandfather's case. In order to do that he needed to deal with the woman who was distracting him. He'd spent the night mulling both the problems and had formulated a rough idea. He just needed to ask a few questions before he implemented his plan.

He was at Anthony DiLeo Automotive for those answers.

Entering through the main office's glass door, Mac took in the spacious waiting area as he made his way to the desk. The woman behind it sat with a telephone earpiece protruding from her right ear. The epitome of efficiency, this woman juggled a call, credit-card approval and a handheld radio that blared out a question about the whereabouts of someone Mac could only assume was a mechanic.

"I want to see Anthony," he said.

She glanced up with a pleasant smile. "What do you want to see him about?"

"Personal."

She pressed a button on a switchboard. "Anthony, there's a…" She glanced at him expectantly.

"Mac Gerard."

"…Mac Gerard here to see you about something personal."

He knew he'd been granted a meeting when the woman stood, leaned over the counter and pointed down a hall leading out of the reception area. "Straight down there, second door on the right. If you get to the garage you've gone too far."

Anthony DiLeo's office was no less upscale than his customer-waiting area, with an elaborate computer set up and streamlined office furniture that would have looked equally at home in a bank. Clearly the man was doing his bit to dispel the grease-monkey image associated with his industry. He sat at a desk scattered with stacks of what looked like invoices.

"Thanks for agreeing to see me," Mac said.

"Curiosity. So what's your deal, Gerard? Should I be surprised you showed up in my office today?"

On the drive over, Mac had considered how best to play this interview. He'd been leaning toward the up-front approach and decided to go with it. "I want to know about your relationship with Harley."

"What's it to you? Last I heard she was looking to run every time she saw your face."

Mac cocked a hip against a chair and laughed. "She's still looking to run. I've decided to chase her."

"Really?"

He nodded.

"If you're so interested in the status of her personal relationships, why don't you ask her?"

"Because I want a straight answer."

"You don't think she'll give you one?"

Mac shook his head. "She'll tell me you've been married since you were eleven if she thinks it will make me back off."

"What's the problem then. Can't you take the hint?"

"Taking no for an answer isn't one of my best qualities."

"Hate to burst your bubble, man, but you're not playing with someone you can push around. You're playing with Harley and she likes to do the pushing."

"I got that part already. What I don't have a handle on is who you are to her."

"And you think I'll answer you straight?"

Mac shrugged. "Not really. I had a choice between the devil I know and the devil I don't. Figured my chances were better with the devil I don't. I got the impression this morning that you didn't want me stepping into your turf."

"You don't pull any punches." Anthony shook his head. "The princess told me all about you. I thought she was exaggerating. But you really are that big of an asshole." Leaning back in his chair, he hooked his hands behind his head and eyed Mac with open amusement. "She doesn't like you, man. What makes you think you stand a chance in hell with her?''

''She might not like me, but she's attracted to me. That's why she's running.''

That stopped Anthony cold, and Mac guessed he hadn't expected quite so much honesty. He folded his arms across his chest and waited. The ball was in Anthony's court now and how he played it would reveal a lot about who Mac was dealing with. And he found it particularly interesting that the man still hadn't confirmed that he and Harley were an item.

Suddenly Anthony shot his chair back from the desk and stood. ''All right, you want straight. You got it.''

Mac watched as he covered the distance to a private entrance and pushed open the door. ''Take a look out here.''

Curious, Mac went to the entrance of the auto-repair shop that opened to a side lot filled with all sorts of haphazardly parked vehicles. He immediately noticed Harley's car.

''Harley's having car trouble?''

Anthony nodded. ''Transmission's gone. I'll have it back up for her next week.''

Well, that explained why she'd been driving the chopper. ''What do you want to show me?''

''See that bird?'' Anthony pointed to a cherry-red Firebird with a white hard top and gleaming side pipes parked close to the property's security fence.

He nodded. ''I see it. It's as well kept as your bike.''

Anthony nodded, acknowledging the compliment but never taking his eyes from the car. ''I took her virginity in the back seat when she was seventeen.''

Mac wasn't sure what got him more—Anthony's satisfied expression or the thought of Harley naked in the back seat of that car. One thing was sure—he'd never wanted to punch anyone more in his life. His hand burned with an urge so strong, he found himself actually clenching his fists.

He bit back the impulse to make some remark about back seats opposed to beds. "Seventeen was a long time ago. That doesn't tell me if you're still together."

Anthony shifted his gaze back and Mac recognized the annoyance there. "We've been on and off for the last *ten years*. We *always* get back together."

Now it was Mac's turn to smile. No matter how long Anthony and Harley had dated, broken up and gotten back together, they weren't together now.

Which meant he had a shot if he acted fast, because that look on Anthony's face said *always* was about to happen again.

5

HARLEY HAD HELD UP fairly well through the day, considering the combined effects of a late night and uncustomary alcohol consumption. The acetaminophen was just wearing off by the time Josh called them into his office late in the afternoon to discuss Stuart's case.

She'd been giving the thefts a good deal of attention throughout the day and had conducted some preliminary research on the company. She wished she'd chosen any other night to tie one on—although she supposed two drinks technically couldn't be considered tying one on, but as she *never* drank... Turned out she'd needed all her faculties today because greed kept making her think about ways to solve the Nice and Neat thefts and recover the stolen goods.

Generous cash rewards would work right now.

Making her way into Josh's office, she half sat on the desk with her back to Gerard so she didn't have to look at him. As much as she hated to admit it, she owed him one. The last thing she'd needed was to have driven the chopper after she'd been drinking. Gerard had saved her from making a stupid move. And she couldn't honestly say that she'd have stopped him if he'd kept on touching her last night, either....

This week kept getting better and better.

"All right, team, let's get it on the table." Josh leaned back in his chair. "We've got a decision to make."

"Did you get through to Miss Q?" Gerard asked.

Josh nodded. "And several of the other victims. It's basically what your grandfather presented—the old folks have banded together to solve a mystery and protect one of their own."

"Can we expect them all to cooperate?" Working for so many clients on one case could be tricky.

"If I'm reading Miss Q right, and I am, we can expect them to grab binoculars and conduct surveillance." Josh rolled his eyes and Harley swallowed back a laugh at the image of these senior citizens staking out Garden District mansions.

Must be the hangover. She wasn't usually punchy.

"As you said yesterday, Harley," Josh began, "I don't see another way to do this except inside surveillance. Thoughts?"

"The obvious way would be to penetrate Nice and Neat as employees," she tossed out. "I researched the employment history and it seems that no matter how upscale, a cleaning service is a cleaning service, which means staff turnover."

Josh didn't look convinced. "I see you making a convincing cleaning person, but Mac? How many men do they employ?"

"None that clean houses, I'm afraid, but I do like the idea of him scrubbing toilets."

Gerard arched a brow in one of those superior looks that never failed to irritate her. He'd touched her last night, damn it, and she'd let him.

"Scrubbing toilets isn't the problem—timing is," he said. "Nice and Neat doesn't send staff members into the Garden District until they've been with the company for a probationary period. It'll take too long to establish our cover and infiltrate the theft ring. The thieves could clean house by the time we get close. No pun.''

Josh agreed. ''The chances of recovering any stolen items lessens each day. If we decide to take this case, we can put word out on the street and maybe a reward for information, but given what these thieves are stealing, they can be fencing the goods anywhere. It doesn't look good and time is a key issue.''

Gerard nodded. ''The best way to get in is to set ourselves up as a decoy. I'm willing to bet the thieves can be convinced to hit us a lot faster than they can be convinced to trust us.''

Harley watched Gerard, pleased that he'd started using his head. One step closer to being capable of working his cases without her. A good thing, no matter how she came at it.

''You've got an idea?'' Josh asked Gerard.

''We need to set up a household in the Garden District,'' he said. ''We fill it with high-ticket goodies and then hire Nice and Neat. We'll wire the place and see what happens.''

''What's our cover?'' she asked.

''Newlyweds. We'll be the new Mr. and Mrs. Gerard.''

Josh laughed. ''Harley undercover as a bride? I have less trouble seeing you scrubbing toilets.''

She scowled, which made Josh laugh harder.

''I see real possibilities here,'' he said, turning to Gerard. ''If I can get past the fact that you two will be undercover as a couple. Have you considered this means being together twenty-four/seven? You'll have to sleep sometime, Mac. Do you trust her not to shoot you when you close your eyes?''

Now it was Gerard's turn to laugh. ''Got a lock on it.''

''Oh you do, do you?'' she asked dryly.

He nodded. "I know where you keep your gun."

And since she didn't want him *accidentally* mentioning the one she slept with under her pillow, which would invite embarrassing questions about when he'd been in her bedroom, she implemented diversionary tactics.

"To make decent targets," she said, "we'll need visibility or else this could take as long as infiltrating the theft ring."

Gerard had the grace to concede her point. "We'll have to draw attention to ourselves."

"How do you plan to do that?"

"No offense, Harley, but you'll do the trick nicely. You don't swing in the same circles as the Nice and Neat clientele."

Which was a polite way of saying she wasn't his pedigree.

Normally Harley would have laughed at such a distinction. If pedigree produced idiots like this one, she'd count her blessings, thank you. But right now, sitting next to both these men in their custom-made suits that probably cost enough to pay her exterminator, she just felt exposed and raw.

Must be the hangover. She wasn't usually so touchy.

She knew exactly what the sneaky bastard was up to. He was manipulating her into a fling. Unfortunately, she couldn't call him on it in front of Josh.

"Stop dancing around and get to the punch line." She needed three more geltabs, fast—*before* her head exploded.

"Our social differences will attract attention and give us mobility," Gerard explained. "We'll be able to move between the victims' world and the thieves' world. We can set ourselves up as a target and investigate without risking our cover."

Oh, this was getting better and better. Not only did she have to live with his references to her drinking beer from a bottle, but she'd been demoted from a licensed P.I. with a degree in criminology to a thief while she was *still* paying off loans.

"Gerard, you're acting like you know something about my life and you don't."

"I do," he surprised her by saying. "While you spent your day researching Nice and Neat's employee records, I spent my day researching you." He flashed a dimpled grin that made her heart leap into overdrive. *Damn.*

Josh hooked his hands behind his head, leaned back in his chair and settled in to enjoy the show.

"Follow me on this, Harley," Gerard said. "I'll buy us a place to live. It so happens that half of the house in front of yours is up for sale. It was split into a duplex years ago, but given the square footage, it'll work."

Harley had several questions crowding her head at that particular moment, but only one made it past her lips. "You'll *buy* us a place to live?"

"I'll be the husband. That's my job."

When she continued to stare, he exhaled heavily and said, "I'll sell it after we dissolve the marriage. I'll make out on the deal, so think of it as an investment."

Harley wasn't thinking anything at the moment except that she'd grossly underestimated this man's determination—to help his grandfather and to get into her bed. "Dissolve what marriage? You're not suggesting we make this legal, are you?"

Gerard nodded.

Josh barely managed to swallow back another laugh.

"Don't be ridiculous." She'd wanted to say stupid but

managed self-control in front of the boss. "Since when do we actually have to do the deed to live the cover?"

"Since we're private investigators," Gerard said matter-of-factly. "Without a marriage license on record, I won't be able to make purchases in both our names. It'll be too obvious we're setting ourselves up as decoys."

She couldn't exactly argue that point now, could she? *Double damn.* "I thought you were a lawyer. Can't you use your connections to slip a fake license into the system?"

"Aside from the fact that what you're suggesting is illegal, I'm not willing to risk blowing our cover. If anyone finds out the marriage isn't legal, we'll have wasted a lot of time." He frowned. "I'll have my attorney draw up documents to protect us both, if that's what you're worried about."

That wasn't what she was worried about. He had a lot more at stake financially than she ever would, and the fact that he sounded so calm and reasonable irked her.

"You're asking me to play Cinderella and I don't want to." She didn't give him a chance to comment, just glared at Josh. "And where are you right now? You haven't said one word."

"I've got two—good job." He shifted his gaze to Gerard. "You take point on this case, *if* you can convince Harley to play your bride."

Well, she hadn't been expecting *that*. She reminded herself that if Josh thought Gerard was ready to handle his own case, she was another step closer to losing him as a trainee. She couldn't quite get past her surprise. Running an operation meant he'd be giving orders and she'd be following them.

Gerard inclined his head in silent acknowledgment of Josh's praise. "I can't emphasize how important it is to recover my grandmother's wedding set. And I do appreciate that this is above and beyond the call of duty, Harley, so in addition to putting on this show, I'll waive my share of the professional fee and any rewards. After our expenses are covered and Josh gets his cut, you keep what's left."

Harley blinked, had to swallow to find her voice. "You're talking about a chunk of change."

"I'm talking about a big favor."

He didn't have to say she owed him, the implication was there. If that wasn't enough—and it wasn't because she hadn't asked for his help last night—he was talking about enough money to pay off Anthony, catch up on her lagging mortgage and still have change to put toward the exterminator.

Damn.

Harley couldn't keep up the pretense of standing still. Pushing away from the desk, she headed toward the window. Josh was curiously silent and she didn't trust herself not to say something that might annoy him. She couldn't even look at Gerard. The bastard had backed her into a neat corner.

Could he possibly know how neat?

Parting the vertical blinds, she stared through the window. No one knew the gory details of her finances except Anthony. He would never talk. Especially after the way he'd acted this morning.

No, Gerard was most likely arrogant enough to think she was so beneath him that she'd do anything for a price.

And the kicker…she was. As much as she loathed facing the ugly truth, she was Cinderella, and the fairy godmother had waved her magic wand and given her a chance to change her luck.

When she finally turned back around, Harley found both men watching her expectantly. "So what? You're not going to get down on your knee and propose?"

HARLEY HONESTLY HADN'T thought about getting married in recent memory. She'd bought her home knowing it wasn't family sized and had planned to live in it for a long time. But when she'd been very young and much more fanciful than she'd grown up to be, Harley had imagined a big Italian wedding with Anthony as the groom.

Anthony wasn't the groom today. In fact, she could barely bring herself to look at the man who was.

Mac Gerard.

She had to fight the urge to back away from Judge Bancroft's desk and run from the courthouse. If she did she'd be taking Miss Q with her, as that one had a death grip on her arm.

At first she'd been surprised when Stuart and Miss Q had arrived to stand as witness for the nuptials, but like Gerard had said...they were the victims. And to make matters worse, Stuart had arranged the service to be performed by Judge Bancroft. Just her luck the judge remembered her. Although Harley supposed that shouldn't come as a surprise, given how often she'd been in the man's chambers once upon a time.

"Harley Price," he'd greeted her when they'd walked through the door. "It's been a long time. Look how lovely you've grown to be. And successful, too, from what I hear."

"Been keeping tabs on me, have you?" she'd asked.

The judge had smiled, looking pretty much the same as he had the last time she'd seen him—the day he'd cut her loose from the state's child welfare system ten years ago.

His bristly gray hair still stood out like steel wool on his head; his grizzly brows still needed a serious trim. Given his grin, he still found her amusing—a fact that had saved her on more than one occasion. "Of course I keep tabs on you, Harley. And I'm sure you're still involved with the DiLeos. How are they faring nowadays?"

"Everyone's doing well, thank you."

Judge Bancroft wasn't the only one amused. Stuart and Miss Q had laughed, finding humor in a place Gerard had apparently missed, if his strained expression was any indication. He looked as if he wanted to know if she had a criminal record but couldn't come up with a polite way to ask.

Of course she didn't volunteer any information, just allowed herself to be dragged into a ceremony that seemed to be amusing everyone but the bride and groom.

Money, money, money, money, money, she chanted silently to convince herself she could handle this humiliation to catch up on her mortgage, fix her vehicle and free her home from bugs.

Unfortunately, while she could handle running into Judge Bancroft, she couldn't seem to bring herself to look at her groom. Even more unfortunately, Harley could feel him towering above her, his muscular body pressed close, as though he, too, hovered to make sure he could catch her if she bolted.

She jumped when he reached for her hand, his long fingers slipping possessively around hers, all warm and strong. He placed a wedding band on her finger.

Money, money, money, money, money.

She tried not to glance down at the ring, couldn't help herself. It was a simple gold band, tasteful. She wondered if he'd picked it himself or if he'd had Jewelers "R" Us deliver the daily special.

She wondered why the thought even crossed her mind.

"I don't have a ring for you." She unintentionally interrupted the judge, who lifted those bristly brows before looking at Stuart as if to ask, "What did you get me into?"

He probably thought she *had* to get married. At least then she'd have had a solid reason for becoming Gerard's wife. The fact that she was doing her job simply wasn't making her feel better. Gerard might feel obligated to his grandfather, but she didn't. She'd never have accepted this case if not for being so pitifully desperate for money.

Her pride stung because she'd had no choice but to walk right into Gerard's line of fire, knowing he wanted to wear down her defenses to get her in bed. Her pride stung even more because she couldn't control her damn attraction to him. She didn't even trust herself in close quarters with the man.

Reaching into his pocket, he withdrew another band, obviously the mate to her own and said, "You have a ring."

She jammed it on his finger. "With this ring, I thee wed."

"Then with the power invested in me by the state of Louisiana, I pronounce you husband and wife." The judge shot them a wry look. "You don't have to kiss to make this marriage official. Just sign the papers."

"Where's the pen?" Kissing Gerard in front of Judge Bancroft and the old folks would push her right over the edge.

Especially when she glanced up to find herself the target of a video camera. She'd forgotten the secretary who stood in the back of the room, taping the ceremony at Stuart's request.

She sealed the deal with brisk pen strokes and crossed the room before her new husband caught her to do something *husbandly,* like put his arm around her or whatever husbands did when thanking the judge who'd officiated their wedding.

Stuart and Miss Q cornered her in the middle of the room, though, and blocked off her escape.

"Leave it to Mackenzie to bring home a bride as pretty as his grandmother was," Stuart said.

Miss Q laughed. "She'll certainly liven things up around your place, don't you think, Stuart?"

Harley found herself the recipient of good wishes, hugs and kisses in a ritual she couldn't quite figure out why these people bothered. They were paying seriously good money for her and Gerard to conduct this ruse. Why were they acting as if she was some welcome new addition to the family?

One glimpse of the secretary videotaping the ceremony answered that question. *Documentation.*

Gerard suddenly appeared and, before Harley could make her getaway, he slipped his hand around her. She instinctively pulled away, but he locked his fingers inside the strap that secured her shoulder holster and trapped her with his body.

She stopped resisting, glanced at the video camera instead, leaned into her new husband's warm chest and forced the giddiest smile she could muster.

There, documented.

6

MR. AND MRS. MACKENZIE Gerard's first official performance as husband and wife wasn't off to the greatest of
starts and it technically hadn't even started yet. Mac stood
in front of Harley's closet, searching for an outfit to meet
his family in.

Leather, leather and more leather.

They needed to be across town at the mayor's ribbon-
cutting ceremony for a new women's shelter, a project his
sister had spearheaded. He'd intended to wear a tux.
Looked like he might have to downgrade to a suit, which
meant traveling across town to his place, which meant they
were going to be late. They'd temporarily set up shop at
Harley's and, until he closed on their new house, he'd be
living out of a garment bag.

"Help me out here, Harley. Don't you own anything that
won't make you look like a gang member?"

She shrugged, her expression so closed he couldn't tell
if he'd offended her. "What did you expect? I don't swing
in your circles, remember?"

Okay, so he had offended her, but now wasn't the time
to figure out how to make amends. A simple apology
wouldn't do the trick. That much he knew.

Then the sight of something *not* black caught his eye.
Digging his way to the back, he exhaled in relief when he
found the dress she'd worn to the wedding. "Wear this."

She eyed the gown and her mouth puckered in a kissable moue. "I can't wear a holster."

"You can't be armed at this function."

"I'm licensed to conceal."

"Not around the mayor you're not. Trust me. You'll wind up spending the night explaining yourself to the security people."

She frowned harder but didn't argue. Apparently she was willing to take him at his word. A miracle.

Plucking the hanger from his hand, she headed for her bathroom. The door shut. The lock clicked. Mac was left to dress alone while stemming his disappointment for a missed opportunity to see some skin.

He dressed, mulling the best way to present Harley to his family. Their marriage would come as a shock—something of an understatement, given what they'd heard about her. Mac hadn't said much, but he hadn't hid they weren't getting along.

The success of this ruse depended on people accepting their marriage and he'd been counting on his family to start the ball rolling, which meant a plausible reason for the change of heart.

Attraction was the only plausible reason.

A fact that hit him hard when Harley emerged from the bathroom a short while later. His blood temperature soared from comfortable to slow burn in the time it took him to glance from her head to her toes.

She looked softer around the edges. She'd pulled her hair back in a sweep that left wispy pieces curling around her face, drawing his attention to her neck and making him want to press kisses there.

His head filled with images of peeling away her dress, of spreading out on the bed with her naked body wrapped around him, her wild hair blocking out everything but the two of them, their rapid breaths and the promise of sex.

Suddenly the seam of his trousers bit into his crotch uncomfortably, through no fault of his tailor. No, the fault was all Harley's, with her deep blue eyes and too kissable lips.

In a quick move, he covered the distance between them.

She pulled away, and the only thing that saved him was the dress. Not only was she unarmed, but the narrow skirt precluded her from using her best defense moves.

Taking total advantage of the moment, Mac caught her before she got away and tucked her against him. He ran a fingertip along the curve of her neck, trailed up to her ear, brushing aside soft wisps of hair and tracing the shell of her ear.

She shivered, one of those full-bodied numbers that brushed her against him. "Gerard."

"Yes, my beautiful bride."

"Knock it off."

His crotch gave a rebellious throb, but he let her go, deciding not to push her—not when he was so pleased with her response to him. Her chest rose and fell on rapid breaths and, though she protested, she'd reacted in a big way. He knew it. She knew he knew it because she didn't make one smart remark all the way across town.

"I'll handle my family," he said as he maneuvered into the line in front of the women's shelter to await a valet. "You smile and agree with whatever I say."

"You don't want much, do you?" she said, and while she might have been quiet on the drive over, she was back in form now. "I never agree with anything you say."

"Until tonight. If we can get my family to buy our marriage then we'll be home free with the rest of New Orleans."

"Doesn't it bother you that you'll be lying to them?"

"I'd prefer to take them into my confidence, but I won't risk our cover. We need their varied reactions to give us credibility with the rest of my friends and acquaintances."

She conceded his point with a shrug. "Won't they be angry?"

"Once we wrap up the case and recover my grandfather's things, I'll explain and apologize. They won't be happy, but they'll understand why I handled the situation this way."

There was another reason Mac wouldn't take his family into his confidence, a reason he wouldn't share with Harley. Most of his family already questioned his sanity because of his recent lifestyle changes and he didn't want to start the whole debate again. Marriage was a done deal. The family would have no choice but to accept that Harley was now a part of their lives. No one need know the situation was only temporary. Not yet, anyway.

After arriving at the valet station, Mac escorted Harley down the runway toward the shelter, greeting acquaintances in the crowd and members of the press.

The ribbon-cutting ceremony provided the perfect place to present his marriage. A public place made them visible and limited his family's reactions. That limitation turned out to be a good thing.

Just as his sister climbed the front steps with the mayor, Mac caught up with them. He presented his mom, dad, brother and sister-in-law, and both his great-aunts, who'd accompanied his grandfather. "This is Harley," he said, a casual introduction because there wasn't time for anything else.

"You work with Mac, don't you?" his mom asked.

"Yes, I do," Harley said politely.

But her reputation had preceded her and everyone stared

as if expecting a nine-millimeter to sprout from her forehead.

"Your grandfather said you had a surprise for us, Mac," his dad said. "Is Harley our surprise?"

"She is indeed." He'd explain the finer points later.

"I don't think Harley joining us tonight is our only surprise." His aunt Camille—great-aunt Camille technically, as she was his grandfather's younger sister—gifted them with her airiest smile and proved the timetable wasn't to be his. "She and Mac are wearing matching wedding bands."

"Can't get anything past you, Aunt Camille." Mac laughed and reached for Harley's hand to reveal their rings for inspection. Now was as good a time as any, he supposed. "Harley and I decided to stop fighting the way we feel for each other."

A silence that should have been impossible given the size of the crowd fell heavily, or maybe Mac just felt it because all eyes were riveted on him for an explanation.

His father recovered first. "This is a surprise. When?"

"This afternoon. Grandfather stood up for me."

"I see." He shifted a suspicious look between Mac and his grandfather, obviously working hard to reserve judgment.

His mom followed suit. Fixing on her most gracious smile, she took Harley's hands. "Welcome to the family. I look forward to hearing all the details."

Stuart elbowed Harley and winked. "I knew they'd love you."

That was an exaggeration, but Harley played along and he inhaled his first decent breath—a breath that only lasted until Aunt Frances—another great-aunt as she was his grandfather's older sister—scowled. "Are you pregnant, young lady?"

"Of course she isn't," Mac said.

"What do you mean, *of course*, Mackenzie. I don't know this girl from Eve. How am I supposed to know whether she'd get pregnant before marrying you."

There was no rebutting that argument and he braced himself when she turned that imperious gaze onto Harley. "Well, young lady, what do you have to say for yourself?"

"Aunt Frances, we'll explain everything later." He tucked Harley more closely against him.

But Harley wasn't one to let him run interference. She lifted her chin proudly. "I'm not the kind of girl who gets pregnant before the wedding, ma'am. I'm a gold digger. I married Mac for his money."

Another silence fell, even more complete than the last. Mac marveled at the way she used sarcasm more skillfully than a gun. The effect on his family was complete.

Aunt Camille burst into laughter. His parents, brother and sister-in-law decided to go along for the ride and smiled, although Mac didn't think they were amused. His grandfather shot her another conspiratorial wink, and the tension finally drained away, leaving Aunt Frances watching them all as if they'd gone crazy.

"Courtney's going to speak." Mac drew their attention to the ceremony that was about to begin and steered Harley around to watch, relieved to be past the initial interview.

"Relax," he whispered into her ear. "It's over."

She lifted her face to his and he watched, fascinated as relief flashed in her beautiful face, a flicker that shone for a split second before being replaced by a dry smile.

"That went *very* well," she said.

Mac heard the sarcasm, but suddenly recognized it as so much more than a derisive take on the world.

A defense, that's what it was. Harley used sarcasm the way she used her shields. She might take on the world with a scowl and a gun, but confronting his family had unsettled her. He felt it in his gut, even though it seemed to contradict everything he knew about her.

"Open your eyes, Gerard, and see all the possibilities," Harley was fond of instructing about his investigative work. *"Try to look past the way things relate to you."*

Mac had thought he'd understood her point, but he'd also considered her advice as much of an insult as it was sound investigative technique.

Harley believed he was nothing more than a self-indulgent bastard who thought of himself before he thought of anything else. Mac had dismissed her opinion offhand, placing the fault with her. She was a too-tough woman who looked for things to criticize him about. But when had he ever considered why Harley came at him from such a tough position?

He hadn't. Not once. Just as he hadn't considered that she'd have to defend her character tonight. He'd only thought about how their lifestyle differences would affect their cover.

But now, as he stood in the crowd, watching his sister pass the ceremonial scissors to the mayor, Mac didn't like that Harley had needed to defend herself against him and his family.

No more than he liked that she'd been right about him.

HARLEY HAD SURVIVED stints undercover among gang members and drug dealers with less emotional wear and tear than she had a night at a ribbon-cutting ceremony with Gerard's family.

Just the memory made her bristle, sending goose bumps down her arms, despite the hot shower spray that had turned her bath into a steam room. She *hated* social functions, hated being out of her element in situations where she didn't know the rules, wasn't sure what to expect.

Leaning back into the water, she rinsed the shampoo from her hair and tried to clear her head of the night's events. With the exception of a few stellar moments, Gerard's family had been decent for having him spring a bride on them. They'd stood graceful and united in the face of a social disaster—and finding out Mac had married her had to qualify as a big one.

Gerard had been surprisingly decent, too, all things considered. After the ribbon-cutting ceremony, they'd moved inside the shelter for a reception where he'd introduced her to New Orleans high society. Or what had felt like a significant portion of it, anyway. He'd led the conversations so she hadn't once wound up staring at strangers not knowing what to say. He'd provided her with flutes of lime-laced mineral water and hadn't made one crack about bottled beer.

Now if he'd only stay on his good behavior.

Blinking water from her eyes, she peered around the side of the shower curtain to check the bathroom, found the room exactly as she'd left it. She'd not only locked the door but pushed the hamper in front of it, in case Gerard got any brilliant ideas about barging in. The hamper would give her a chance to grab her gun, which sat within easy reach on the toilet tank.

He'd made one too many comments about the *wedding night* for her not to take precautions.

The man couldn't really think she'd give into this attraction no matter how much she might want him. However, it usually wasn't about what *she'd* do but what *he* wanted.

Hence the hamper.

Resuming her shower, she scrubbed every inch of her

skin as if she could wash away the lingering remnants of tonight's events to fortify herself for what was still to come. Gerard's lawyer had apparently worked a miracle and moved up the closing on their new house. Gerard had arranged for movers to pack up his place and unload it as soon as they were able to take possession and when she'd commented that he'd gone through an awful lot of effort for their temporary arrangement, he'd just shrugged. "The movers do the work. All I do is write a check."

Must be nice.

By the time Harley had finished showering, dressed for bed and belted her robe tightly around her, she felt ready to take on Gerard again. Grabbing her gun from the back of the toilet, she checked the safety then unlocked the door. But she'd barely pushed the door open before Gerard got the drop on her.

He had her gun out of her hand and her body locked ineffectively against him before she could react. Once he got ahold of her, there was no point in resisting.

Sometimes size did matter.

"All right, Gerard, what do you want?" She'd try to reason with the man, because reasoning was the only tool she had in her arsenal right now.

Gerard didn't want to reason.

Flipping her into his arms as if she weighed no more than her gun, he strode across her room, set her gun on her dresser and dropped onto her bed with her pinned underneath him.

"Gerard," she managed to squeak out. "What are you doing?"

He didn't answer. He didn't have to. The handcuffs he yanked from his pocket answered her question loud and clear.

For one wild instant Harley struggled, not sure what was panicking her more—the feel of his hard body crowding her into the mattress or the realization that if he cuffed her she'd be at his mercy. She maneuvered hard, tried to knock him off.

All she did was make him laugh.

"This is my bed, Gerard. I don't want you in it."

"I'm really sorry about that." He slapped a handcuff around her wrist with a practiced move. "But it's my wedding night. Skin's supposed to factor somewhere."

Click. "Not my skin, damn it."

Again he didn't bother with a reply as he dragged her arms above her head and leaned over her to... She tipped her head back to see what he was doing, realized that he'd fastened a belt around the bed frame so he'd have a place to restrain her. *Her* belt, damn it.

"Do you want the robe on or off?" he asked.

"What?"

He raised up enough to lock his thighs around hers, hard muscles anchoring her beneath him. Threading his feet around her ankles, he held her even more securely before leaning up to peer into her face. His crystalline eyes glinted and she came up hard against the fact that she'd underestimated this man.

"The robe," he repeated. "Do you want it on or off? Once I lock these handcuffs, you won't have a choice."

"Then don't lock the handcuffs."

He flashed her one of those dazzling smiles that always made her feel naked. "With your penchant for firepower, you really didn't think I'd close my eyes without some sort of protection, did you?"

Well, when he put it like that... "Do I need my robe?"

"It won't protect you. But..." He raked his clear gaze over the tangle of wet hair fanned out over her pillows.

"You have my word I won't do anything that you don't ask for. Deal?"

"Argh! You are such an arrogant bastard." She bucked hard to emphasize her point.

"I'll take that to mean you feel safer with it on."

She didn't feel safer with her robe on, but she wasn't going to willingly give up a layer of clothing that gave the illusion of added protection.

But unfortunately Gerard was right—the robe meant nothing. Not when he threaded the handcuffs through the belt one-handed and then brought it home around her free wrist. He had her restrained in her own bed and she hadn't seen it coming.

The weekend from hell had definitely stretched into midweek.

7

NO MATTER HOW HARD Harley willed herself not to look, she couldn't help herself. She would take a guy in a pair of jeans any day, so worn and comfy that they'd frayed at the seams and rode low on his hips. *Mmm-mnm.* Which did *not* explain her reaction to Gerard in his dressy tux as he climbed off her bed in a burst of muscular grace.

She needed to clear her head and calm down in case some opportunity to reason presented itself. The thought of spending the entire night with her arms cuffed above her head made her cringe—she'd be crippled by morning.

He picked up her gun from the dresser. "Jeez, Harley. You had the safety off."

"You've been working with me all these months and haven't figured out I don't pull my gun unless I'm ready to use it?"

His gaze cut across the distance between them and he didn't look so much surprised as he did thoughtful. That look irked her. She wasn't quite sure why. Then again, her irritation might have had more to do with the handcuffs.

"I assume you already took the gun I keep under my pillow," she said, an attempt to assert some control over the situation, lame though it might be. "Obviously, I can't check."

He inclined his head, a regal gesture that made his dark hair gleam in the light of her bed-table lamp. "I'm putting them both in your top drawer. Safety's *on.*"

Her panty drawer. Why not? At least her guns would smell pretty. Or maybe her panties would smell like gun oil. She supposed either would come as a surprise to whoever got close enough to one or the other.

Clearly Gerard thought he should be the one to get close. He'd already shrugged out of his jacket. It crossed her field of vision to land in a careless heap on a chair.

The bow tie followed.

For a man with a good education and blue blood, he sure could be obtuse. A *real* gentleman would have availed himself of the facilities to undress. Not Gerard. He was performing a bloody striptease. As if she hadn't seen enough of him in that towel yesterday.

Not that she'd minded Anthony walking in to find a nearly naked man in her bedroom, but she very much minded facing a whole night in bed with him.

She didn't think for one second he'd do the gentlemanly thing and sleep on the couch. No, he was going for shock value, because it didn't take any reasonably healthy man this long to unfasten his cuff links.

Gerard was *way beyond* reasonably healthy.

This was a performance, plain and simple. He challenged her with each glimpse of those tanned fingers working the buttons at his throat. He pulled away the collar to expose his neck, unfastened the last button and started peeling away a sleeve. Fingers flexed. Shoulders shifted. Biceps bulged, and suddenly a long, tanned arm shot out to start the process all over again.

He wore a white undershirt that had to be silky and soft given the way it clung to the ridges of his chest. And though she'd never imagined an undershirt could be sexy, something about the bright white against his tanned skin made the sight even sexier than if he'd been naked.

A crazy swooping dropped the bottom out of her stom-

ach and Harley swallowed hard to smother a groan. This
was so unfair. She didn't want to want this man. Even if
he wasn't as big an idiot as she'd thought he was, he was
still an idiot—one way too attractive for his own good.

For *her* own good. She should just close her eyes.

And let him know he was getting to her? Harley raked
her gaze over him and gave a haughty sniff as if his striptease wasn't doing a damn thing for her.

Right. Just watching him hike a long leg onto the bed to
take off his sock was a sight. He had feet as tanned and
strong as the rest of him and, even though she'd never been
one to notice feet, she noticed his.

He whipped the undershirt over his head with a burst of
bunching muscles and treated her to a full frontal of defined
pecs and rippled tummy with a line of silky dark fur.

That swooping sensation kick-started an ache inside her.

From a purely analytical angle, Harley could appreciate
how much work his toned physique must take to maintain.
She'd devoted herself to the martial arts, which made working out pleasurable, but Gerard was a club boy, a man who
weight-trained and swam in the upscale privacy of his club.
She knew he liked to play golf, but aside from some fishing
excursions she'd heard him talking about with Josh, she
hadn't heard him ever mention another sport.

Trouble was, it was hard to stay analytical when a handsome man unbuttoned his fly. Her thoughts scattered as he
shifted his hips and shoved his slacks down, down...and
down.

Damn, if the man didn't have the best legs...all strong
and straight and perfectly hairy, as opposed to *too* hairy.

And why, oh why couldn't he have been a boxer man?
She hated boxer men, with those baggy bottoms hiding
their thighs and making their *parts* look like tent poles. No,
Gerard had to be a brief man, with all that nice white cotton

molding his hips and snuggling his *parts* into a suggestive bulge that seemed to be *bulging* the longer she stared.

Harley's pride took another hit when her breasts grew tight in response to the sight, her nipples peaking until she could feel her light cotton pajamas like a whisper against her skin. She was glad she'd kept her robe on, *really* not wanting to give this man proof of how she reacted to him. He was arrogant enough already, thank you.

But then Gerard pulled out all the stops, effectively claiming the prize in their little contest of wills. Turning back around, he hooked his fingers in the waistband of his briefs and gave a tug. Not even pride would make her take on *that*. Closing her eyes, Harley buried her face in the pillow.

Gerard laughed. The rich sound filtered through the quiet like a bayou breeze, grazed across her senses like a caress.

"I sleep naked."

"Of course," was all she said, refusing to open her eyes.

He gave another chuckle then the bed bounced as he climbed over her and started tugging the comforter from beneath her.

"I don't want you in my bed," she said in a would-be-reasonable voice. "No one will ever know if we really sleep together or not. We don't have to put on a show."

"It's our wedding night," he said as if that explained everything. Then he went to work on the sheets. "Roll over."

That did it. Her eyes shot open. "Roll where? I'm handcuffed to this bed, or are you blind?"

His gaze slid up her arms and back again. "I'm not blind."

She was so glad she'd kept the robe.

But her robe didn't do much to protect her from Gerard when he'd finally wrestled the sheets out and slid in beside her. For one thing it was only September and her robe, for all that it reached her ankles, was still made of lightweight cotton, which meant exactly nothing when he pulled her into his strong arms and curled around her, all big and hard and *male*.

His chest pressed so close to her back that she rode each rise and fall of his breath. His thighs fit beneath hers, acquainting her with how very much he enjoyed their closeness.

She waited for him to make some smug comment about how he finally had her where he wanted her, but he only rested his chin on the top of her head and held her. His body relaxed.

She finally couldn't stand the silence. "The only reason you suggested this whole marriage ruse was to get me in bed."

"That was only one of the reasons," he said, a throaty burst far too close to her ear. "The other reason was to help my grandfather. Killing two birds, you know."

"Murdered birds. Oh, that's real romantic, Gerard."

A beat of silence. "I didn't think you wanted romance."

"I don't."

"Then what do you want?"

"You to remove your rock-hard erection from my butt."

"Turning you on, is it?"

She gave a laugh. "You wish."

Suddenly he moved and his lips fluttered around her neck, gusting warm breaths below her ear in a place she hadn't realized was quite so sensitive.

"I don't wish. I know."

What was she going to do—deny it? She'd only look stupid with her pulse jumping beneath his lips. So she kept her mouth shut, which he clearly interpreted as an invitation. His mouth brushed her skin again, a whisper of a kiss.

Every nerve ending from her ears to her thighs began to tingle, crazy bursts of sensation that made her aware of the way his body heat penetrated light cotton as if it didn't exist. So aware of the hardness nestled against her bottom.

"You're killing me here, Gerard."

"Really? Want me to unlock the handcuffs? You can't jump me when you're all tied up."

"If I have sex with you, you'll let me go?"

"That would be coercion."

"You really are hard up for a date."

No reply but a sweep of his lips in that sensitive place where her neck scooped into her shoulder. "I'll remove the handcuffs if you agree to let me hold you while we sleep together. That way I'll know if you go for your gun."

"*Every* night?"

"Every night until we finish the case," he repeated. "But first you have to answer a question."

"You don't want much, do you?"

"I want you."

He held all the cards right now and she hissed out an exasperated breath, couldn't tell if he was bluffing. Would he really handcuff her every night until this case was over?

Determined bastard had gotten her into bed, hadn't he?

"What kind of question?" she asked.

"A personal one."

Of course, her favorite kind. "Deal. Shoot."

"How do you know Judge Bancroft?"

A *really* personal question, although now that he'd asked, Harley should have guessed the subject would come up. Naturally he'd be curious why the judge had kept tabs on her.

This wasn't any big secret, not in the conventional sense, but Harley didn't talk about her past. She didn't even think about it if she could help it and she'd been on such a nice roll until coming up against the judge today.

It had been a long time since anyone had asked about her past. Her relationships with men usually never went beyond the need for vague generalities. Anthony already knew all the gory details. Now that she thought about it, one of the last times she'd had to explain herself had been when she'd stood in front of Judge Bancroft.

"Why do you keep running away from your foster families, Harley?" the judge had asked. *"You're not giving them a fair chance before you run to the DiLeos."*

"That's because they love me and want me with them," she remembered explaining.

"I know they petitioned to adopt you, but Mrs. DiLeo is a widowed mother with six children of her own. She's having trouble making ends meet."

Harley hadn't quite understood what difference money should make. *"But they love me and want me to be with them."*

"I was a juvenile delinquent, Gerard," she told him.

"Really?"

"Oh yeah. A real troublemaker."

He chuckled, a sound that was even more effective at sparking those tingles along her skin. "That would explain the guns. How many times did you go in front of Judge Bancroft?"

"I already answered your question."

"I haven't unlocked the cuffs yet."

She exhaled hard in resignation, forced to dredge through memories she'd purposely forgotten. "Twelve, maybe thirteen."

He gave a low whistle. "You were bad news. And you didn't wind up in a juvenile detention center? Bancroft's not known for his patience."

"No, I didn't." But she hadn't wound up in the home she'd wanted to be in, either.

Gerard's arms tightened around her. Now came the part when he'd say something patronizing—one of the reasons she never discussed the past. But Gerard surprised her. He didn't give her one of those worn-out responses she hated. He asked yet another question. "Did coming up against Bancroft do the trick?"

"What trick?"

"Get you past the delinquency phase?"

"Yeah, I suppose you could say that."

"Good." He snuggled closer. "Otherwise you might be in jail right now and I couldn't hold you like this. You feel good."

She resisted the urge to roll off the side of the bed. Sure, she'd get away, but she'd likely break both arms in the process. "I thought you couldn't stand me."

"That's not true, Harley. I like you."

"You just want to sleep with me."

"That, too."

She didn't know what to say to his calm-voiced admission, so she didn't say anything at all. As it turned out, she didn't like it when Gerard gave her answers she didn't expect. The usual arguments were okay, but anything else threw her. So Harley just waited for him to make good on his promise.

The man might be arrogant, but his mama had raised him to keep his word. He finally slipped away, forcing her to close her eyes to avoid sight of his naked self as he leaned over her to retrieve a key from the bedside table.

"You're warm," he said while he unlocked the cuffs. "Sure you don't want to lose the robe."

She *was* warm, but that had more to do with the fact that

she could feel him kneeling over her, knew if she opened her eyes, she'd get an eyeful.

The cuffs slipped off and she rolled away. "I think I will."

But his hands were suddenly there, helping to draw the robe off her shoulders. He slid it down her arms, a move that seemed very intimate in the moon-soaked darkness. They were in bed together. He was naked. She wasn't much more than naked.

And she'd agreed to lie here while he held her.

HARLEY'S FIRST DAY as Gerard's fake wife started off with a bang. She had no intention of giving in to his challenges, but that didn't stop her from waking up wrapped around him like a twist tie. She'd turned sometime during the night and now her head nestled in the crook of his shoulder, an arm over his stomach, a thigh hiked across his. He apparently didn't mind, because he cradled her close with both arms, his cheek resting on the top of her head.

No matter how determined she was to resist this man, no matter how valid her reasons, she wanted him. Even in this hazy half-awake state, she couldn't ignore the way her skin glowed everywhere they touched. A slow ache pulsed between her thighs, her body aware in places she didn't even know could be aware. She liked him wrapped around her, all warm and naked and hard.

Harley supposed if she hadn't gone so long without sex, she wouldn't be going to pieces around a man she didn't want to go to pieces around. Talk about paying the price.

"Good morning," he said sleepily.

She rolled out of his arms, and took a deep breath of Gerard-free air. What was it about men that made them smell in the mornings? Not a body-odor type of smell, but a...*male* smell, as unique to each as a fingerprint.

"It is a good morning. For you. No bullet holes."

He chuckled, a throaty sound that made her glad to make an escape. She slipped over the side of the bed and got to her feet. If she'd been thinking, she would have made for the door, but Harley wasn't that awake yet. She glanced at him stretched out on her bed. The comforter only reached his waist, leaving his broad chest bared and his tanned skin looking dark and tempting against the white bedding.

Looking at his face was an even bigger mistake. His features were relaxed in a way she wasn't used to. His glossy hair spiked around his head at odd angles, only lending to his sleep-tousled look, and his heavy-lidded eyes made her think of sex.

"I need coffee." *Badly.*

To Harley's relief, Gerard didn't follow, and as she set up the coffee to brew, she heard the shower turn on. Grabbing a scraper from her drain board, she set to work chiseling away a section of wallpaper in what had become a morning ritual. Slowly the wallpaper was peeling away and, eventually, she'd strip every inch of the nasty avocado floral print so she could start mud work to repair the drywall.

She didn't know what she wanted to do with the room yet. Once she saw how the walls shaped up, she'd decide on paint or wallpaper. And that all presupposed she had money to buy supplies. At the rate she was going...

The smell of coffee soon filled the kitchen with an aroma that jump-started her drowsy senses. After pouring a mug, she headed back into her bedroom to get her clothes. She'd dress out here since the man had commandeered her private bath.

As she passed the desk, Harley noticed the flashing telephone recorder light. Depressing the play button, she sipped her coffee and listened to yesterday's messages.

Mama DiLeo's Italian-accented voice rang out. "*Cara*

mia, Anthony mentioned you'd gone to a wedding last weekend. I told him he must have mixed up the dates because I know you wouldn't embarrass me by going anywhere when you're *three weeks* overdue for a haircut. You book an appointment so I don't have to send someone after you.''

Harley smiled, not doubting for an instant that Anthony's mom would send out the hit squad. She deleted the message and made a mental note to call.

An unfamiliar male voice spoke next.

''Ms. Price, this is Harry from All Parishes Pest Control. You haven't gotten back to us yet, so I thought I'd call to let you know I just got word from corporate headquarters that we're starting a no-interest, no-payments-until-next-year special. I reviewed your extermination and repair estimate and it looks like you qualify. All you need to do is sign the papers and I can send a crew out to start work. Give me a call at…''

Harley stared. She blinked. Then she remembered to breathe.

''Hot damn!''

She didn't remember meeting Harry, but she slammed her mug down on the desk hard enough to slosh coffee over the rim, snatched up the receiver and dialed his number. A recorder answered and she left a message telling him to fax the paperwork to her office. If they were willing to extend *her* credit, she'd sign her life away, no questions asked.

She kissed the receiver and whispered thanks to Lady Luck. Anthony was right—something did break. With this unexpected turn of fortune, she could take the money she'd earn from this case and any cash bonuses to catch up on her mortgage and pay for her transmission so he wouldn't have to foot the bill.

The rest she'd put on her credit cards. If she could get them down, she could swing her loan payments, and if she could get her head above water now, she could pay off her loans by next April and divert that money to paying off the exterminator.

Harley sopped up spilled coffee and headed into her bedroom, so relieved that not even the sound of the running shower or the man inside her bathroom could wipe away her grin.

She was still grinning when Gerard showed up in the kitchen, barefoot and bare-chested and looking all damp around the edges.

And he was wearing jeans. The worn, comfy kind that looked soft to the touch and clung to his thighs and hips like an old friend. A memory of the way he'd felt wrapped around her made her grow warm inside, but she just handed him a mug of coffee and went back to peeling her wallpaper, too happy to let anything spoil her mood. Even chemistry she didn't want to feel.

"Home repairs, Harley?" he said, coming to stand close enough so she could smell his freshly washed skin. "I'm surprised. I thought you spent all your free time in the dojo or at the gun range."

"Not all my free time. I find these types of projects relaxing."

"I like what you've done around here."

"Thanks."

He stepped away and sipped his coffee. "We need to discuss today's schedule."

"Shoot."

"First item of business is returning the chopper," he said. "My wife can't drive her ex-lover's motorcycle."

"My car's in the shop and won't be fixed until next week."

"I have an SUV. We'll swing by my place later and pick it up so you'll have it if we need to split up." He made it sound like splitting up wasn't likely to happen.

Not even that thought threatened her good mood. "Okay. What's next?"

"We've got the morning and early afternoon to shop for your new wardrobe and pick up supplies for our new house."

"What new wardrobe?"

"The one that's not leather." He grinned over the rim of the mug. "Not that you don't look great in leather. I've had fantasies about peeling your clothes off piece by piece."

The promise in his sexy morning voice made her breath catch. Harley pulled a strip of wallpaper off so hard she brought a chunk of drywall with it. Damn.

"As your new husband, it's my job to outfit you for the sorts of functions I'll be taking you to."

"You're going to town with this madness, aren't you?"

"This is my first official case. I want to impress you."

The amusement in those clear gray eyes sent her dodging for cover. She headed across the room and tossed the drywall into the trash. "What supplies are you talking about?"

There, she sounded almost normal.

"You do eat, don't you?" The man whipped open her fridge and peered inside, giving her a prime shot of long legs and tight butt in the process. "All I saw in here the other night was peanut butter, green grapes and a bottle of Tabasco sauce."

There wasn't anything but peanut butter, green grapes and a bottle of Tabasco sauce there now, and the grapes were probably on their way out. "Protein, fruit and vegetables—everything a healthy girl needs. What were you doing in my fridge?"

"I was hungry." He took out the peanut butter. "Mmm, breakfast. Do you put this on something or eat it straight?"

Harley reached into the silverware drawer and withdrew a spoon. "Straight. It's the crunchy kind."

"Add a trip to the grocery store on the list."

"So what are tonight's plans? Not another family function?"

Leaning back against the counter, he swallowed a mouthful of peanut butter and chased it with coffee. "No family functions until the weekend. Tonight it'll be just you and me."

"What do you have in mind?"

"We need another official appearance as a married couple. I got us noticed at the shelter last night. Tonight it's your turn. Any ideas where we can go to get noticed?"

"How about out in the Quarter?"

"To the Pleasure Dome?"

A sex dungeon. Why wasn't she surprised? "If you already had an idea, why'd you ask for my input?"

Gerard shrugged. "I wanted to be PC. You said you were a real troublemaker and I was hoping you'd get me into trouble."

"You are so not funny."

"I'm not trying to be a comedian. I'm trying to get laid."

She turned back to her wallpaper. "You want to get noticed, Gerard? I'll get you noticed. Be dressed to go clubbing at ten."

"It's a date."

No, it was *work*.

8

"WHY LOVE CAJUN STYLE?" Mac asked as he grabbed a parking ticket from an attendant in a private lot he used when visiting the French Quarter. "Why not the Pleasure Dome? I heard it's more upscale as far as sex dungeons go."

"You heard wrong," Harley said from the passenger seat. "And they're not sex dungeons, they're private social clubs. Members only, you know—*legal*."

"Then what's the problem with the Pleasure Dome?"

"It has more bells and whistles, but the guests are paying for the extras, trust me."

Harley had dressed for a night on the town and as Mac drove to an upper floor, the lot lighting sliced through the darkness, flashing him glimpses of the sparkles she'd dusted into her hair, the glimmery makeup she'd used on her eyes. It was an exotic look that suited her black leather minidress, better than any look he'd seen so far.

It was a look that made his blood course hot.

"You're worried about the money?"

Harley gave a snort of exasperation that told him he was still missing something here. "I'm not talking about money. I'm talking about security. It doesn't exist at the Pleasure Dome. Bobby Lee Slick likes hidden video cameras. He rolls the film on his customers without their consent then bootlegs copies to all the porn shops and makes a killing. Josh and I worked a case to recover one of those tapes before it hit the stores and ruined a man's life. Really ugly."

"Why don't the police shut him down?"

"They do, but he's not known as slick for no reason. He's like grease—nothing sticks. He sets up shop, runs it clean, starts up his nonsense until he gets busted again."

"And you know Love Cajun Style is clean?"

"Yes."

One word. Unfortunately, that one word made his already-heated blood rise to a boil in a totally unexpected way. Mac backed into a free space, trying to figure out how to ask the question he wanted an answer to.

How did she know Love Cajun Style was clean?

He wanted to hear her say she'd found out while working that case with Josh, but his imagination kept serving up visions of Anthony DiLeo instead. When he couldn't think of a way to ask, he opened her door and escorted her out of the lot.

The French Quarter at ten o'clock at night was in full swing with people looking to party. Lights from the shops and street clubs glared through the darkness and music blared loud enough to feel the vibration in the concrete beneath his feet. Mac wound the way through the crowds of partying tourists and locals, keeping Harley close.

Of course, he knew she'd have insisted she didn't need protection. She wore a thigh holster, surprisingly well concealed. He could barely see the bump in the line of her dress. An argument for wearing leather. She looked like walking sex with that short, short black dress hugging her curves and those long, long legs flashing shimmery hose with every step. And Mac wasn't the only man looking as they wound their way toward the club.

From the outside, Love Cajun Style might have been any club with the doors thrown open to attract the night crowds.

It occupied a three-story building on a side street a few blocks off Jackson Square, far enough away from Bourbon Street to avoid the tourists who didn't know this club catered to special interests. Even from the street he could see the sign by the doors that read: *Private, Members Only.*

And from the length of the line at the door, lots of people in New Orleans were members with special interests tonight.

Harley bypassed the line entirely and led him toward the front door. Mac followed without comment, more interested in keeping his eyes on the partygoers who glared from the line.

Grabbing her hand, he dragged her closer as some jerk wearing a lot of gold leaned over the cordon and yelled, "Hey, sugar, who are you to cut in line?"

"A VIP," she shot back with a narrowed gaze. "So why don't you lean back over that rope so you don't lose your place."

Mac stared the jerk down, the butt of his gun cutting reassuringly into his waist and making him appreciate the decision to bring it along. Harley's motto, Never Leave Home Without It, apparently applied to her nearest and dearest, too.

"Long time no see, Cha Cha," the bouncer moved away from the door, scooping Harley into a hug so fast Mac had to release her or risk dislocating her shoulder.

The guy had to be six-six if he was an inch, and he sported a silver piercing every place Mac had ever thought could be pierced, plus a few he hadn't thought about. As he spun Harley around, her sparkly hair whipped out around her.

"Hey, Bear." She laughed. "Keeping the crazies in line?"

"Shit," he drawled the word on a long breath as he

unhooked the cordon to let them in, glaring at some dissenters in the front. "Cajun Joe's behind the bar. Let him know you're here."

Harley nodded. She never even glanced at the *Members Only* sign before leading Mac through the doors of his very first sex dungeon and past the registration desk. He assumed she must be a serious VIP and he'd been vouched for by association.

The club opened up around him, a surprisingly earthy looking place of dark wood beams and winding stairways. A live band played music heavy on the fiddle with a pulsing accordion beat in the familiar hand-clapping, foot-stomping Cajun rhythm.

Harley led him on a winding path toward the bar, while he tried to reconcile the slim woman in the tight black leather with a woman who would have VIP status in a club like this.

He couldn't. Mac didn't know what it was about the tumble of red waves bouncing down her back or the swing of her hips, but there was something about Harley here that didn't work.

Then again, how much did he really know about her? Not much. He'd researched the basics while pulling together his marriage plan, but he hadn't dug deep enough. She had termites, money grief, a sometimes-lover named Anthony, an interest in home improvement and a taste for Tabasco sauce. By her own admission, she'd had a less-than-stellar childhood.

He filed the thought in the back of his brain for further consideration when he wasn't skirting a dance floor where people wanted to two-step through him.

In the meantime, meeting her friends helped put together the pieces. The owner of Love Cajun Style was clearly a good friend. A middle-aged man, Cajun Joe sported a beard that matched his long gray hair, a beret and a cheery red bandanna he wore around his neck. His bar didn't serve alcohol but a menu of specialty coffee drinks to rival Starbucks.

He spotted Harley right away and plunked a blender onto its base and leaned over the bar to pinch her cheek. "Looking as gorgeous as ever, Cha Cha. What brings you to my love hole in the dark? Hungry?"

Harley laughed. "I need a room, Joe. Got anything for me?"

"You always got a room here, Cha Cha. You know that." Cajun Joe sliced an incredulous look his way. "With this guy?"

Mac met the man's gaze steadily. He'd bet money the surprise was real, which meant grappling with the fact that all Harley's pieces weren't fitting into place the way he thought they should. Not only was she on a first-name basis with the owner of Love Cajun Style, she apparently availed herself of the facilities with an exclusive someone.

He didn't need to ask who that someone was.

"Mac Gerard, Harley's husband," he introduced himself.

"Husband?"

Harley gave a curt nod.

Cajun Joe let out a whoop that drew the attention of everyone at the bar and even from the dance floor, people who shouldn't have been able to hear anything above the throbbing music. He tugged a towel from his jeans and tossed it down before making his way around the bar to scoop Harley into his arms with the same familiarity the bouncer had displayed.

"Delilah won't believe this." Then he turned to Mac and thrust out a hand. "You want a private or semiprivate room?"

They shook. "Private."

Harley scowled so hard that Cajun Joe laughed. "All right. I knew that. You gotta give me some lead time to get your honeymoon suite ready."

"No problem," Mac said. "I'll dance with my bride."

"Ooowee, if you can get Cha Cha to dance, I just might like you, babe." He turned back to Harley. "You need to bring your new man by the next munch to meet everyone. It's Saturday."

"Yeah, yeah, I'll pencil it in before my workout."

Mac didn't know what a munch was, but Harley's sarcasm told him he wasn't likely to find out on Saturday. Cajun Joe obviously got that, too, because with a laugh he headed back behind the bar to pick up a phone. His beautiful bride was still scowling when he led her onto the dance floor.

"Brides are supposed to look happy," he said.

She looked up at him with a deadpan expression. "Oh, joy. We're dancing again."

"I like dancing with you." Especially when the upbeat music slowed to a jazz tune that gave him the perfect excuse to pull her into his arms. "You've got some interesting friends."

"Cajun Joe served a few terms as mayor a long time ago. He doesn't like to talk about it."

Mac shot a glance back at the bar where the alleged former mayor juggled four shot glasses for his appreciative patrons. "I voted for him. He fixed the potholes on my street."

Harley gave a snort of disgust and he provoked her further by pulling her so close her thighs parted to make room for his.

"Gerard," she said in a warning voice.

He buried his face in her sparkly hair, inhaled deeply of

her subtly spicy fragrance as he dragged his mouth over her ear. "Yes, Harley?"

"You're holding me too close."

"You like it." He tugged on her earring with his teeth.

She growled low in her throat, but to his immense satisfaction, she shivered while she did. His body gave a corresponding tremor, so incredibly sensitive to the feel of her against him. Her slim fingers twined through his. Her breasts pressed against his chest, making him ache to peel the skimpy dress away and taste their pale softness with his mouth.

His thigh nestled in the juncture of hers, close enough to imagine he could feel her heat through his trousers, which drew his attention to the way her stomach cradled the body part that only needed permission to become an erection.

"We have to establish our cover as newlyweds," he said. "Just relax and enjoy yourself. Everyone is having a good time here." He skimmed his gaze across the dance floor where couples ground sensuously together to the sultry music and laughed around the bar and huddled together at tables....

Mac did a double take. "There's a woman on her knees under that table, giving some guy a blow job."

"Probably an exhibition fetish."

Mac looked down into her bland expression. "I thought you said this place was legal."

"It is."

"Since when is oral sex in public legal?"

"Since this is a private club and the oral sex is between two consenting members."

Mac danced Harley around to get another glimpse of the bobbing brunette. The consenting recipient of her attention leaned back in the booth and made no pretense of hiding his pleasure while two mugs of coffee sat untouched on the table.

"You want to take a picture?" Harley lifted her head, and her eyelids shimmered exotically beneath the low lights.

"Live and learn."

"You've been sheltered. Consider yourself lucky."

There was subtext in that statement and Mac regretted every comment he'd ever made about their lifestyle differences. He'd broken his engagement and ditched his career to start enjoying his life. He'd expected a challenge in his new career. He'd expected wining and dining women not hung up on prenups. He'd expected to lose the discontent that had plagued him for so long to explore the full range of his emotions. He'd expected to learn what it felt like to have his blood simmer for a woman.

And he'd found all of these things—in Harley Price.

Wasn't life full of surprises?

Mac was surprised. He'd judged her without getting to know her. Until they'd kissed, it had never even occurred to him he could be attracted to her. She was a different breed from any woman he'd known and, while he'd claimed to want different, he'd dismissed her as *too* different.

"You've helped me broaden my horizons." And she had. She'd intrigued him enough to look past the surface.

"I'm glad I could help you slum."

He'd had about enough of the sarcasm tonight. Moving close, he forced her backward until she gasped, had no choice but to bend over his arm in a low dip, a move that raised her beautiful leather-clad breasts high for his viewing pleasure.

"Who said anything about slumming, Harley?" he

asked. "You excite me. You have since we met. I was too blind to realize it at first."

"The sight of that guy getting a blow job excites you."

He wedged his knee between hers, forcing her legs wider. He stared down into her face. "It's the sight of you underneath me that I find exciting."

He held her poised beneath him to emphasize his point before finally pulling her upright. He was sure he'd have gotten an earful if Cajun Joe hadn't appeared with a key.

"Come on, Cha Cha. You got the penthouse."

Harley didn't need directions. She knew the way to the third-floor room with its thick red carpet, mirrored walls and black leather furniture.

Sultry jazz piped in from hidden speakers and candles flickered in holders, casting reflections in the mirrors and layering everything in a hazy glow. Two steaming mugs occupied a warmer on a sideboard, along with a tray of fresh fruits and cheeses, a fondue pot of what smelled like chocolate and a big bottle of Tabasco sauce.

The Tabasco clued Mac in that this buffet was meant especially for Harley and he watched as she plucked a green grape from a vine and popped it into her mouth, a soft smile playing around her lips.

"I'm surprised Cajun Joe managed to find us a room with such short notice," he said.

She reached for a mug, sipped, and her eyes fluttered shut appreciatively. "This is his private room."

"So what's his deal?" He couldn't bring himself to ask about another man's *fetish*. So much for broadening his horizons.

"Joe's a savvy businessman. He keeps up with the times. He renovates and reopens to stay on the trends, but all in all, he's a man with simple tastes. He likes strippers."

Suddenly all the wide leather chairs made sense and Mac

recalled a rather fond memory of a particular blond lap dancer he'd encountered at a co-worker's bachelor party.

"That would explain why there's no bed," he said, forcing a calm he didn't feel when he wanted to know why Harley was so familiar with Cajun Joe's likes and dislikes.

Loosening his collar, he made his way to the sideboard. Between the heat on the dance floor and his own skyrocketing body temperature, he was choking.

"Did you think we'd need one?" she asked.

"I thought I might luck out since you're a VIP member."

"Well, that's not your first mistake," she said, dismissing him with a glance and taking another sip from her mug. "We came to Joe's because it was safe. We can pretend to enjoy the facilities and not have to worry about blowing our cover."

"So that's why you brought me here."

He had no right to sound annoyed. Whatever Harley had done before their visit to Judge Bancroft's chambers yesterday wasn't his business. But his tolerance level for sarcasm and mysteries seemed to have taken a sharp decline.

Mac had no idea he could get so frustrated with one tiny redhead. He'd had to coerce her into marriage. He'd had to restrain her to get her into bed. What would it take to get her to make love to him?

He had no answer. Worse still, he was fresh out of ideas.

Yet he didn't doubt for a minute that she wanted him so much that she was fighting harder than she'd ever fought him before. Why?

Because she had tastes she didn't think he could satisfy?

That thought slammed him hard with his own deficiencies. He'd had exactly the same complaint about his life. He'd walked the straight and narrow, had rarely, if ever, deviated from the norm and had always done what was expected of him.

Reaching for a mug off the sideboard, Mac took a swig of what turned out to be thick Cajun coffee. He barely noticed it scald his throat on the way down. Harley had taken to pacing the length of the room, her slim body and long-legged strides reflected in the mirrors, haunting him from every angle.

"What's the real problem here, Harley? I want you. You want me. It should be simple."

"You're arrogant, Gerard. Do you know that?"

"So you keep telling me," he said. "I'm not wrong about this. So what's the problem?"

She didn't reply, but she did stop pacing. Half-sitting on the arm of a chair, she asked, "What did you see happening between us with this marriage? Did you think it would entitle you to privileges?"

That was a loaded question and he should have been smart enough not to answer. Honesty wasn't always the best policy with this woman. Sometimes it gave her another reason to shut him out. Which was why he couldn't keep his mouth shut—it didn't matter what he said, or didn't say, Harley wasn't going to let him in either way.

"I wanted a chance to seduce you without your mechanic getting in my way."

If it was anything, she looked surprised. "This isn't a real marriage even if we did sign papers."

"I knew you wouldn't date him and pretend to be married to me at the same time."

"That's something, I suppose. I keep getting the impression you're surprised I haven't fallen into bed with you."

"You want to. I'm not wrong about that."

"How the hell do you know what I want?"

"I don't." The admission irritated him but he wouldn't deny the truth. Leaning back in the chair, he stretched his legs before him, locked his hands behind his head and kept affecting that calm he didn't feel. "I don't know nearly enough about you, but I'm starting to pull the pieces together."

"You think so?"

"You're a VIP at a sex dungeon. Excuse me, a *private social club*. That tells me something."

"Right again, blue blood. Joe has owned this place for over twenty years and I've been coming here every one of them. I remember this place when it was still a strip joint."

"Is that where the *Cha Cha* comes in?"

His reference to her nickname wiped the offhand expression from her face. Mac didn't know what it was about his question, but it took her off guard. Something about the way she drew in on herself, the way she squared her shoulders and lifted her chin proudly, made her seem completely untouchable.

Completely *vulnerable*.

It was a rare glimpse of the woman beneath the shields. A reminder of how she shored up those defenses so no one could get in. He remembered her revelation about Judge Bancroft... Had she danced at this club when she was younger? Had she danced for Cajun Joe?

The thought blindsided him...and the feeling that went along with it. The same urgency he'd felt when first meeting Anthony DiLeo. It was that feeling more than anything that had prompted him to suggest marriage as a way to solve his grandfather's case, that *possessiveness*—was this jealousy?—that made him slam his mug down on the sideboard and propel himself from the chair.

Harley clearly didn't miss his intensity and shot him a

surprised glance as he bore down on her. She set her own mug aside, freeing up her hands to defend herself.

But her defense *was* the problem. Mac wanted around her defenses so he could understand why she was shutting him out.

He cut off her escape before she launched herself from the chair, crowding her so their knees tangled together and she was forced to tilt her head back to meet his gaze.

"What do you think you're doing?" she asked.

"I want an answer from you." He hated the rough edge to his voice. "Why you won't even give me a chance?"

"I don't want to."

He supposed it was something that she sounded nearly as raw. "Why not give us a chance to see where we go."

Her expression closed off so completely, shut him out so effectively that he realized right then where he wanted this relationship to go.

Beyond sex.

In that moment, as Harley stared up at him with her exotic eyes, her ragged breaths belying her neutral expression, Mac knew his desperation went way beyond wanting to make love. He *wanted* this woman in a way he hadn't known he could want before. He wanted her body, he wanted her to look at him with that same sense of longing that was eating away at him.

The room could have blown up, and Mac couldn't have stopped himself from threading his fingers into her hair, anchoring her head in his hands as he leaned over…

His mouth caught hers hard, their breaths colliding in a way that answered all of his questions, proved just how blind he'd been. He wanted this woman with a fierceness that staggered him by its intensity. Yes, his blood scalded through his veins with his rushing pulse. Yes, his tongue thrust deep inside her warm mouth, exploring, tasting, savoring…but the *need* was so much more than physical. It was all-consuming, almost overwhelming.

Like a hunter with his prey, he'd targeted her the moment they'd met. He hadn't understood what was happening, but Harley, with her sharp survival skills, had sensed it from the start.

And she'd been fighting him every step of the way.

She desperately didn't want to be caught—as desperately as he'd wanted to catch her. And any question he might have had was answered when she kissed him back.

He tasted her sigh, the sweet taste of her resignation rolling over his tongue in a hot wave. She was as helpless as he to resist this intensity between them.

Mac wanted to lose himself in her body, feel her skin surround him. He wanted to sink deep inside her until he heard nothing but the sounds of her pleasured moans, felt her need when she arched that sleek body against him.

And when she ran her hands up his back, touching him of her own free will, for one blinding moment, he lost himself. He made love to her warm mouth with his tongue. He absorbed her breaths bursting softly against his lips. He cradled her head in his hands, experienced an almost tender rush of desire along with the need. He wanted to be inside her, around her, a part of her.

For one awesome moment, he knew she wanted that, too.

She hung on to him as if he was her anchor. She tangled her tongue with his, drank in his taste as he drank in hers, explored his mouth with a kiss that not only accepted what he gave, but challenged him to offer even more.

"Let me make love to you." He breathed the words against her lips.

Her denial burst out as a sob, as desperate and broken as he felt. Then she tried to pull away, but he held on, curled his fingers around her head, locked his thumbs beneath her chin. He forced her to look at him, searched her beautiful face for some clue as to why she wouldn't let him.

"Tell me what you want and I'll give it to you," he said.

"I want you not to touch me."

He heard the words, but they weren't reflected in her expression. Her face reflected the panic she struggled so hard to hide. Was she afraid of what she felt for him?

Bending low, he pressed a kiss to the soft skin of her neck, felt her pulse flutter against his lips. When she shivered in reply, he felt a surge of pure triumph at proving her a liar.

"You don't want me to stop touching you, Harley. You're afraid of how much you want it."

She pulled out of his arms. She slid over the chair arm and scrambled away so fast that he rocked backward. "You can't give me what I want."

"Try me." A challenge.

He was letting his pride get in the way. He knew it, but he couldn't stop himself. "Your body responds to me. Do you think I didn't notice the way your nipples got hard when we were in bed? The way your body melted against mine when we danced? Do you think I can't see how flushed you are right now? You want me and it scares you so much you don't know what to do except push me away. But I'm not going anywhere."

"You don't scare me, Gerard."

"If you weren't scared, you'd let me make love to you."

He could see the instant he'd pushed her too far. He recognized the look from defense training, knew it meant she was planning to teach him a lesson.

This was a lesson he'd been waiting to learn.

Everything about her seemed to melt in that incredibly

sensual way he'd only glimpsed before. The candlelight flickered, sparking off her hair, and she pointed to the chair she'd just vacated and gave him a slow, erotic smile.

"Have a seat, Gerard, and I'll show you what I want."

9

GERARD WOULD GET his show all right. As far as Harley was concerned, she owed him for his performance the night before. He'd had no business handcuffing her to the bed, no right tossing her attraction to him into her face.

She owed him for assuming the worst about her tonight.

There was no doubt in her mind that he'd drawn his own conclusions about her status at Love Cajun Style. He'd been blowing emotion all over her ever since she'd suggested they come here. But what else could she do? He'd devised this plan that relied on them becoming fast, visible targets. They'd needed someplace to party and she wouldn't go to Bobby Lee Slick's place. She wouldn't explain herself either.

And she owed him for the way she felt right now.

Hurt because he'd assumed the worst.

She shouldn't even care. Arrogant man. He sat in a leather chair built for two, looking as entitled as a king with his arms folded across his chest, his eyes eager for her to make the next move. To give him what he wanted.

Her.

He'd become obsessed and she was convinced sex would only complicate the situation. But she'd tried everything to push him away and he was only getting more obsessed.

Turning her back, Harley breathed deeply, cleansing her mind and relaxing her body in a ritual she always performed before training. She erased worries about her control. She allowed the music to filter through her senses, to wipe away distractions and free her head of thoughts.

All except one—her power over Gerard.

The climate-control system cycled on, kicking a burst of air across her face, over her bare arms, grazing her with the sensation of cool when her skin felt flushed. Awareness rippled through her, as if his anticipation was a warm caress along her body, a light touch that ignited her nerve endings in its wake. Arousal, despite its intensity, was a familiar sensation. She'd been aroused before.

This would be just another fling.

A familiar calm tamed her thoughts, bringing her to that peaceful place she went to train, to retreat from the world, a place where she knew only an intense awareness of her body.

And the man who watched her.

There, she took another deep breath, feeling much more in control. Now to get comfortable.

Her heels forced her to an unnatural posture, so she bent at the waist and reached down, stretching the muscles along her lower back, her thighs. The hem rode high on her butt, nearly flashing Gerard a glimpse of her goods. She took her sweet time unfastening the clasp.

After slipping out of the shoe, she repeated the move, savored the way her muscles eased as she regained her balance, enjoying the fact that she could suddenly hear Gerard's breathing, a new strain woven in with the jazz.

The tight dress was the next to go. Sweeping aside her hair, Harley reached an arm behind her, slowly peeled the zipper down her back. The leather parted and she thought she heard the hiss of an indrawn breath and resisted the urge to smile.

Hooking her fingers into the thin straps, she guided them down her arms, peeled away the bodice and freed more skin to the cool air. She wasn't wearing a bra. She hadn't needed one. The cut of the dress had held her breasts up nicely. Now the air grazed her skin. Her nipples puckered, a response from the cool air and the knowledge that Gerard was seeing her like he'd never seen her before—not only was she nearly naked, but there were four walls of mirrors reflecting her from every angle.

Definitely a hiss of indrawn breath.

This time she couldn't resist the smile. Harley had always enjoyed taking him off his guard, giving him a shock.

She worked the leather down her hips, down her thighs…let it slide to her feet. She half expected to feel Gerard's hands on her bottom when she bent over to drag away the dress.

But he seemed to be containing himself, and she glanced at his reflection from beneath the fall of her hair, found him sprawled in his chair, so internally still she recognized the control he exerted to maintain the pose.

Good for him. They'd been working hard on this skill in the dojo and she was pleased to see the lessons paying off. He'd need all the control he could get tonight because she couldn't have dressed better if she'd planned this seduction.

The only place to conceal a gun had been on her thigh, which had forced her to wear a thong and thigh-high hose that left enough skin exposed her holster didn't slip around. Some women might not mind panty hose and thigh holsters.

Harley wasn't one of them.

And she was glad. Hunger sharpened Gerard's sculpted features and made her feel decadent, all skin and black thong and shimmery thigh-highs. Her gun holster rode in between, almost reassuring with her bottom lifted high in the air.

She wanted him to feel the full impact of her show as much as she'd felt his last night. But Harley hated dancing, so she'd have to put her own twist on this striptease. Taking another deep breath, she began the moves of the kata she performed when warming up to train with Damon. She turned, pressed her open palms against her legs and bent slightly at the waist, keeping her eyes on Gerard as she made her formal bow.

Be careful what you wish for....

His expression made her feel the hungry gaze he shifted down her face, her neck, her breasts...lower. His nostrils flared and his long fingers gripped the chair arms deeply enough to make impressions in the leather.

Her skin tingled in reply.

Harley tried to dispel the sensation by beginning her moves, letting the familiarity of her routine fuel her boldness, refused to let her arousal escalate and make her feel vulnerable. It was that feeling she hated, the feeling that her reactions and her emotions were beyond her grasp, as if she'd presented them to Gerard like some erotic gifts.

She hadn't. She wouldn't.

Giving in to her body's demands didn't mean she'd let him touch her emotions.

She couldn't.

She focused on the precise movements she practiced so religiously in karate, instead. Her movements weren't sinuous or graceful like a dance but each move flowed into the next, her whole body in motion, all her muscles controlled. She shifted, stepped, turned, reached, sometimes fast, sometimes slow, sometimes held intentionally to give Gerard a nice clear shot.

She managed to keep her face a blank mask, but his every drawn breath, the fingers that hadn't stopped clutching the chair, tested her control. Her skin glowed with her exertion, with how completely exciting she found him wanting her. He radiated a fiercely held restraint, his body so tense she expected him to bolt up and grab her. And Harley couldn't resist pushing to see how far she could....

Stepping up her pace with more forceful moves, she faced him with her breasts swaying heavily, her hair whipping around her face, her fists pivoting out as her breaths came harder. She thrust out her leg, a kick that brought her heel within inches of his face and gave him the mother of all crotch shots.

He didn't flinch. He didn't blink.

He smiled, one of those roguish smiles that flashed his dimple and melted her insides into a hot puddle, a feeling so powerful that she came to a stop in front of him, forced to stand still to manage the sensation.

Staring down at him, she braced herself against the longing in those thickly fringed eyes. Something deep inside her stirred, made her fight an almost overwhelming urge to melt into his lap, to wrap her arms around his neck and kiss his mouth.

To let herself go. To let him do what he wanted with her. Hunger like Gerard's promised so much...which was precisely why she had to hold back.

Harley couldn't trust him. He wanted her way too much for his own good. It had been driving him, *obsessing* him...she'd thought denial would eventually deter him so he'd move on to friendlier pastures and accept they had nothing in common. They didn't even like each other.

Oh, but how wrong she'd been.

Denial had only challenged them both. Now she was as hungry as he was and barely hanging on.

Hooking her fingers into the straps around her hips, Harley worked the thong down, unhooked it when it snagged on her gun. She stepped out of the skimpy circle of silk, exposing her mostly shaved sex for his pleasure. He was very, *very* pleased. A vein jumped in his throat. His crotch bulged so much it flattened the pleats of his slacks.

She might have been pleased, but she had nothing to be arrogant about. She was struggling, too. She had to stay in control, couldn't risk losing herself in this man. Gerard wasn't the man for her. He would never be. She could have a fling, like she'd had others, but she wouldn't let herself care, not in any way that mattered. She would only care for Anthony that way. She knew what to expect from him.

But not from Gerard. He was from another world and could never understand who she was.

He reached for her. She didn't consider options. She didn't think, because only one thing mattered in that instant—not letting him touch her. Not when she was this close to falling into his arms and losing herself.

His expression barely registered surprise before she had her gun pressed beneath his jaw.

"Don't touch." Her voice came breathless and hard, a stranger's, because she'd never heard herself sound so needy.

His gaze flickered to the safety—off. He frowned.

She didn't move. She leaned over him, her breasts plumping forward, so exposed he could have touched them, dragged his tongue across her nipple.

"You can *watch*," she said in that stranger's voice.

Her command hung heavily between them, almost palpable in the jazz-soaked quiet. She saw understanding register deep in his eyes, comprehension that she'd drawn a line in the sand.

Some dark, dangerous part of her hoped he wouldn't listen, wanted him to take the control away from her so she could give in to this ache. Only Gerard ever made her feel this way.

She tightened her grip on the gun.

His gaze captured hers and, to her amazement and alarm, she didn't see surprise in those clear gray eyes. He seemed to be looking inside her, seeing all sorts of things she never let anyone see, deciding that she'd have never drawn her weapon unless he was the one wielding the real power.

"I won't touch." He settled his hands on the arms of the chair.

He'd play by her rules.

But Harley found that the sight of her gun pressed against his throat reassured her, aroused her, *reminded* her she was fighting an opponent bigger than she was—her desire. She wanted Gerard. And it was nothing more than rebellion, an absolute refusal to give in to her desire that made her draw the gun away, set it on the bar behind his head.

She lowered a knee onto the chair beside his, followed with the other until she was straddling his lap in a variation of the formal Japanese sitting position. She bowed, a slight bending at the waist, then leaned back, keeping her posture erect, her breasts thrust outward.

The fire in his gaze flared. His breaths burst softly against her skin, and her body betrayed her, performed for him with her breasts feeling heavy and tight, her nipples puckering. Her parted thighs spread her across his lap, exposing her most private places to the cool air, to the realization that she was so very wet.

His slacks pressed along her silk-clad legs and she could feel the fabric abrade her bare bottom. She wanted to touch him, to strip away his shirt and reveal all those tanned muscles below, to press her breasts to his hot skin and satisfy this ache.

She needed to distract herself, so she began to move. Not

a dance. There was no place to go wedged as she was against him in the chair, but she moved to the rhythm of the music, to the pulsing of her own heated blood.

Dragging her bottom across his thighs, she rose on her knees and lifted her arms high above her head, swaying before him, gifting him with a view of her body, arching forward to taunt him with her nipples close to his mouth.

He traced her thighs with his outspread fingers hovering a hint above her skin. He didn't touch, just tortured her with the warmth of his hands sparking brush fires in their wake.

He trailed his almost touch upward over the curve of her bottom, over the swell of her hips, as if he were memorizing her body, marking a trail he'd come back to explore later. He grazed her abdomen, stirring the air in that sensitive juncture between hip and thigh. Her muscles contracted and she sucked in a surprised breath, amazed at her body's response to *not* being touched.

This man was fire. He dared her to back away when he molded his fingers around the curve of her sex, not quite brushing the neatly trimmed hairs covering the intimate folds below.

Desire pooled between her thighs with the promise of his hand. Such intimate contact that promised everything she wouldn't let him give.

He brought his face into the game, glancing his mouth toward her breasts, close enough to gust warm silky breaths across her skin. She shuddered, a full-length shiver that made his lips tip upward in a smile. He knew he had her. Harley glimpsed herself in the mirror, eyes heavy lidded with desire, mouth parted, body curling above this fully clothed man. She looked so decadent, so aroused, so *needy*.

For the space of several heartbeats, Harley didn't trust herself to keep from dragging his face toward her breast.

Her sex throbbed just out of reach of his skin and the only thing stopping her from sinking down onto his hot fingers was the irony that she'd devised her own torture.

She'd drawn the line in the sand. Wouldn't he just love it if she was the one to cross it?

Sheer stubbornness saved her.

This tortured look was the one she wanted to see on Gerard's face, not her own. Especially when the man hadn't even touched her. And with that thought spurring her, she arched backward, putting the safety of distance between them. She sank back onto his lap and reached for his zipper.

She hadn't established any rules about *her* touching *him*.

Now it was his turn to suck in one of those gasping breaths as she worked on unzipping his fly, careful not to harm the goodies below, enjoying a moment of satisfaction that she'd managed to turn the tables.

His fingers were digging into the leather chair arms by the time she'd freed his erection from the tangle of slacks and briefs and she couldn't help but smile at the sight.

"Ah, Gerard, you are pretty."

And he was. His erection was as sculpted and beautiful as the rest of him, all smooth, perfectly shaped thickness.

Her sex gave another moist clench and she rose up on her knees and arched above him, wrapping her fingers around that hot length. He gave a low growl that echoed through the room. He sank against the chair, visibly fighting for control, head tossed back so she could see his face.

Exactly the tortured expression she'd been hoping for.

She stroked him along her heat, making herself tremble with the taste of his hot skin against her creamy folds, a sample of what that hardness would feel like inside her.

Lord, she wanted him.

This time Harley did dance, or as close to it as she could given the constraints of their positions. She started up a sinuous rhythm, body swaying with long smooth motions, each stroke riding the head of his erection, pressing it into her wet folds just enough to make her tremble.

Each tremor built the ache inside, fired her even hotter, drenched her even wetter, made her sex clench to urge him inside. She fought the need to sink down on that hard length.

Gerard never closed his eyes, he watched her through those thick black lashes that made his clear eyes even clearer. He didn't hide how much he wanted her, how hard he was struggling not to lose control, or to *take* control.

How much it was costing him to play sex her way.

She had the vague thought that his restraint was better than she would have expected from any man. He still clutched the chair arms, even though she could see the veins bulging in his hands, his knuckles white with effort.

She could feel his thighs vibrate and still she didn't let up her grip, didn't slow her pace. She arched her hips to press his hot shaft against that tiny bundle of nerve endings that was pulsing with want, to hold it there, the pressure feeding the wave of sensation that was swelling inside her.

His gaze never left her face as she gasped out her orgasm, a huge, rolling wave of sensation that made her chest rise sharply, her breasts quiver, her bottom never slow its erotic motion.

He watched with that hungry expression, that dimple peeping out to show her how very pleased he was to watch her come.

Then he lifted his hips and thrust inside, proving how easily he could have taken control all along.

Harley moaned, the feel of him filling her so unexpected and intense. A huge shudder rocked her, made her brace her hands on the back of the chair to steady herself.

The instant Gerard was in, he proved that he didn't need

his hands to make her burn—just his lethal erection and those strong thighs lifting him to plunge inside her.

The stroke caught her exactly where she needed it, dragged another low moan from her throat and suddenly the power struggle was over. He lifted up again, started his own rhythm. Again, and again, and again.

The next thing Harley knew, she was digging her fingers into his broad shoulders, anchoring herself as she rode him with sleek strokes, rising up, then sinking back, strokes that crushed the air from her lungs, made her sob out each breath.

His body began to vibrate, his muscles tightening for the explosion. She cried out when he pounded into her with driving thrusts that dragged her into the blowout with him.

Gasping for breath, she collapsed and then, only then, did he break her rules. Pressing his mouth into her hair, he showered her with soft kisses that stunned her with their tenderness. Wrapping his strong arms around her, he cradled her close as she lay sprawled across his body, her sex still clenching his erection in fading bursts.

Their hearts pounded in time. Their broken breaths drowned out the sounds of the smooth jazz.

Or maybe it was just that none of Harley's senses worked anymore, not when she was overwhelmed with the horrible, horrible truth that she was so in over her head with this man.

MAC WASN'T ENTIRELY SURE he'd be able to stand when he pushed himself out of the chair. His heart still hadn't resumed its normal rhythm and his legs felt weak. Straightening his trousers, he zipped his fly with an unsteady hand.

Harley had leveled him. Since their first kiss, he'd known making love to her would be an event, but he'd *never* expected anything like this. His wildest fantasies hadn't hinted at the intensity he'd felt with her tonight, still felt.

Harley had taken control, had established the ground rules and, in doing that, had revealed so much about herself that Mac was still trying to pull it all together.

And he needed to make some sense of what had happened. He'd never in his life felt such conflicting emotions. He wanted to drag her back into the chair and hold her until they'd recovered enough for another round. But he was afraid—simply and honestly afraid. The wrong move would start up the struggle all over again. He wanted to hold her, not dodge her bullets.

He wasn't surprised that she'd scrambled out of his lap almost as soon as they were through. He understood her rush to get away. They'd lost themselves in each other and, while that event amazed him, it frightened Harley.

A lot, if he was reading her right.

And Mac thought he was. He was becoming proficient at recognizing when her shields went down—and now was one of those times. She seemed so tiny, so exquisite with all her pale skin and red hair reflected in the mirrors around the room.

So *rattled*.

He wanted to say something, but didn't have a clue what would span the distance between them. One wrong comment would put her back on the defense faster than he could blink. So he didn't say anything at all, just retrieved her gun from the sideboard and brought it to her.

She accepted it, avoided his gaze. Some women would have been self-conscious to be standing nearly naked while he was fully dressed, but he didn't think that was Harley's problem. She seemed very comfortable with her body. No, Mac suspected she was uncomfortable with losing control.

Which brought him up against the real mystery here—why she lived in defense mode.

He supposed he should take it as a good sign that she felt he was such a threat. That was something at least, but it didn't do much to erase this feeling of ignorance, of not knowing what to do or say to make her understand how much tonight meant to him.

He retrieved her clothes from around the room, fingering the silky thong, smoothing out the soft leather dress. And after replacing her gun in the holster, she glanced up, seeming surprised to find him standing there with her clothes.

"Thanks" was all she said before donning her dress and covering her beautiful curves from his view.

The need to touch her hit him so strong it was physical, so he brushed her hands from the zipper and completed the task. Miracle of miracles, she didn't resist.

He pressed the thong into her hand. Her deep blue focus dropped to the scrap of fabric. Maybe the thong was symbolic of their closeness, because Harley's expression seemed to crumple before his eyes, proving that she was hanging on in much the same way that he was.

"It was just sex, Gerard," she said.

He could have argued the point, but he just pressed a kiss to the top of her tousled hair and went to find her shoes.

Until five months ago, Mac would never have found himself inside a sex dungeon with a co-worker. But he'd changed his life, looking for challenges. He'd found one—he'd fallen in love with a woman who wouldn't admit she had feelings for him.

10

HARLEY KNEW she was in serious trouble before Gerard ever drove his Porsche into the driveway of his family home. The place looked like a damned palace, one of those Garden District mansions that would fit right in on the fantasy house program on the Home and Garden Network.

Sinking back into the seat, she stared out the window at blooming beds of late-season annuals as he parked behind someone's Mercedes. Sunday dinner in this place with his family was exactly what she didn't need.

Sex with Gerard had thrown her for a loop and, even though days had passed, she wasn't steady on her metaphoric feet yet. The memory of her last meeting with his family was still sharp and she felt nerved out and edgy, as if she had an audience with the royal family rather than a simple Gerard get-together.

These damn social gatherings so weren't her thing.

She reminded herself that this was a case, but after the sex…being within a five-mile radius of Gerard didn't feel anything like work.

Her *lover*.

Her *husband*.

Their marriage was just a cover, justified, rationalized. But she'd had sex with the man. He *really* was her lover. And her husband. While she hadn't reconciled herself to sleeping with him again, Gerard had transitioned into a fling neatly. He'd crawled into their bed each night, wrapped his arms around her and wouldn't let go. He'd brought her coffee to wake her up in the mornings. He'd even shown up in the bathroom while she was showering today to chat about how best to conduct a search of his grandfather's apartment during their visit.

He'd made it loud and clear that he liked his new status in her life and, short of shooting the man, Harley knew he wasn't going to disappear. She just wished her new status as *his* lover didn't make her quite so jumpy.

She'd known giving in to this man would be trouble.

But she couldn't complain. He'd agreed to keep their sex public for the benefit of the case, which had bought her a reprieve until the next time they went to Love Cajun Style.

It was bad enough when Gerard clung to her like a monkey in bed. She couldn't handle having him roll over in the night and start up a seduction while she was half-asleep and vulnerable to a bunch of stupid emotions she shouldn't be feeling.

This was sex, damn it, not a freaking romance.

Harley would do whatever it took to keep the differences straight. Falling asleep in Gerard's arms, drugged by the kind of sex they had, would definitely not support the cause.

Luckily he'd agreed to respect her wishes. He'd even made sure she was dressed appropriately for the occasion today. He'd pulled the vest and pants set from the closet himself, said it complemented his sports jacket. She liked the outfit. The embroidered vest wasn't fussy and the deep blue color worked with her hair. The hem of the vest covered her belly holster nicely, which was always a plus.

Of course the outfit had cost more than she'd spent renovating her master bathroom, but what the hey?—if Gerard was itching to spend his money...

Suddenly the car door swung open and he appeared, towering above her with the sunlight silhouetting his broad shoulders and his too-handsome face.

There was something so different about him since they'd slept together, something more possessive about the way he took her hand and helped her from the car, something less...overbearing. He seemed too calm almost, at peace with her in a way he'd never been before.

Then again why shouldn't he? He'd gotten what he'd wanted. He'd indulged his obsession with her and maybe she'd even luck out and he'd finally satisfy his desire for her.

Which was exactly what she was hoping for.

Especially after she got a good look at the inside of his family home, which was...well, *awesome*. The doorway opened onto a great hall with an ornate frieze of twining leaves and huge columns. A graceful marble staircase led to the upper stories, and showcased beneath the curving stairwell was a marble nymph that looked like it should have been in a museum.

"Why don't you live here?" She had to ask.

"Too crowded," Gerard replied as though that should have been obvious. "My grandfather has the second-floor apartment and my parents live up on the third. Ben moved out when he got married, but Courtney still lives here."

"A real tenement." Harley thought Cajun Joe's entire staff and their families could have moved in, but who was she to argue? Rich people obviously had a different idea about what constituted adequate personal space.

Glancing up, she shot him her best high-beam smile. "So where do the folks hang out? You'll have to navigate. I left my map in the car."

He frowned but she ignored him. The sooner they got on with this function, the sooner they'd be waving goodbye. Hopefully in one piece, she thought, after hearing a strident voice call from the bowels of the house, "Pearl, did someone just arrive?"

Within minutes, Harley had been introduced to the Gerard family's housekeeper and learned that their royal audience officially began with mimosas on the gallery. She drank coffee.

Gerard's parents were cordial and Stuart seemed genuinely pleased to see her. He patted the seat beside him on a porch swing. "Come sit with me, my dear. This was my Julia's favorite spot in the house. We swung on this gallery for sixty years, watching the sunsets while our family grew." She sat beside him and he took her hand. "Now, tell me all about your new home and how you and Mackenzie are settling in."

Harley enjoyed talking with him, answered what she could and left Gerard to handle the rest. As he had at the ribbon-cutting ceremony, he stepped smoothly into the breaches when she wasn't sure what to say.

She found it ironic that she kept relying on him to fill the gaps. He sat there sprawled on a bench with his sister, as comfortable as you please, talking about this whole made-up marriage as though he were a bridegroom in love.

She'd had no idea he was such an impressive actor—a skill that came in handy in their line of work. Somehow she'd missed this in all their months of training and she couldn't help but wonder if she'd missed it because she'd been so busy trying to ignore his pretty face.

At work, she'd been in the position of mentor. But now she was forced to take a back seat to his expertise. What struck her was how graciously he shared that expertise.

She'd never been so gracious. She'd resented him from the day he'd stepped foot inside Eastman Investigations, which begged her to ask why—because Gerard was an idiot or because she'd been too attracted to him?

A week ago, she'd have insisted the man was an idiot.

Now she wasn't sure, which rattled her almost more than their sex had.

"You don't scare me, Gerard," she remembered telling him at Cajun Joe's.

"You're a liar. If you weren't scared, you'd let me make love to you."

Harley had thought he was taunting her, but had she been so threatened by their attraction that she'd blinded herself to everything about him, even professionally?

That was a hard question, which meant she wasn't going to like the answer. Just looking at Gerard bore this up. He laughed at his father's comment, an easy laugh that relaxed his sculpted jaw and made his dimple appear.

When his gaze found hers, as it seemed to so often since their arrival, she recognized approval in those startling eyes, knew he enjoyed having her here surrounded by his family.

And there was no denying her body's response, the way her breath caught in her throat, the way her heartbeat quickened.

She must have shown something in her expression, because the next thing she knew, Gerard was working his way toward her, making her budge up on the bench. He didn't say anything. He just slipped his arm around her shoulder, as if he had every right in the world to touch her, and chatted with his grandfather until they were called in for the meal.

Unfortunately, the dining room quickly became an interrogation room, when Aunt Frances zeroed in on her with questions about her family—Harley's very favorite topic.

"I want to know more about the girl," Frances insisted, when Gerard and Stuart, to Harley's surprise, kept trying to get her out of the hot seat.

She appreciated the effort, but questions came along with working undercover and weren't something they could protect her from. She had no choice but to step up to the plate. "My father was in electronics here in New Orleans," she told the unrelenting aunt. "He owned a business."

"Owned? Did he retire?"

She shook her head. "He died. A long-term illness."

Well, alcoholism was a disease, which made cirrhosis of the liver a long-term illness.

"And your mother?"

"She died when I was young. An unfortunate accident."

Harley had been young when her mom had gotten so terrorized by her abusive husband that she'd run away and left Harley behind. It had been very unfortunate that she'd hooked up with another violent man who'd accidentally killed her.

Gerard eyed her warily, as if he couldn't decide whether to believe her. She smiled—see, acting came in *very* handy in their chosen profession.

"You went to school in town?" Aunt Frances wasn't through with her yet.

"The university." Which wasn't exactly Harvard, but she'd earned her degree in criminology fair and square and was proud of that degree. Of course, she didn't mention that in order to get into college she'd had to take a high-school equivalency exam and three semesters of remedial courses that had cost her a fortune and hadn't contributed one credit toward that degree.

Ah, life could be so unfair sometimes. But it could also throw you a lifeline when you least expected, too. And Courtney Gerard providing her a character reference was about the last thing Harley had expected.

"At the reception the other night, I knew I'd heard your

name, Harley, but I couldn't figure out where," Courtney said.

Gerard's older sister was a beautiful woman who looked a lot like him with her shiny hair and her big gray eyes. "It wasn't until days later that I remembered. You won the United Way Volunteer of the Year award last year."

Every eye targeted her as if she'd sprouted a bull's-eye on her forehead. God, she loved being the center of attention.

"You did?" Gerard asked, before she had a chance to reply.

Aunt Frances plunked her fork back on her plate and said, "An argument for a longer engagement, don't you think?"

"Who wants to know everything up front?" Aunt Camille waved a delicate hand. "Where's the mystery? Don't you agree, Mac?"

"I do indeed, Aunt." His gaze swept over Harley so possessively she actually shivered.

Had to give the guy credit. He wasn't shy about wearing his heart on his sleeve around this bunch. Given the circumstances, she understood why they all questioned his sanity.

Except perhaps for Stuart, Aunt Camille and maybe even Courtney.

"So, tell me about this award," he said.

Harley felt exposed when she should have been pleased to throw him a curve. "I do some pro bono investigative work."

Courtney frowned. "Margaret Baxter told me that you do *a lot* of pro bono work. She said you're not only conducting background research on domestic-abuse cases, but that whenever a father skips town to avoid support payments, you find him."

Harley gave a light shrug, not sure what to say. Margaret Baxter was an ageless virago who'd devoted her existence to improving the lot of children who were victims in domestic-abuse situations. She had to be pushing seventy, yet she still ran a private care facility called Angel House that transitioned abused mothers into safe houses, and children into the state social services system if both parents were deemed unfit.

"That's the only reason I remembered your name." Courtney continued. "My nominee and I were seated at the banquet with Margaret. She was thrilled when you won. She accepted your award because you couldn't be there."

"I couldn't make the ceremony." She'd *refused* to make the ceremony. Social events didn't happen if she could find any way out and Margaret hadn't pushed hard enough. Now Harley felt guilty. She'd known the award was an honor and had appreciated being nominated when so many contributed so much.

"Margaret spoke highly of all you do for Angel House."

"Margaret appreciates any help she can get," Harley said. "Her government supplements don't make a dent in the program and private contributions don't cover everything. She needs help."

Gerard had leaned back in his chair. "That's got to be *a lot* of work, Harley."

She shrugged. "Can't spend all my time in the dojo and on the gun range."

"So you know Margaret Baxter, young lady." Aunt Frances eyed her with a look that suggested this was the first thing she'd done worthy of notice. "For how long?"

Ever since Judge Bancroft had sent Harley for community service after getting busted for shoplifting a bra. She couldn't suppress a wicked thrill at the thought of Aunt

Frances's reaction to hearing *that* story. The great-aunt would probably swoon over her plate.

"Quite a few years now," she said, and luckily the arrival of the next course segued the conversation into talk about the ribbon-cutting ceremony and Courtney's next project. The spotlight swung in another direction and Harley was grateful when the meal finally ended.

On cue, Stuart invited her to tour his apartment, so she and Gerard accompanied him upstairs for a search of the cold crime scene. They hadn't expected to find anything, but once they were alone, Stuart informed them he'd been hit again.

"That Rolex your father gave me for my seventy-fifth birthday. I can't tell you if it disappeared during this week's cleaning-service visit. I only noticed it gone this morning and I'd completely forgotten the thing when I did my inventory."

"Didn't you check your list against the insurance company's?"

"I did, but I might have missed it." He spread his hands in entreaty. "Mackenzie, you know I never wear the thing."

The missing Rolex gave them a place to start looking and Harley relished getting back to work. She'd had her fill of social for the day, thank you very much. She'd much rather search a crime scene than try to impress a great-aunt.

It wasn't until later, after they'd said their goodbyes, that she was back to dealing with the one Gerard who made her dislike socializing more than the rest of the family combined.

Who would have thought *any* man could make her more nervous than a dinner party?

"Let's go home," he said.

"I'm sorry they hit your grandfather again," she said

once inside the car, keeping the focus on the investigation, a safe zone. "I don't think anyone questioned our cover so the outing was successful in that regard."

It was a *done* outing, the very best kind.

Night had long since fallen, layering them in a darkness that made the low-slung interior of Gerard's sports car seem intimate. He hadn't yet turned on the lights and the faint glow from the display illuminated his upper body and his face in profile, the long fingers he held loosely on the steering wheel.

"Does Josh know you do pro bono work?" he asked, his voice a rich whisper that filtered through the quiet, drew her attention to how close they were in the car's tight interior.

"He helps me sometimes."

"I had no idea."

She shrugged. "I'm chock-full of surprises."

His gaze cut through the darkness, a trick unique to him. Those crystalline eyes saw things inside her that no other eyes could. "Why do you keep them surprises?"

It was a simple question, but one she couldn't easily answer. Explanations weren't necessary with the people she cared about, and others—co-workers, boyfriends and acquaintances—all came and went so she never worried about impressing them.

Harley supposed she simply didn't share herself easily, not the good stuff or the bad. She never talked about her past, didn't even think about it when avoidable.

But she couldn't admit any of that to him without inviting all sorts of questions she didn't want to answer. "What difference does it make?"

"I want to know about you."

Damn, but one calmly issued declaration had the power

to make her go all soft and stupid inside. "Don't you think you're taking this too far?"

"How? I want to know about the woman I married."

"But this isn't a *real* marriage. There's no place to go except divorce court. Can't we just enjoy the trip there?"

"There are other places for us to go."

"No, there aren't. And it's crazy for you to even think that. We're on a case. Just because we've let some personal sneak in doesn't change the fact that we're working."

"Life is about more than work."

"Not for us it isn't. We don't swing in the same circles. You said so yourself, and you're right. I don't want to understand you and you will never understand me. You wanted a fling. You got one. Now let it be enough. Maybe in your world it's polite to observe the niceties while you're having sex, but it's not a corequisite in mine. We had sex. No more, no less."

"What if I want more?"

"You can't always get what you want. It's a fundamental rule of life. Be grateful you've escaped it this long."

That clear gaze cut the darkness, searching her face, promising so much more than Harley had bargained for.

"All I ask is that you try to keep an open mind," he said. "You told me I'd never take point on a case, and here we are with our trap all set. Sometimes what seems impossible turns out not to be so impossible after all."

Damn, if that didn't feel like a threat. And like all good threats, it wasn't something Harley could draw on and shoot.

11

Despite acquiring an unexpected husband and lover, Harley's week was off to a much better start than the previous one. While her own wheels weren't back on the road yet, she'd sealed the deal with All Parishes Pest Control. Work would begin on her house just as soon as she dropped off her key.

The movers had unloaded Gerard's things over the weekend so they'd finally spent their first night in their new home. She'd set up a consultation appointment with Nice and Neat just this morning, and had been running background checks on the employees ever since.

She and Gerard had divvied up the list of the top-tiered employees who serviced the Garden District homes. These particular staff members had means and opportunity, which left them searching for potential motive through various public, civil and criminal databases. Any convictions or indictments were of interest, along with payment delinquencies, bankruptcies and records of substance abuse.

By lunchtime, Harley had acquired a lot of information and even a couple of red flags.

Mercedes Del Torres had signed up with a credit counseling service to intervene with the financial institutions she owed significant totals.

Charlotte Bouvier had had recent dealings with a local bail bondsman to spring her deadbeat boyfriend from jail.

Allie Kimble had just completed community service

hours for a traffic infraction that had cost her driving privileges for a year.

While these leads were all starting points, they were nothing to get excited about. Harley was in the preliminary stages of her research and it took time to piece together a clear view of a person's life. Each database search peeled away another layer and, combined with the way the rest of Gerard's trap was neatly shaping up, they were making progress.

Josh had arrived in the office this morning to announce that he was also pleased with how they were establishing their cover. News of their marriage had been spreading through their circles of friends and acquaintances. This lent their marriage credibility, even if it did come with an unexpected side effect—wedding acknowledgments and gifts had started arriving.

Harley had told Melissa to store them in the file room. Miss Manners online gave them a full month to reply with a thank-you, and by then this case should be over. Gerard could ship every one of the gifts back and make explanations. She had no idea what excuse he would give, but she supposed his impromptu marriage and quickie divorce would support what most people already suspected—the man was losing his mind.

Here was a positive to *not* swing with blue bloods.

Harley would just tell Cajun Joe she'd grown tired of her new husband and dumped him. He'd laugh and tell her she'd been a fool to get married in the first place. While she might not rack up goodies from her friends like Gerard did, life seemed a whole lot simpler without having to write all those thank-you notes.

"Change of plans." Gerard materialized in the doorway of her office and she glanced up from her computer screen to find his arms filled with takeout from her favorite Chinese restaurant and a thick manila envelope.

He'd strolled into her office nearly every day of the past five months since coming to work for Josh, but somehow he looked different now. Somehow the *handsome* that she'd been trying to ignore had taken on a whole new level of *virile*. Her stomach did such a ridiculous flip-flop that she almost growled out her greeting.

"I think I might be on to something," he said, handing her a bag. "I need to make some calls. Mind if we eat here?"

"No shopping for jewelry on our lunch hour?" She tried to sound heartbroken. Peeking inside her bag, she found an order of egg rolls, hot mustard and a small carton of roast pork fried rice. One of her standard in-house luncheons, which meant Gerard had asked Melissa to order. "So what have you found?"

Dropping the envelope in front of her, he half-sat on the edge of her desk and dug through his own bag for a big carton and a fork. "Evangeline Wilson, the maid who serviced my grandfather's apartment on Friday. Given the Rolex's disappearance, I looked into her employment history. She's been with Nice and Neat for the past two years and services my grandfather's apartment at least once a month. She has had a lot of hits through the credit bureaus recently, so I want to look into her money trouble as a potential motive for the thefts."

"Good for you. I've got a few leads of my own here to follow up on. But since we're not jewelry shopping, I think I'll take a break first and head over to the pest control office to drop off my house key—"

"Not so fast," he said. "We still have to jewelry shop."

Okay, so he'd figured out she wasn't heartbroken. Bully

for him. "I thought you said you didn't want to leave the office."

"Reina sent some brochures from her private collection."

Harley leaned back in her chair to put distance between them and dragged an egg roll from the bag. "Her private collection, hmm, sounds so...*highbrow.*"

"She's a jewelry artist."

"Is this jewelry artist a friend?"

Had she been focusing her attention where it should have been—on her egg roll—she'd have been too busy chewing to have asked the question. It had just sort of popped out. She wasn't exactly sure why, because she didn't want to know about Gerard's love life. Especially while being momentarily trapped in it.

But the damage was done. He chewed his...chow mein with a smile that made her stomach do that crazy swooping thing again, which meant he'd interpreted her question to mean she was interested.

"Reina is a friend's wife."

"Great." She dunked her egg roll into the mustard container and tried not to scowl. "Do you mind my asking why we need custom-designed jewelry?"

"We're killing two birds with one stone here. Now that we've successfully set ourselves up as a decoy, we need to plant something attractive to steal. I don't want to wait forever for our thief to take the bait. Every day that passes lessens our chances of recovering my grandmother's rings. Reina's jewelry is high-ticket and different. It'll draw more attention and be easier to track down if it's fenced."

She would have asked exactly why Reina's jewelry was different but figured she'd find out soon enough. And Gerard had clearly given a great deal of thought about how to run his case so she didn't want to second-guess him. He was covering all the bases. She had the urge to tell him so, but managed to resist the impulse in favor of a bland, ''Makes sense.''

She couldn't recall ever paying the man a compliment, and she wouldn't start now. He might think she was mellowing out because of the sex.

Or worse yet—the marriage.

She took a big bite of her egg roll to keep her mouth too busy to ask any more personal questions or give in to any wild impulses to pay compliments.

Of course, she almost wound up choking on said bite when Gerard spread out the full-color glossy brochures and Harley got her first look at the private collection.

''Whoa, Gerard. You said jewelry. Those are sex toys.''

''Reina is an *erotic* jewelry artist.'' She didn't miss a flash of dimple that told her he was amusing himself at her expense. Stabbing his fork into the carton, he set it aside and picked up one of the brochures.

''Oh, yeah. I like this one.'' He pointed to a piece displayed artfully across a mannequin's bare breasts. ''I'll fantasize about you wearing this.''

Harley surveyed what looked like a long tennis bracelet dangling between two shiny gold nipple clamps. ''You better enjoy that fantasy because you won't be seeing the show live.'' Dropping her gaze to the blurb listing the details of the piece, she blinked. ''Correction—*really expensive* sex toys.''

''It's the pink diamonds,'' he said.

Harley had no idea what the significance of a pink diamond might be and wasn't going to ask. Besides, Gerard wasn't paying any attention anyway. He was too busy perusing the brochures.

''Would you like to make a selection?'' he asked.

''You're the boss.''

"Well then, I like this one…" He pointed to the pink-diamond nipple clamps then flipped the page to show her a beautifully crafted cloisonné bracelet. "And this."

There had to be a catch. The piece was too innocuous with its tiers of bright cloisonné, so she scanned the history to discover the double bracelet flipped apart to create handcuffs.

"I can make love to you without worrying about getting shot," he said, his husky tone conveying that he was remembering the last time she'd drawn her gun on him.

"I haven't put a bullet hole in you yet," she said dryly. "I have handcuffs if you're that worried."

"You keep them in the trunk of your car. You can wear this bracelet all the time and await my pleasure." He shot her a look of pure sex. His clear eyes lasered through her, promising her that he'd make awaiting his pleasure *very* worth her while. Harley felt heat pump into her cheeks.

She was in so much trouble here.

"If I wear the bracelet, how is our thief going to steal it?"

Gerard trailed a finger along her temple, brushing aside wisps of hair. She refused to pull away, refused to give him the upper hand, although her hot cheeks made any bravado a lie.

"That's why I'm buying two pieces," he said.

Damn, but she'd walked right into that one.

"No objections?"

"What's to object? It's not like I'll be wearing the stuff to *await your pleasure.* If you want me, Gerard, you can have me—at Cajun Joe's."

"I find it interesting that you'll only make love to me in a controlled environment. How should I interpret that?"

"I don't care how you interpret it. This is a job. You

want to screw, then we screw in the sex dungeon where it counts."

A beat of silence passed. Harley forced herself to stand her ground, but what she saw in his clear eyes only fueled the heat in her cheeks.

Gerard wasn't buying anything she said. "I thought you said Cajun Joe's was a private social club."

"Whatever." She dropped her egg roll back onto the wrapper. Appetite gone.

He reached for the phone. "Then the nipple clamps and the bracelet restraints it is."

"Have at it, Gerard. It's your money."

She focused back on running Mercedes Del Torres's immigration records, but concentrating was a lost cause when she sat six inches from Gerard's thigh and could overhear his half of the conversation with the erotic jewelry artist.

The brochures hadn't listed all of the prices, which should have been her first clue that if one had to ask the price of a piece, one couldn't afford it.

But *five* figures for nipple clamps?

She didn't care if they were pink diamonds. Just the thought of that kind of money made her head swim. Especially when he added another five figures for the bracelet.

With that kind of money, she could have paid off the exterminator, every cent of her student loans and *still* have enough left over to buy a new transmission.

Unable to resist the urge, she glanced up at him, sitting casually on her desk, rattling off his credit card number by heart. His custom slacks and Egyptian cotton shirt screamed money but *how much* money seemed to be the next logical question.

Harley didn't have a clue. She was so out of her league here. The only thing she could be sure of was that Gerard's

family—excluding Stuart, Aunt Camille and perhaps Courtney—was right about him. This man had definitely lost his
mind.

He hung up the phone and reached for his lunch. "Reina
knocked off another twenty percent as a wedding gift."

"I'll add her name to the thank-you list." To Harley's
amazement, she actually delivered that with a straight face.

Scooping up the half-eaten egg roll, she stuffed it into
the bag. "I'll finish lunch later. I've got to swing by the
exterminator's."

She was out the door before he could say another word.

MAC LEFT THE OFFICE after placing phone calls to Josh's
contacts in the national credit bureaus that purchased records from banks and retailers detailing financial activities.
He'd waited until lunchtime, because contacts talked more
freely when upper management was out to lunch. Harley
had taught him that.

She'd also taught him to keep digging until he'd answered all his questions. And it just so happened he had a
lot of questions about a woman with VIP status at a sex
dungeon, who volunteered enough time to a domestic-abuse
shelter to earn the United Way Volunteer of the Year
award.

So he'd added investigating Harley to his to-do list and
headed into the Quarter to visit Love Cajun Style. Employees also talked more freely when their bosses weren't
around. He suspected Cajun Joe wouldn't be around this
time of day.

The club lost a good deal of its luster in the daylight.
The building was like so many others in the Quarter, historic and architecturally attractive but weathered and in
need of constant maintenance.

He found the front doors unlocked and walked inside,

ringing a bell on the registration desk. Within minutes a middle-aged woman with waist-length graying blond hair appeared from the room behind the bar, a kitchen, Mac assumed.

"What can I do for you, doll?" she called out as she circled the bar and crossed the dance floor. She might have looked like a throwback from the seventies with her long hair and flowy clothes, but as she approached, Mac realized she was still a very attractive woman in her hippie sort of way.

"I want to book a room for tomorrow night."

"Fetish night." She eyed him closely. "I don't remember seeing you here before. Are you a member?"

"I came last week as Harley Price's guest."

The woman did a little hop-skip to get behind the desk, then stood back to survey him. "So you're Cha Cha's new hubby. I heard all about you, and let me say that you are living up to the press. I'm Delilah." She thrust a hand toward him and he took it within his own, then brought it to his lips.

"Mac Gerard. A pleasure."

She actually giggled and Mac returned her smile, glad he'd made a good first impression.

"So what's your fetish? Not many choices left, but I've still got a couple of rooms available."

"What room did Harley like best when she worked here?"

Always appear to have more information than you need. Another of Harley's lessons.

Delilah glanced up from the computer, surprised. "I don't know that she had a favorite, doll. She was too young to care what the guests were paying to do around here. Cha Cha was usually so wiped out by the time she got to Joe that she was just happy for a hot meal and a place to crash.''

The image of a *too* young Harley wiped out and needing a hot meal and a place to crash wasn't what Mac had expected. He shot her what he hoped was a puzzled look. ''I must have misunderstood what she told me. I assumed she was older when she worked here.''

Delilah shook her head.

''What did my beautiful bride do here when she was young?''

''Cha Cha helped her dad do the electrical work when Joe bought the place back in eighty-two.'' Now it was Delilah's turn to frown. ''What'd you think she did here?''

Mac did the math and realized Harley would have been only seven or eight, which invited more questions, but he didn't want this woman to suspect he was interrogating her. Reaching into his grab bag of Harley investigative tricks, he played stupid.

''You know, Delilah.'' He shook his head and gave her a lame smile. ''I never even thought to ask until right now.''

Her chuckle told him she bought it. ''Well, now you know. Cha Cha used to help her dad do the wiring whenever Joe decided the place needed a face-lift. A smart little thing.''

''I knew her dad had owned an electronics business. I just didn't realize she worked with him.''

Delilah gave a sad smile. ''She worked *for* him sometimes. Joe would've cut the unreliable bastard loose a long time before he died if not for Harley.''

Mac realized two things. Delilah's open hostility meant that the man's character must be common knowledge. This woman clearly cared for Harley and wouldn't speak so freely if she'd have been worried he'd repeat their conversation. Which led to realization number two—Harley must have shared a similar opinion of her father.

Following up on a suspicion, Mac said, "She doesn't talk much about her dad. He must have died a while ago."

Delilah nodded, appeared to think hard. "Yeah, Cha Cha was what…about eleven, I guess. A *long* time ago."

Mac smiled. "I can't wait to tell her we met, but, Delilah, before I go I have to ask—why do you call her Cha Cha?"

She considered him thoughtfully for a moment and Mac got the impression that she felt sorry for him, as if he didn't know something so simple about his own wife.

"Okay, doll, first you gotta picture Cha Cha as a little girl," she said. "A teeny tiny thing with all this red hair. She was gorgeous. This place was a strip joint for years and the strippers used to tease her that she'd grow up and put them all out of business. Whenever she was here, they'd try to teach her how to dance, but she'd run out that door, saying she wouldn't cha-cha for anyone. Joe thought it was a hoot and started calling her that. The name just stuck."

Mac laughed, but it was a laugh that came straight from his mouth because there was nothing about him amused.

Delilah smiled. "She was a cute kid, doll. We all love her. Especially Joe. Speaking of…" She glanced at the computer screen. "He doesn't have his penthouse booked for tomorrow. I know he'd gladly give it to Cha Cha. Otherwise, I've only got the waterplay, the waxworks and the bondage rooms left."

"Put us down for the bondage room." Restraints might help him get some answers.

After saying goodbye, he crossed the street to his car, but didn't drive away. Mac sat there staring into the sun-washed afternoon. While most of the clubs catered to night crowds, the French Quarter stayed on twenty-four/seven.

People milled around busily during the day, sightseeing or heading to the many eateries for lunch.

He couldn't shake the image of a *too* young Harley covering for her father on the job.

"What brings you to my love hole in the dark? Hungry?" Mac remembered Cajun Joe asking on their first visit to the club.

"I need a room, Joe. Got anything for me?"

"You always got a room here, Cha Cha. You know that."

Why had Harley needed a place to crash? Why hadn't her father been working and caring for his daughter?

"He died. A long-term illness," she'd told his great-aunt.

"And your mother?"

"She died when I was young. An unfortunate accident."

Her father had apparently died when she'd been young, too. What had happened to her after his death?

It wasn't much of a leap to put Judge Bancroft and her pro bono work together.

She'd somehow been involved with the state's social services.

Mac leaned back against the headrest and closed his eyes, as if that might block out the view of a *too* young Harley running down this street to get away from a bunch of strippers.

"I do not dance," she'd told him at the wedding.

He'd never thought to ask why and now it came crashing in on him how much he didn't know about her. So much that he didn't even stand a chance at figuring out how to win her heart.

Or earn her trust. He was beginning to think that trust was the key issue here. Harley trusted Anthony DiLeo. She trusted Cajun Joe. She trusted Josh.

She didn't trust him.

Had he ever done anything to earn her trust?

No.

Amazing how fast that answer came. How much the truth hurt. No, he'd never done a thing worthy of her trust.

He'd challenged her instead. When they were at work, or in the dojo or even during the teamwork training session. After he'd realized they were attracted to each other, he'd challenged her with their attraction, too. He'd wanted a fling so he'd cornered her into marriage for a chance to seduce her without Anthony DiLeo's interference.

He'd only thought about what he wanted. He hadn't once stopped to consider what Harley might want, or *need*.

It hadn't been hard to figure out that she couldn't foot the bill for the termite extermination—not after overhearing her conversation with Anthony. He'd put two and two together, made some calls to local pest control companies and found out she was ten grand shy of exterminating her pests.

But it hadn't occurred to him to look any deeper to understand why she was so shy on cash. Instead he'd used her need as leverage to force her into marriage to help his grandfather and get a shot at a fling.

Mac had been so concerned with what he'd wanted, it had never occurred to him to ask why she was fighting him so hard. He knew she wanted him and that was all he'd cared about.

Now he realized she'd most likely seen his challenges as threats, his actions as self-serving. She didn't trust him, so she'd fought him and bumped up her efforts the closer he got.

And he'd kept pushing, believing she'd ultimately give in. And she had—she'd made love to him with a gun in her hand and without letting him touch her. Then she'd refused to make love again unless she was in the safety of Cajun Joe's dungeon.

Harley had accused him of being arrogant.

Mac was guilty of a lot more.

12
_____

AFTER THEIR INTERVIEW with Caroline Thompson, Harley walked the granddaughter of Nice and Neat's owner to the front door, handed her a house key and confirmed their first appointment for Friday.

"We'll take good care of you, Mrs. Gerard," Caroline said with a smile. "I've got my list of everything you'd like done. If you have any questions or problems, you give me a call."

She handed Harley a business card then headed across the portico and down the steps to a van with the Nice and Neat logo on the side.

Harley watched her drive away, pleased with the interview. She'd toured the woman through the house, detailing what she wanted the maid service to clean with emphasis on the bedroom where they would plant Gerard's expensive sex toys.

This part of the job had been kind of fun. Having a maid had been a dream of Harley's for as long as she could remember. She could spend three solid days sanding down the woodwork of a room and never have it feel like work, but scrubbing a floor...it had never done much for her.

Housecleaning was one of life's ironies—if one wanted a home, one must clean it. Unless, of course, one swung in Mr. Blue Blood's circles. Then one simply wrote a check.

Stepping back inside, she found Mr. Blue Blood himself standing on the bottom riser, arm draped casually over the balustrade, looking remarkably like the king of the mansion for a man who'd moved into his house less than a day ago.

"Are you all right, Gerard? This is your investigation and you let me conduct that interview. Are you sick?"

"I'm not sick."

Harley wasn't sure she believed him. Something was up and had been ever since she'd returned to the office from the pest control company. "Weren't you happy with the interview? Caroline answered every one of our questions."

"The interview went very well." But he didn't say anything else, just kept watching her.

She wanted to ask what the hell he was up to, but closed the door and kept her mouth shut instead. She didn't need to get into anything with him before they headed out to an art auction with his brother Ben and his wife.

She didn't need the stress. The sex toys had pitched her over the edge before lunch. Now the thought of sitting in a room, afraid to cross her legs or sneeze while some auctioneer ran his mouth...Harley could only hope she didn't freak and start twitching or something else equally stupid that would wind up with her as the new owner of the Mona Lisa.

Attempting to sound casual, she swept toward the stairs and said, "Well, come on. Let's get started placing those remote receiver video cameras. It'll take us hours to get every foot of this place wired. By then it should be about time for you to dress me so I look like I fit in."

THE NEXT DAY Mac came face-to-face with another clue to the depth of Harley's loyalty to the people she trusted. During a conversation in the office about their defense training, she'd mentioned to Josh that her own trainer had recently opened a new facility. She hadn't criticized their current training situation and it turned out she didn't have to. Their boss was dissatisfied enough to ask about hers.

When Harley had told him how long she'd been with her trainer, Josh had wanted to make a trip to meet the man. So Mac found himself back at Anthony DiLeo's place, climbing the stairs to his brother Damon's dojo.

"*Do not,* I repeat, *do not* say one word about our fake-o marriage to Damon," Harley cautioned on the way up.

"You haven't told your friends?" Mac knew he shouldn't be surprised, didn't think surprise was responsible for the jealous, ugly way he felt right now.

"There was no point. My friends are no help or threat to our cover. They don't swing in your circles and they're not thieves, either."

"Not a problem for me," Josh said.

Mac didn't like being her nasty secret to people obviously important to her, but given her on-again, off-again relationship with Anthony, he supposed the reason he'd given his own family—the truth ironically—wouldn't have gone over well.

He'd play by her rules. This was about Harley dealing with people she cared about whether he understood or not. And Mac didn't understand. Was the no-commitment, be-available-when-it's-convenient relationship Harley had with Anthony really all she wanted?

He kept his mouth shut and followed her inside.

Damon DiLeo was a younger version of his older brothers. He shared the same golden Italian fairness and dark eyes, but this DiLeo wore his hair halfway down his back. His dojo was new with a few subtle touches that Mac recognized as observations of formal ceremonial customs, despite his informal attire of worn sweatpants that revealed an aggressively physical frame.

"Hey, Red." Damon strode toward them and gave Harley a quick hug before she performed introductions. He shook Josh's hand. "So you want a show. Timing couldn't be better since Red hasn't been in to practice all week."

"I've been busy on a case," she said. "I'll go change while you dazzle Josh with your credentials."

She disappeared down a hallway and Mac noticed she hadn't brought her gear, which suggested she stored her things here. Here was one more DiLeo she trusted implicitly and apparently knew very well because Damon did indeed have the credentials to dazzle. When Josh had finished grilling him, Mac asked a few questions of his own—about Harley and how long they'd been training together.

"Man, you want to laugh?" Damon said with a smile. "And I swear it's the God's honest truth. We've been training together since we were six years old. I tried practicing my Bruce Lee moves on her and she hauled off and gave me a bloody nose. I've been polishing up her technique ever since."

Josh laughed and Harley reappeared, dressed in pink sweats with a muscle shirt that molded to her upper body like a second skin. "Did he tell you I can still bloody his nose?"

Damon scoffed. "So she's been telling herself for the last twenty-plus years."

These two were obviously very close, but when they faced each other across the mat, their whole mood changed. They became competitors who knew each other's strengths and weaknesses and played to win.

He and Josh kicked back to watch the show and they weren't two minutes into the performance before Mac realized that five months of defense training with Harley hadn't given him a glimpse of the true depth of her technique.

She was at home in this dojo in a way that he—or Josh,

judging by his comments—had never seen her before. She was at the top of her form working with her lifelong trainer and the two of them did indeed put on quite the show.

She was so impressive, a bundle of controlled energy and lightning-quick motion, and they weren't the only ones who thought so. Mac caught a reflection in the mirror and turned to find Anthony silhouetted in a doorway from a hall that must have led to his shop below.

Once again he wore his work uniform and he was watching Harley and his brother with a slight smile, as if he was remembering a lot of years with these two going at each other. Then he caught Mac's reflection.

"You came with an audience, princess," he said.

"I brought my boss," Harley replied breathlessly as she dodged Damon's heel and pivoted sideways.

"Josh, Mac, my brother Anthony," Damon said. "So what do you want, big bro? As you can see I'm trying to impress potential clients."

"*Trying* is right. Not much of a show with just you and the princess here."

Damon gave a grunt of laughter, a distraction that cost him because Harley took his legs out with a sweeping kick that sent him down to the mat. She was on him in one skillful roll before he tossed her back off again.

Anthony laughed.

"Don't laugh too hard," Damon said. "You spent more time on your back than on your feet the last time you played with Red."

"What are you saying, Anthony?" Harley said with mock innocence, though she never took her eyes off Damon. "That it takes two big DiLeo boys to bring down little old me?"

Josh leaned back in his chair with a laugh because Harley's challenge had an immediate and equal effect on the two big DiLeo boys. Damon lunged for her and suddenly Anthony was kicking off his shoes and pulling off his socks.

He headed onto the mat, looked askance at them. "If you want a real show, you've got to challenge the princess."

The princess backed away and squared off against her opponents, clearly challenged and clearly loving it. "So I ask again—it takes two big DiLeos to take on little old me?" Her eyes flashed as she assumed a combative stance.

Raising her arms, she motioned her opponents toward her. "Then come on, boys, challenge me."

Mac watched three people who'd obviously been playing this game a long time face one another across the mat. Anthony bowed. Damon grinned. Harley tossed her head back, her clear laughter ringing through the dojo, a sound that rushed him with the same intensity that she rushed her opponents.

Josh leaned forward, elbows on his knees, obviously enjoying the show. "You've been a friend of my wife's for a long time, Mac, and I consider you a friend now, too," he said in a voice low enough not to be overheard. "So I'm going to give you a piece of advice." He slanted Mac a sidelong glance. "Unless you tell me you don't want it."

"Shoot."

"You need to make the effort to get to know Harley. Give her a chance. You might just be surprised."

Mac shifted his attention back to the floor and watched her. Every move was a display of controlled motion. Her chest rose and fell sharply with her exertion. Her skin was flushed. Her eyes sparkled. She looked more challenged, more alive...*freer* than he'd ever seen her before.

Mac knew then that this was the woman he had to reach, the woman who rarely came out from behind the shields.

He didn't bother looking at Josh when he said, "I know."

A DECENT WORKOUT, drumming up new business for Damon, and a solid connection between a Nice and Neat employee and a local pawnshop did wonders for Harley's mood. She felt more centered than she had for days.

A good thing since she was facing Fetish Night.

Gerard had made the arrangements himself and she tried to decide whether that should scare her as he escorted her inside Love Cajun Style for another night of sex. She decided to continue doing what she'd been doing all along— ignoring it.

But Gerard wasn't easy to ignore. His hand rode low on her waist as if it belonged there. Fortunately, greeting Bear provided a decent distraction and finding Delilah behind the registration desk diverted her further.

"How did Joe get you to work at night?"

Delilah had been Cajun Joe's companion for as long as Harley had known them, a reoccurring couple not unlike her and Anthony. But whether they were on or off, Delilah was Joe's right-hand person in business. She didn't do grunt work.

Circling the desk, Delilah hugged her and smiled big at Gerard. "I didn't want to miss you. I danced all over Joe's head last week for not calling me when you came in."

"You're in bed at nine, Delilah. You'd have danced all over his head if he had called you."

"I'd have gotten up for you and your new hubby, Cha Cha." She laughed then reached up to pinch Gerard's cheek. "You caught yourself a cutie. We had a nice chat and picked out a fun room for you."

Harley eyed them warily. "What's my poison?"

"Bondage," Gerard said offhand as he kissed Delilah's hand in a move that made her visibly melt.

Sheesh. "Can't wait." Good thing the pantsuit she wore had a jacket to hide her shoulder holster, because if the man intended to restrain her, she'd definitely be using it.

When they finally made it past Joe at the bar and into their room, Harley was primed and ready to draw her weapon if Gerard took one step toward her before they established some rules. He didn't seem worried enough for her peace of mind as he sauntered over to the sideboard, helped himself to some coffee.

He looked like he always did when he went out at night to a nonformal function, tailored sports jacket, shirt and slacks. But somehow seeing him standing inside a room with a *huge* bed, lots of mirrors and chains dangling from the ceiling gave her a new slant to his tall, dark and handsome self.

Or maybe it was anticipating how he'd look without those clothes, how he'd feel inside her. Or that he wanted to use some of those chains...

"We've got to talk, Gerard."

Inclining his head toward the sofa and table that created a conversation pit in one corner—the corner next to the wall with an assortment of whips and paddles—he said, "Have a seat. We'll talk."

Harley didn't sit. She prowled the perimeter of the room. He just shrugged off his sports coat, poured a second cup and got comfortable.

"Come sit," he said again. "I want to tell you something."

She didn't want to hear but sat to keep things civil. He turned to her and scooted closer, close enough to toy with her hair where it draped over the sofa back.

"Is this foreplay?" she asked.

His smile made her breath catch. "I'd like it to be."

"I thought that's why we came."

"We haven't come yet, but we will if you let me touch you."

She rolled her eyes, not sure who to be more disgusted with—him for his stupid pun or her for walking into it. Didn't matter. He was making her jumpy and he knew it.

"Why are you suddenly being so nice? You didn't need my permission the last time we were here. You provoked me until you got what you wanted."

"Yes, I did."

"You admit it?"

He nodded, and wrapped that lock of hair around his finger. "When I booked this room with Delilah, I thought I'd need restraints to make love to you without a gun to my throat."

"I got that part loud and clear. You bought the designer handcuffs, remember?" She held up her wrist to reveal the handcuff in question, an innocent bracelet that wasn't.

"I don't feel that way anymore."

"How do you feel?" She was breathless. There was an intimacy between them that had never been there before, that made it hard to keep her distance.

"I don't want to screw. I want to pleasure you."

"Are you trying to freak me out?"

He laughed softly, tracing his thumb down her cheek, along her jaw. "I'm not trying to freak you out."

"You're doing a damn good job."

"I want to make love to you tonight. I want you to let me."

"You're asking?"

He nodded. "I haven't given you any reason to trust me. I understand that. I'm asking you to trust me anyway."

"What if I say no? Will you use your designer handcuffs and make me?" Just the thought of Gerard *making her* sent her stomach into a nosedive. An ache started between her thighs, a hot liquid pulsing that made her crotch grow warm in her leather.

"I'll respect your wishes and let you run the show. Even if you pull your gun and tell me not to touch."

Okay, now he had her. She could handle this man when he challenged her. She could handle fighting him during training. She wasn't sure she could handle him all intimate and…*agreeable*. She expected him to be an idiot.

She *counted* on him being an idiot.

This sudden affability reminded her of when he held her in bed at night. Sleep dulled the edges, and there was just him and her and the quiet. It was all right because they didn't talk. She didn't need to defend herself against his stupid remarks or her own vulnerability. But they were awake now. He didn't want to screw, he wanted to make love.

Big difference.

"Why should I trust you?"

"I owe you."

"Really, what for? Last I looked you lent me your car, bought me clothes, gave me a place to stay while my house is being exterminated and offered to turn over your share of our professional fee and rewards. You even bought groceries, Gerard. What could you possibly owe me?"

"Courtesy and respect."

He wasn't talking about *stuff*, and she desperately wished he was. *Stuff* was so much easier.

"We've been working together for five months," he said. "We've gotten married and slept together. But I haven't made any effort to know you. I judged you a long time ago, not understanding how I felt. I wasn't fair. Not to you or to me. I want to change that, if you'll let me.''

His honesty was killing her. She avoided his eyes and reached for her cup to have something to do with her hands. "You don't want to know me. You don't feel anything but horny.''

"I do.''

"It won't make any difference.''

"I'll take my chances.''

The earnestness in his voice told her he meant exactly what he said. And she wondered at the implications of *that*. She was reasonably certain she couldn't handle the truth, nor would she want to. "What do you want from me?''

"Only what I told you. I want you to keep an open mind. I'll do the rest. Tonight...'' She could hear the smile in his voice. "I want to pleasure you.''

Pleasure.

That ache between her legs swelled with the promise in his voice. He was coming at her from a whole new angle, one that she wasn't up to coping with. Before they'd had sex, she'd have laughed in his face, but now...now he was hitting her in all the places she felt fragile and that wasn't funny.

Suddenly he was plucking the cup from her hands, drawing her back against him in the corner of the plush leather sofa.

"I haven't been any fairer to you, you know,'' she said breathlessly. "We're square.''

"No. We owe each other,'' he whispered into her ear, a warm burst of sound that made her shiver. "You let me make love to you. I'll give you pleasure. *Then* we'll be square.''

He made it sound so simple. So easy. As if she could close her eyes and tell him to have at it.

That ache urged her to give in. The heat slogging through her blood and the sight of his tanned hands around her middle made her need his touch in a way she'd never needed before. And he was being such a gentleman. She couldn't let him assume all the responsibility for being unfair, could she? She'd been just as unfair to him, hadn't cut him a break once, or even praised him for how far he'd come in his training.

And what would be the point of denying him...? They were going to have sex tonight anyway.

"Have at it, Gerard," she said in a thick voice that didn't sound like her own.

He gave a rumble of pleasure deep in his throat, swept aside the hair from her neck and bent his head low.

Every hard inch of his body curled around her. His chest created a protective shelter and the bulge of his growing erection pressed into her bottom. His mouth sucked and nibbled a path from collar to ear, his hot breaths tickling her skin. He seemed in no particular hurry. He breathed in her scent. He threaded his fingers into her hair. He explored her as though he'd waited forever for the privilege.

She'd half expected him to strip her down and get on with it, but quickly realized that Gerard had meant exactly what he'd said. He wanted to pleasure her.

With those strong fingers twined in her hair, he urged her head back against his shoulder, her neck arching to expose her throat. He sucked softly on the pulse point beating with languid throbs, slow erotic pulls that she could feel echoing through her body like a velvet tremor.

He made love to her face with his hands, exploring each curve, every line, tracing her brows, her eyes, her nose, her lips as if he wanted to memorize her features. His fingertips and palms rasped along her skin. His mouth followed in the wake of his hands, nuzzling, tasting...his brand of pleasure drugged her. His every touch fueled the ache inside that needed him to trail those magic fingers from her hair and her face and her neck...*lower.*

But what surprised her the most was how Gerard savored each touch, as if he felt more for her than attraction, as if touching her wasn't just a new and clever way to get past her defenses. Each touch was so careful, each kiss so tender, she might have actually thought he cared.

But she knew better. He was playing her. He knew she struggled to resist him and, like any good opponent, he'd zeroed in on that weakness, used it to his advantage.

And she let him, because she didn't have the will to resist, didn't want to resist. Not now when his touches felt so...*right.*

But Harley wouldn't forget this was one battle. Even though his mouth and his hands made it so difficult to remember the war still raged on...

Gerard paused in his exploration long enough to peel away her jacket, to expose her bare arms, her gun.

"Unfasten your holster."

She let her eyes flutter closed, swallowing back the urge to tell him she'd rather unfasten her pants.

"Trust me," he said simply, his voice throaty and earnest. He pressed a kiss to the top of her head and waited.

If nothing else, he was playing fair and she respected that. Harley didn't *trust* it, but she did respect it. Unfastening the buckle at her waist, she let him slide the belt from her loops. He withdrew the holster and dropped it into her lap.

His breathing resounded in the quiet, each breath deepening as he parted her bodice, realized there was no bra to obstruct him. The bulge nestling against her butt swelled greedily, attesting to his control as he peeled the leather away, exposed her shoulders, her breasts to the air.

Her nipples prickled almost uncomfortably, stretching full and tight with expectation, but he didn't touch her there. He molded the curve of her shoulders instead, grazed his fingertips down the length of her arms, making her yearn and want and anticipate. Harley soon discovered that Gerard's control wasn't the control in question tonight.

She wanted to slide her arms around his neck and pull his face toward hers until she could reach his mouth, could hide from this need in a kiss. She wanted to act, to abandon reason with passion. All this leisurely exploration was killing her.

Every slow stroke of his hands along her arms, every brush of his lips against her jaw, her neck, her shoulder, was undoing her bit by bit. Her sex had grown so warm and moist that she couldn't stop squeezing her muscles tight to feed the ache, yearned to shed the hot leather prison of her clothes.

But Gerard only lifted her arm, brought her hand to his mouth and explored even that with exquisite thoroughness. His breaths burst against her palm. His tongue trailed through the web of each finger, traced the wedding band. He worked his way down her wrist, his lips caressing her skin, igniting a need she hadn't known could be so intense.

He caught the bracelet with his teeth, clamped down hard, a bite that hinted at the cost of his own restraint. The sound echoed through the quiet and the fierceness of it made her breath catch, a gasp that could only prove she'd fallen under the spell of the moment as well.

She expected him to press his advantage, but he only lifted her arm higher, ran his tongue along the delicate skin underneath. One long stroke that made her shiver.

He brought her body to life with anticipation, with pleasure. And only after he'd explored every sensitive inch of her arm did his hands snake lower. His fingertips grazed her ribs, teased the undersides of her breasts until she clutched the gun, an anchor to cling to when she wanted to grab him, a reminder that she still had control if she wanted it. Which was the problem...she didn't. She wanted nothing more than to let Gerard satisfy this ache.

She wanted to feel him spread out naked against her. She wanted to explore him with the same thoroughness he used to explore her, she wanted to take him apart at the seams until he trembled.

But she was the one trembling. He found her nipples and rolled them between his fingers, tugged the sensitive tips. Her sex pulsed so hard she could only rock her hips back against him, inspiring his erection to greater proportions, feeding the demand that throbbed with his knowing touch.

Then his hands cupped her breasts, hauled her back against him, the seam of the pantsuit catching her in exactly the right spot to feed the ache. And when he plucked at her nipples again, she went to pieces right there, exploded, her body spinning out of her control.

He rocked his erection against her, rode out her climax, his own struggle evident in the gathering of his muscles, the kisses he raged along her shoulder and neck.

But Gerard didn't stop there. He didn't give her a chance to recover, to think, to catch her breath. He just left her gasping, left her drinking in the scent of his skin, his hair and he slid out from behind her. Sinking to his knees, he swept his hot gaze over her as she collapsed into the cushions, weak and wanting, still gasping for air.

He didn't smile or look smugly triumphant at all. He just knelt before her like some freaking sex slave and slipped the heels from her feet.

"I want to see you naked."

The gruff need in his voice made her crotch throb all over again and she bit back a moan and dodged his needy expression as she swiveled around bonelessly to accommodate him.

Gerard needed no further permission. His hands urged her to hang on to her gun as he leaned over her, helping her lift up so he could tug the pantsuit over her hips, taking her panty hose along with it.

"You're beautiful," he said in that throaty voice that sounded like sex, and she braced herself for his next move, expected to feel his hard body against hers, some reward for bringing her pleasure.

But Gerard stood. He tugged her up and lifted her into his arms. She was forced to hang on, to bury her face against his shoulder, as much to avoid their reflection in the mirrors as to avoid his hungry but almost gentle expression.

"Do you want to bring your gun?" he asked, no humor or condemnation in his voice, just a simple question.

She could stand up to his challenges, but it had only taken a few orgasms to learn she couldn't bear up to his tenderness. At least not when she was feeling so raw herself.

"Do I need to?"

"Only you can answer that, Harley. I'm no threat."

But he was a threat and to admit she needed her gun was tantamount to admitting how big a threat he was.

"Leave it."

He carried her to the bed and lay her out before him wearing nothing but his bracelet and his wedding band. He stood above her, so terribly handsome with his hair gleaming in the candlelit darkness, his strong features softening as he swept his gaze over her, his expression intense.

"What happens now?" she asked, needing to hear a voice, even her own, to fill the silence.

He sank to the edge of the bed, all fluid muscle and

grace, dragged his palm along the length of her thigh. "I find more ways to pleasure you."

"Another orgasm like that and you might kill me."

He paused, hand hovering above her neatly shaved sex, the heat from his palm making her skin tremble. "I won't kill you."

She gave a desperate laugh. "That's probably a good thing. Otherwise, I won't be able to reciprocate."

He brushed his fingertips along the curve, his gaze dropping to her stomach as it contracted sharply in reply. "Tonight isn't about reciprocation."

"Is this some deep, dark fantasy of yours? I honestly never imagined you as the sex-slave type."

"I'm not. But tonight I'm all about pleasing you. That's my fantasy."

Harley flinched beneath such honesty, beneath the look in his eyes that backed up his statement and made pleasing her seem like some noble life accomplishment.

She couldn't analyze that statement, *wouldn't,* even if she could think with his eyes burning into her, his light touches making her insides vibrate. Fortunately, she couldn't, except for one inescapable thought—she'd rather be succumbing to his climaxes than having this conversation.

So she arched her hips and parted her thighs enough to invite him inside. "Then have at it, Gerard."

And he did. He leaned nearer, one hand bracing him into a half sitting, half kneeling position over her, a position that blocked out the chains above his head, the mirrors. A position that narrowed her focus until he was her whole world.

She wasn't sure why he hadn't undressed, unless he thought his clothes provided an added layer of protection, physical proof that he was no threat, that he could control himself.

His clothes made her feel so incredibly naked.

Especially when he caressed his fingers into the creamy folds of her sex, slow, sleek curls that started up the whole achy, needy thing all over again. He bent low, raining light kisses along her stomach, her ribs, her breasts. Making it damn near impossible not to sink her fingers into his hair and drag him against her, to rock her hips against his hand to feel him slide his fingers deep into her wetness.

He latched onto a nipple, and that wash of hot sensation made control impossible. Her fingers speared into his silky hair, held him locked against her. His name tumbled from her lips as he drove her wild with his mouth.

Pleasure…she felt pleased as he dragged his lips over her skin, across her nipples, over her breasts, down her stomach and back again. His fingers teased and took liberties.

Pleasure…she was pleased that his touches drove all thought away, protected her from the emotions inside, making her yearn to act crazy, totally and desperately crazy.

She wanted to lock her ankle around his and flip him beneath her. She wanted to strip off his expensive clothes to reveal the gorgeously tanned body below. She wanted to assume control of this need, wanted to feed it by exploring *his* body, by savoring *his* urgent responses, hearing *his* throaty growls of pleasure as he came unglued.

But she'd promised to trust him, to let him please her.

To do anything else would be admitting she wanted more than to feel his erection inside her.

She wouldn't, *couldn't* do that.

So she clung desperately to him instead, arching into his touches, dragging her fingers through his hair. She explored the terrain of his broad shoulders, his strong back, her hands searching anything she could reach until the pleasure became so extreme she feared she might explode.

But he wouldn't bring her to completion. He kept spurring her higher and higher, his thumb circling that bunch of nerve endings. His long fingers teased, gliding sleekly along her folds in a trail of her body's moisture.

Pleasure so intense it was becoming torture…and not only for her. Gerard finally broke away, raising above her to catch her mouth with his, a kiss of such urgency that Harley couldn't doubt she was the only one close to losing control. His tongue speared inside. Their breaths collided. She was struck that this urgency was so much more than sex.

Now it was her turn to break free, rolling away from him and his lethal mouth, naked and not caring, her breasts swaying heavily as she rose to her knees. She could read the surprise in his eyes, the want that was as great as her own.

Tugging the bracelet from her wrist, she tossed it at him. He caught it neatly in midair, his gaze on her as she stretched her arms up toward the chains dangling from above.

"The restraints, Gerard," she said on the edge of a gasp. "Use the restraints."

Otherwise she would do something stupid like rip his clothes off and pull him against her. She'd kiss that mouth and snuggle into those arms and drag his erection inside to take a ride on his hard body.

She would let him glimpse what he couldn't possibly see—that she was losing herself in him.

13

SLIPPING THE CUFFS through the chains, Mac clicked them around Harley's wrists and watched as she collapsed against them, pale curves gleaming, beautiful breasts heaving, upper body stretched toward the ceiling in a position of such powerful vulnerability, she threatened his control.

But he'd promised to pleasure *her,* not lose *himself,* and she'd trusted him enough not to bring her gun to bed. He would keep his promise, no matter how much he ached to grab her, pull her beneath him, sink inside…especially when she'd gifted him with her trust.

But as Mac swept damp hairs from her cheeks, he gazed into her face, into her relief…relief he didn't understand. Those restraints left her vulnerable, left her exposed to him.

He stared deep into those candlelit blue eyes, searching for answers, needing to understand his effect on her, needing to know if he was the only one in danger of losing himself.

And when she lifted her chin defiantly, met his gaze straight on, a bold gesture that sent wild red hair tumbling over her shoulders, Mac suddenly understood the significance of those restraints…they were another shield.

Harley wouldn't make love to him anywhere but Cajun Joe's. This dungeon was a shield—a place that differentiated screwing from making love. The restraints were another—they might leave her vulnerable to him, but they prevented her from responding. He could touch her but she couldn't touch him.

Harley trusted him more than she trusted herself.

Disbelieving, Mac searched her expression, the desperation still lingering behind the bravado. He glimpsed his first real hope that he might affect her as deeply as she'd affected him.

The realization made him close his eyes and rest his forehead against hers. He breathed in her scent, her taste, the moment powerful, overwhelming.

"It won't make any difference," she'd told him earlier, and he'd known she meant it.

"I'll take my chances."

And he would, because knowing that she felt enough for him to need restraints meant he had a chance. Harley might fight. She might decide not to let her feelings make any difference, but the fact that she *felt* for him meant he was making headway. And he wanted to see the woman she could be if she trusted him, wanted to be worthy of her trust.

Pressing a kiss to her temple, he retreated. He didn't want her to see how impacted he was or give her any reason to feel threatened. He'd said he would pleasure her, and he would do exactly what he'd promised.

He undressed, gratified that her focus kept shifting to the mirrors to catch his reflection as he peeled away his shirt, stripped off his trousers.

"You sure are pretty, Gerard."

He saw right through her bravado. "The view's fine from where I'm standing, too."

The view was downright unreal from where he was standing. All pale gleaming curves and wild red hair, Harley knelt before him like some vision from a fantasy with her hands bound, her breasts speared high in the air.

Fetish Night.

Who knew he would enjoy a fetish? Not Mac for sure, but as he admired Harley's slim curves stretched out for his pleasure, he knew an overwhelming gratitude that he'd thrown off his past life to open himself to new experiences. Otherwise he'd have never known that he could feel such an ache to make this woman respond to his touch, to have her willingly submit to restraints because he tested her control.

Kneeling on the bed before her, Mac pressed his thumbs and fingers to the mattress, forming a triangle. Bending low, he touched his forehead to his hands and executed a formal sitting bow, a show of respect he hoped would reassure her.

Harley had taught him the move during defense training, and she'd also taught him the word *Onegaishemasu*. He repeated it now, in effect saying, "Please, let's teach each other."

She'd been teaching him. Not only investigative and defense techniques but also about how he'd been limiting himself from life—not only with his circumstances but also with his selfishness. He'd blinded himself to possibilities, which had limited his choices.

He wanted to teach her, too. He wanted her to relax those shields and enjoy herself without worry or fear. He wanted her to explore her life without being buried beneath financial troubles, so termites and transmissions didn't weigh so heavily. He wanted her to know that he appreciated those glimpses of the woman she hid from most people, the generous, caring woman who inspired so much loyalty in those who cared for her.

He wanted her to open her mind about him, too, realize he was changing. He wanted to be a man she placed her trust in and not just when he was kissing away her defenses in bed. He wanted to be a man she could trust to love her, to look out for her interests, never to hurt her.

And earning Harley's trust suddenly seemed a worthier goal than anything he'd ever aspired to before, made a joke out of job titles and portfolios and expensive toys.

His hands actually shook as he skimmed them along the delicate curve of her face, tracing the lines, awed by the power of his own need, awed by the proof of hers in her heavy-lidded eyes and her parted lips.

He dragged his mouth across hers, unable to resist. He wove a path of glancing touches and light kisses down her neck, along her shoulder, over her breasts. He worked his way down her body, cherished her with touch, memorized every inch of this woman who'd inspired him to live, and love.

Mac suddenly found himself kneeling before her. Hanging as she was from the restraints left her wide open, so he slipped his hands beneath her, hiked her onto his shoulders, a position that brought him level with her sex in all its wanting glory.

Dragging his tongue along the trim tuft of red hair at that juncture between her thighs, he tasted her warmth, her body's moist response to him.

Harley bucked hard against her restraints. Her smooth stomach contracted, her breasts swayed with the motion, her gasp filled him with the sound of her desire.

It suddenly seemed that Mac's whole life had boiled down to this moment, to his ability to make her experience the same intensity he felt. He abandoned himself in her sweet softness, in her gasping sighs, in her shivers that brought her up against his face to meet the slow strokes of his tongue.

She was incredibly responsive to his touch and he

gauged the effect of his every move in the way her softness convulsed against him. When he drew her sensitive skin into his mouth with a light pull, she moaned and her thighs vibrated, a velvet vise that let him feel the tension building inside her.

He felt each corresponding tremor and his hips bucked against his will, mirrored her body's thrusts. Lifting his head slightly, he forced himself to breathe, to try and regain some control. But the position change was enough to let him run his eyes up her naked body, to admire the visual feast she presented with her arms bound above her, her head tossed back, hips swaying erotically as she rode his mouth.

Just the sight of them together almost cost him his battle, and he groaned in the purest relief when she gasped out, "I need you, Gerard. I need you inside me."

She needed him. It was a start.

Maneuvering her off his shoulders, he eased her down the length of his body, savoring each silken glide of skin against skin, easily bearing her weight as he urged her to wrap her legs around his waist.

She clung to him, letting him see her urgency without hiding behind her shields. And Mac watched her reflection in the mirror, the way she rested her head against his shoulder, the way she closed her eyes and let her expression melt as he stroked his erection against her wet heat.

He drove upward, watched her tense as her body welcomed him and it was that look of surrender on Harley's face that finally undid him. All his control, all his vows to think of her pleasure before his own disintegrated in the face of her need. He was lost in her body rocking against him and her soft sighs that told him she was reaching for climax again.

Mac lost it. He thrust upward over and over, pushed toward the edge of pleasure, a desperate place where one tough, tiny redhead held his happiness, his future, his whole life in her delicate hands.

And when she came, her cries broke against his mouth and her body exploded, the hot grip of her orgasm dragging him right along with her.

AFTER ONLY FOUR HOURS of sleep the previous night, Harley was more than ready to head home at the end of the workday. She and Gerard had spent the day on the road, running from parish office to parish office, checking out their leads on several key Nice and Neat employees. Somehow the information they'd turned up seemed out of balance for the time spent dealing with long lines, even longer forms and often impatient government employees.

But they were steadily moving in the right direction. After a trip to the immigration office, they'd both agreed to bump Mercedes Del Torres down on their suspect list, shifting Evangeline Wilson into the spot of prominence.

Harley was almost too tired to care. Hopping out of Gerard's car, she handed him her briefcase. "Will you take this in with you, please? I want to drop by my place. The exterminators had to lift my floor to drill into the foundation today."

All Parishes Pest Control had promised not to damage her floor, but after refinishing each antique tile herself, she needed reassurance. She half expected Gerard to accompany her, but he didn't, so Harley took off across the yard, not unhappy with the reprieve from his company before facing a night of playing house.

Yawning widely, she let herself inside, soothed just by the sight of her things, the familiar feel of home. While her flooring had been pulled up all around her walls to drill for subterranean termites, there was no damage to the parquet and she was reassured that her floor would be as good as ever once the tiles were back in place.

Now if she could just make it home in one piece after her stint as Gerard's bride…unfortunately, a concern. Harley wasn't holding up very well under the pressure of dealing with him twenty-four/seven. If the man had been happy with a fling, perhaps, but no, a fling didn't seem to be good enough anymore. He was trying to consume her life.

At least their plan moved along as scheduled. Their first visit from Nice and Neat would happen the following afternoon. But they couldn't realistically expect an employee to walk through the door and take the bait on the first visit, which meant the waiting game was only beginning.

With a sigh, she stopped at her computer desk, where her phone recorder flashed a ridiculous amount of messages. Depressing the play button, she heard a series of hang-ups before a message from Damon. The instant Harley heard his voice she knew something was wrong.

"Red, I've been trying to get through to you all day. You weren't in your office and your cell phone's been off."

More likely her cell phone's battery had died, Harley thought, frowning at the recorder. She'd been too distracted lately to pay close attention to these sorts of details.

"Delilah came into Anthony's for an oil change this morning and told him that you and your new husband have been playing in Joe's dungeon. He freaked, Red. I could hear the fallout in the dojo. He took off on the chopper and no one's seen or heard from him since. Call me as soon as you get this."

Click.

Harley stared disbelieving at the recorder, a cold chill skating along her spine. She clutched at the edge of the desk to steady herself, unsure what to think or what to do.

Damn.

Anthony pissed wasn't a pleasant sight on a good day and he was bound to be pissed, which left her with a very interesting dilemma about what to tell him—exactly why she'd wanted to avoid this whole scene in the first place.

Damn, damn, damn.

She was already raw around the edges from lack of sleep and her head pounded with the effort of figuring out what to tell him—*if* she could get him to calm down long enough to listen.

When the phone rang, she nearly jumped out of her skin. Snatching it off the cradle, she barked, "Hello."

"You're in deep shit, Red," Damon's voice shot back. "Mama called. Anthony showed up at her house nuts. Dominic just got there and I'm on my way. Wanted to give you the head's up."

"Oh no, Damon..." Words stuck in her throat.

"Is it true? Are you really *married?*"

"Damn, damn, damn, damn, damn, damn, damn!"

A harsh laugh on the other end. "I'll take that as a yes. Just my opinion, but it might be better if you get to Anthony before he gets to you. At least then you'll have backup. And I do hope you have a good excuse. You're going to need it."

"I'm on my way."

Harley dropped the receiver onto the cradle, barely able to breathe. This was a nightmare.

She turned to head out the door and realized she couldn't just take off. Her *husband* was waiting for her.

Damn!

Reaching for the phone, she dialed.

He answered on the third ring.

"Something's come up, Gerard," she said, forcing a calm she didn't feel. "I've got to run out for a while."

"YOU DIDN'T THINK I'd find out?" Anthony spat, anger distorting his features until he looked like a stranger.

They'd squared off in the kitchen with his mama, Damon and his older brother Dominic poised ringside like an audience at a title fight.

"What the hell kind of excuse is that?" He slammed a fist down on the countertop, making the glasses in the drain board rattle. "How did you think that you going to Joe's dungeon wouldn't get back to me?"

"I had no idea you took care of Delilah's car."

"I know Cajun Joe."

"I didn't know that. I mean, I know you've met him through me, but I didn't know you actually *knew him*, knew him."

"He owns a nightclub. Did you think you were the only one who'd ever been there?"

Harley winced. Anthony had never taken her to Joe's dungeon, which meant he'd taken another woman. Rachel, maybe? Or Amber? Or any one of the string of flings he'd had through the years. She didn't want to know. He was lashing out because she'd hurt him. But even knowing that didn't make her hurt go away.

"Anthony, *cara mia*," his mama said sharply. "You calm down and think before you open that mouth."

He didn't even glance her way, just thrust his fingers through his hair and glared at Harley. "Damn it. How could you marry this guy and not tell me?"

He didn't understand and she had to make him, had to wipe away that anger from his face.

"I told you, it's not what you think. It's not *real*. This marriage is over as soon as Gerard gets his trust fund," she lied, giving him the most plausible excuse she could think of without blowing their cover. "He offered me a lot of money. What else could I do? I'm behind on my mortgage.

I owe you for my transmission. I've got loans up the ass, termites munching through the support beams of my house and no freaking credit.''

She sounded like a whore. And a hysterical one to boot. Her motivation for marrying Gerard hadn't washed when she'd stood in the judge's chamber and said, "I do." It *really* wasn't washing now. Not in front of the people she cared about. Not with Anthony. She'd hurt him.

"Yeah, you needed the money," he said angrily. "I got that part, but who came up with this idea—you or *your husband?*"

Those words ached the way he said them, even more so when she had to admit the idea hadn't been hers.

"Then tell me something, princess—you going to annul this marriage or do you have to get a divorce?"

The hostility behind the question stunned her. She couldn't answer, didn't have to. Anthony knew her well enough to know.

And the look on his face tore her heart out.

"It's temporary." A weak but plausible reason for taking money, but one that sure as hell didn't explain the sex. The accusation in Anthony's eyes proved it.

"We date other people." She tried to sound calm, rational, as if her heart wasn't breaking. "This is just a fling."

They all knew Anthony had been the one to establish that relationship rule. He'd dated in high school before becoming interested in her, and had simply continued dating afterward. They'd been too young to marry and had both been determined to make something of their lives. They'd had so many wonderful times together and she'd been content to know he loved her, would be there for her when she needed him.

Or had she simply been too afraid to commit, too afraid

to demand more from him, too afraid to lose the only man she'd ever trusted, too afraid to allow any other man to get so close?

Had she been afraid of everything?

The question took her off guard, left her wide open for his next volley.

"This is different, princess. Sure, we date, but we don't *commit*. You *married* this guy. You want to lie to yourself, fine, but don't lie to me."

"It's not *real*." She repeated her only defense, willing him to understand. "It's temporary. Why won't you listen?"

She reached for his arm but he shrugged her off.

"Great. Just great." He turned his back to her, leaving her standing there in the middle of the kitchen, his mama, Dominic and Damon all staring, looking as shell-shocked by the emotions flying around as she was.

She stared at Anthony's broad back, the too-long hair curling over his collar, the strong shoulders so tense that she suspected a good punch might shatter him.

She'd done this. She'd hurt him so much that he wouldn't even look at her. Guilt sucked the fight away. Her eyes started to burn. The knot in her throat ballooned so she couldn't talk. And Harley knew right then that she was going to do the unthinkable—she was going to cry.

Bursting past Anthony, she stormed out the door, an action from her past that felt horribly familiar. She couldn't catch her breath. Despite the thick night air, she couldn't unfreeze her lungs enough to take in the tiniest breath, not without letting loose this anguish, not without *crying*.

Harley hated to cry even more than she hated to dance.

Squeezing her eyes shut, she willed back the tears, willed herself to calm down, willed herself to swallow, to take a breath, a small one to start…then another.

She understood Anthony was hurt because she'd hidden the marriage from him, but once he calmed down, she'd make him understand that this was no different from all the other flings they'd had through the years. Why couldn't he see that?

Because it wasn't, and Anthony knew.

The realization sandbagged her, undermined her efforts to breathe, made her open her eyes to stare unseeing into the night.

She loved Anthony. She'd fallen in love with him in this very yard when she'd been six years old. He was everything that was familiar and safe in her world. He was the man she was going to grow up and marry.

But she had grown up and she'd married Gerard.

Because she'd needed the money.

True, but was that the only reason?

No.

The answer struck her, brutal in its simplicity.

No!

"You want to lie to yourself, fine, but don't lie to me," Anthony had said and he'd been right. She was lying to herself.

Her feelings had gotten away from her. No matter how hard she'd fought it, no matter how wrong Gerard was for her, no matter how much she believed Anthony was the man she wanted to grow old with, she'd fallen in love with Gerard.

She'd fallen in love with Mac Gerard.

Staggering away from the porch light, Harley struggled for air, her head so woozy she thought she might faint. She needed to sit. To think. To figure out how her emotions had gotten away from her. She made her way blindly to the garage apartment that had once been her home.

The garage with its second-story apartment had been

many things to many people through the long years the DiLeos had owned this property. When Anthony's father had been alive, he'd run a side business out of the garage restoring old classics.

After his death, Mama DiLeo had needed extra income so she'd converted the upstairs into an apartment and taken tenants. Harley and her dad had rented the place, which had defeated the purpose because her dad's binges meant he often couldn't work.

But Harley had been raised helping him on his jobs, so she'd learned enough to hold her own on the basics. And she'd worked for him often because she'd have done just about anything not to lose the only family that had ever cared for her, the only stability she'd ever known.

And blessedly, Mama DiLeo hadn't evicted them even when they couldn't pay. The money hadn't been nearly as important to her as Harley's welfare.

Harley had never been more grateful for anything in her life.

Even before her dad's death, she'd been shipped off to foster care and Mama hadn't rented the garage apartment again. The building had become a storage facility that served each of the DiLeo brothers in turn. Dominic used to sneak girls up to the apartment for late-night make-out sessions and Marc's band had rehearsed there, too. Anthony had returned the garage to its roots with his obsession for restoring classics. Damon used the apartment as a dojo and she'd trained with him there before he'd ventured to turn his passion into a business. Vinny, the youngest DiLeo son, followed up the rear by hiding neighborhood strays inside, until Mama invariably caught him and made him find new homes for his furry friends.

Now Harley was back again, making her way up the rickety steps to the stoop of the doorway. She stared down at the patch of grass that had been her front yard of the only childhood home she'd ever known.

Once upon a time, the fence had been desperately in need of repairs and she recalled often being awakened on Saturday mornings to one or another of the DiLeo brothers complaining while they'd replaced a rotted post.

Nowadays they all took pride in making sure their mama's fence always looked brand-new.

Harley might have smiled at how times had changed, but for that damn fence, that smooth, weather-coated wood so strikingly changed from the past. She couldn't wipe away the images of the DiLeo brothers as they'd once been or of herself as a young girl who'd needed them so much. Now they were all grown, all changed, and that realization finally pitched Harley over the edge.

She lowered her face into her hands and started to cry.

14

DAMON DILEO OPENED the front door of his family's home as though he wasn't surprised to find Mac on the front step.

"I'm looking for Harley," Mac said.

He gave a strained smile. "You and everybody else today. Come on in."

Damon led him back through the house to a large kitchen, where he found Anthony standing against the counter beside a small woman with stylishly short hair and a dish towel tucked around her waist. Mrs. DiLeo, he assumed.

Mac recognized the big man sitting at the table. He'd run into Dominic DiLeo during his years with the D.A.'s office. He inclined his head to acknowledge the lieutenant.

"What the hell do you want, Gerard?" Anthony asked.

"I've come to see Harley."

"You've got no business here. She already told us about your bullshit marriage."

Mac didn't give him the benefit of a response, wouldn't let him know this announcement hit him in every place that counted. Mac had wanted to know how important Anthony was to her. He had his answer now.

Important enough to risk their cover.

"Anthony," Mrs. DiLeo warned as she turned to Mac. "Come on in. If Harley cares about you, you're welcome here."

Mac didn't get a chance to respond because Anthony

shot him a scowl of barely restrained hostility and stormed from the room.

Dominic got up from the table. "I'll go talk to him." Then he disappeared, too, leaving Mac with Damon and his mother.

Given the ages of her children, Mrs. DiLeo had to be around sixty, but she was a tiny woman with the same dark blond hair and snapping eyes as her sons. She assessed him with sharp eyes that were trying to see everything.

"You love her, don't you, Mac Gerard?" she asked simply.

"Yes."

Mac saw understanding, and regret, flash in her expressive eyes before she inclined her head toward the stove where a skillet of what looked like sausage and peppers simmered. "Well, she's out back. You can let me feed you while you wait for her to come in or you can go find her."

He forced a smile. "Thank you. I'll go find her."

Heading onto the back porch, he glanced around to find Harley, but found nothing except a dull light that cast the backyard into impenetrable gloom. He couldn't see where she might be in this total blackness...but he could hear her, great gulping sobs that shuddered through the night.

He followed the sound, his vision slowly adjusting from the dull glare of the porch light to the starlit yard. Making his way toward a two-story garage, he circled the corner and glanced up a narrow staircase to find her sitting on the top.

"Harley," he said softly.

Her head snapped up, but he couldn't see her expression, just the glint of tears in her eyes and on her cheeks.

"You shouldn't be here." Her voice trembled between them, heartbroken and shattered in a way he had never imagined to hear her. Her shields weren't just down, they'd been crushed.

"You're upset," he said. "I want to be here for you."

"Anthony knows we got married."

"I know. Delilah called the house to apologize for telling him. She felt bad."

Harley didn't reply; she seemed so lost and alone. Devastated. He still couldn't see her face, just that glint of tears. He didn't tell her he knew she'd told Anthony about their cover, and might have risked their solving his grandfather's case. Not when he couldn't get past the fact she cared so much about the man.

He didn't tell her that her tears were ripping him up because he wanted to be the man she cared for, the man who'd earned her trust. The man important enough for her to risk everything.

He wanted her to want him more than Anthony.

But Mac didn't say a word. This wasn't about him being hurt. This was about Harley finding her way.

So he kept his mouth shut, never realizing he could want so deeply or be willing to pay such a high price for the woman he loved. He hadn't understood his capacity to love at all. Or how much it could hurt.

And it hurt more than anything had ever hurt before, but he said, "After Anthony cools down, he'll listen. You can talk more then."

"He—he's so angry with me."

"Maybe, but I think he's angrier with himself for giving you a chance to get away."

Her renewed burst of sobs filtered through the night and Mac's need to comfort her proved so strong that he knew what to do. On some instinctive level he knew that holding her would be right. So he climbed the stairs, his footsteps echoing dully through the night as he closed the distance between them.

"Gerard—"

"Shh," he said, wedging himself against her on the cramped step. "You're not crying and I'm not holding you."

Gathering her against him, he held her close, just held her, amazed by the feeling of *right* that he only knew with her wrapped tight in his arms.

And miracle of miracles, she didn't pull away. She melted against him, sobbing floods into his shirt, while Mac rested his cheek on the top of her head, kept telling her over and over, "It'll all work out."

She wasn't the only one who needed to believe it.

MUCH LATER, in the darkness of their bed, Mac held Harley in his arms, facing the fact his chances with her weren't good.

She felt something for him. He knew that without question. She might not have acknowledged it to herself yet, but she felt something for him way beyond attraction, something that tested her control and scared her.

But what she felt for him couldn't possibly compete with Anthony, the man who'd known she'd only had three drinks in twenty-two years. The man who was part of a family she loved. The man she'd risk everything for. The man who could make her cry...Harley, who took on life with sarcasm, skilled karate moves and a gun.

She'd done a lot more than cry in Mac's arms tonight— she'd let her heart break.

And he'd felt a totally unfamiliar sense of...*something* in reply, a mix of emotions so fierce they hurt. He wanted to shield Harley from her heartache, wanted to hurt Anthony for hurting her. He damned his own selfishness for putting her in this situation and his own stupidity for wasting *five months* that would have been so much better spent earning her respect and her trust.

He damned Anthony for holding the place in her heart that he wanted.

But she wasn't with him now, so Mac held her close in their bed, trying to figure out how he could prove himself. He didn't think about life after this case, tried not to give in to another emotion he'd never felt before—despair.

He would hold her when she wanted to be held, protect her when she wanted protection. He'd savor each moment, memorizing the feel of her body, the smell of her hair, the silken weight of her against him while she slept.

He wasn't sure how deeply they were into the night, but he noticed the instant her breathing changed, recognized when she awakened. And still he held her, waiting, just waiting.

Finally she turned in his arms. She molded her body against him, wrapped an arm around his waist. Tipping her face up to his, she whispered against his lips, "Are you asleep?"

"No," he gave the word back on a breath.

"Will you make love to me?"

It was a plea in the darkness, though she sounded no less proud for her need.

It was the need that surprised him.

He wanted to ask why she was suddenly willing to make love in their bed instead of a dungeon, and wanted to ask her if she was using him to wipe away her hurt over Anthony. He thought about taking a page from her book and telling her he wouldn't make love in this bed unless he could be sure she was making love to *him*, not running away from her sometimes lover.

But he didn't.

Harley wanted him and her reasons were her own. He pressed a kiss to her forehead, and with an urgent gentleness Mac had never known before, he undressed her until she lay naked, her outstretched arms gleaming pale in the darkness as she reached for him.

There was an unfamiliar dreaminess to the moment as he sheltered her from the night with his body, caressed her sex to find her moist and ready. He positioned himself between her thighs, pressed inside.

Harley moaned softly, her body welcoming him as he sank deep. He shuddered, overwhelmed by the feeling of her beneath him, the honesty in the arms she looped around his neck.

Catching his mouth with hers, she kissed him, her tongue pressing inside, not devouring like she'd kissed him last night. A kiss that sampled the taste of their mouths together, it was almost sweet in its simplicity.

Then she began to rock her hips under him, a slow, smooth motion, which molded their bodies together as though they'd been made to fit, hip to hip, chest to chest, mouth to mouth.

Mac picked up her motion, touched by the way their bodies came together. Each thrust drew him deeper, closer to losing himself inside her. And in this moment there was nothing but their bodies…a need as basic as breathing, the moment too powerful, too perfect not to be awed by holding her close and matching her stroke for aching stroke.

So he made love to her mouth with his kisses, kept pumping inside her as the magic he felt only with her lifted him and he swelled inside. And still he waited. He waited until Harley's breaths came shallow, until her body gathered underneath him and she arched upward, trying to knead her orgasm into breaking.

Only then did he let go. Dragging her hips impossibly

closer, he thrust again and again, as if he could hold her here by the force of his will alone. His climax burst upon him, impossible to control, staggering in intensity.

"Don't stop, Mac, please," she cried out against his mouth as hers broke. He could taste her pleasure in the way she speared her fingers into his hair, anchored his head so he could kiss her as her cries gentled to moans and he tasted tears on her lips.

Mac breathed in her sobs, offered the shelter of his body, stunned that she'd called him by name.

Mac.

And something so simple gave him hope.

To GERARD'S CREDIT and Harley's profound relief, he didn't confront her with the events of the previous night. He didn't mention her fight with Anthony, her hysteria or making love to him in the middle of the night, when she just needed to feel his arms around her, feel him inside her. She wasn't going to dwell on what *that* meant in the light of day.

She was going to work to solve this case. She would review this file that her friend from the university placement office was faxing over on Caroline Thompson, granddaughter of Nice and Neat's owner. Then she would hop in the car to go check out a lead on a wedding band and engagement ring set that a friend in a pawnshop had told her about.

Work—the cure-all for whatever ailed her. So she'd had a meltdown last night. What difference did it really make how she felt for Gerard anyway?

None at all. That she'd finally fallen for him shouldn't come as a surprise, either, given the way he'd been hammering at her for months now, given how hard she'd had to fight to resist. The man had been bad news since they'd met, an arrogant, privileged bastard who only thought about what he wanted.

But the Mac Gerard she'd met so many months ago hadn't been the man who'd made love to her last night. Under her and Josh's tutelage, Gerard had grown from a clueless lawyer into an investigator who used his head under pressure. Harley hadn't admitted how much he'd grown at work, nor had she allowed herself to acknowledge that the man himself was changing. But he had—enough to follow her to Anthony's and hold her in his arms while she'd cried.

Gerard had been changing and growing all along, and getting under her skin in the process. He'd been honest enough, and strong enough, to look at the way he did things and decide to change them. Harley understood those sorts of life-altering choices better than Gerard could ever know. She respected them. And last night had only proved how much he was thinking about her. He hadn't asked questions. He hadn't copped an attitude. He hadn't blasted her with emotion. He'd held her when she'd cried. He'd made love to her when she'd asked. He'd been strong, and solid, and...*there.*

And she'd finally admitted to herself in the darkness of late night, as Gerard lay on top of her, inside her, that she wanted this man in a way she'd never known she could want before. She had let her feelings get away from her. She had fallen in love with him.

Unfortunately, love didn't change a thing between them. Gerard wanted his fling and would enjoy it until they burned out. And it was best that way. Love didn't change the fact that they were worlds apart. Gerard might have grown past making cracks about bottled beer, but he still had to dress her to get her out the door.

Her world would never be his and his world couldn't be

hers. Harley hadn't gone to Harvard, but she'd worked her butt off to earn her degree and was proud of that accomplishment. She hadn't wound up dancing as a stripper, on her back as a prostitute or dead from drugs. She'd moved beyond her circumstances and had made something of her life. She would never choose to surround herself with people who couldn't appreciate that.

But she was fair enough to admit that Gerard's family had been decent given the way he'd sprung a surprise bride on them. Except for Aunt Frances, who clearly didn't approve her pedigree, they'd reserved judgment, giving her a fair chance.

Had she honestly given them the same chance to appreciate how far she'd come in her life?

No.

Had she given Gerard that chance, either?

No.

She never talked about her past—not since the day Judge Bancroft had released her from foster care. She'd taken the people she cared for and some well-learned lessons into her future and had refused to dwell on the past, had refused to give anyone a chance to share it. Being uncomfortable with the Gerards en masse was *her* issue, which had nothing to do with their treatment of her. Harley couldn't handle feeling rejected, out of control or scared.

So she hadn't given anyone a chance. She surrounded herself with people who already knew her past because they'd lived it with her.

Even Anthony, which made him the man of her dreams or her comfort zone?

Argh!

Harley shoved the chair back from her desk and headed into the office to retrieve the school records on Caroline Thompson. She absolutely would not tackle any more questions today. The answers made no difference anyway. Anthony might very well be her comfort zone, but she loved him. She had since she'd been six years old. Simple.

That was it. She wasn't thinking about this anymore. She'd made her choices and would enjoy her fling as long as it lasted. Like she always did. She'd told Gerard that his feelings for her wouldn't make any difference. Her feelings for him wouldn't either. They couldn't.

And right now she had work to do. As usual, Melissa was on top of things, handing her the fax before she even got past the reception desk.

"This arrived, too," she said, giving Harley what had turned out to be Caroline Thompson's credit report.

"Thanks." She headed back to her office, where she put aside all thoughts of runaway emotions.

Emotions didn't matter. Not in a fling. She wouldn't let them.

Caroline Thompson's school records served up an interesting picture of a woman who'd had a strong academic career. She'd been awarded several scholarships, had been heavily involved in student government and had graduated second in her class. Which raised the question in Harley's mind about why she currently cleaned houses for the family business when she was more than qualified to manage the business.

Caroline's credit report was routine by comparison, proof that her family's business had provided her a very comfortable, if not as privileged by Gerard's standards, type of upbringing. Harley suspected that Caroline might be working a stint as cleaning staff as some sort of family training program. She jotted the question down on a notebook she kept handy for such questions.

But Caroline's credit report got Harley thinking about how the acquisition of a ten-thousand-dollar line of credit had affected her own report. She still couldn't believe the pest control company had extended her credit—they must have been absolutely desperate for business. Lucky her.

Spinning toward her computer, she was just desperate enough for distractions to access a credit bureau Web site. It was worth the nine buck fee to take a look. Forewarned is forearmed, and even she had a credit card that would hold nine bucks.

To Harley's surprise, though, there were no new hits on her report although the information should have been posted by now. Frowning, she reached into her file drawer for the contract she'd signed earlier in the week and glanced at the name of the company that had financed the loan.

She searched the Web but couldn't find any information on this financial institution, which was downright strange. Leaning back in her chair, she folded her arms across her chest and stared at the monitor.

What was going on here? There had to be some record of a company that financed people amounts in the five-figures because lending institutions were regulated under federal guidelines.

She tried to ferret out the information through every channel she could think of that bypassed the government. Searching through federal data banks was a nightmare. So much of their information meant making requests through the Freedom of Information Act, which meant waiting.

Reaching for the phone, she dialed the number on the contract for the pest control company. A cheery young woman answered and Harley pretended to be a potential customer asking about the no-interest, no-payments-until-next-year special.

"I'm sorry, ma'am." The receptionist sounded confused. "Are you sure this deal wasn't through another pest control company? I have no information on that special and, to my knowledge, we're not affiliated with any lending companies. Would you like me to put you through to the manager? Maybe he can help.''

Harley glanced at the contract and said, "Yes, please do. I'd like to speak with Harry Smith."

There was a beat of silence on the other end. "We don't have anyone on staff by that name."

Harley double-checked the name on the contract.

Harry Smith.

"I've obviously made a mistake," she said. "But tell me, what's your fax number?"

The woman rattled off a number, which was *not* the number on the contract. "That's your only fax line?"

"Yes."

She thanked the woman and hung up the phone.

What the hell was going on here? One thing was for certain—Harley had to find out. She'd revealed personal information on this contract, which would have made her suspicious of identity theft except that the pest control company was currently working on her house.

Calling her contact with the telephone company, she left a message for information on the fax number—that number would be registered, which would lead her a step closer to figuring out what the hell was going on.

Relieved for the distraction that left her no room for emotional turmoil, she tucked the contract into her purse and dropped by Gerard's office on her way out.

"I'm going to see a friend at the pawnshop," she said. "He has a wedding-ring set that might be your grandmother's."

He glanced up from his computer and the light from the window behind him backlighted his strong face, the sweep of absurdly thick lashes, the straight nose, the full mouth that had kissed her last night in the darkness.

Her stomach gave one of those queer flutters. His expression reminded her that she'd lost herself in his arms last night. She'd allowed him to see her cry, had welcomed his comfort, had let him make love to her in his bed. She'd been weak and needy. She knew it. He knew it. And he'd been gentleman enough not to call her on it.

"I'll come along," he said.

"No. That's okay. My friend won't talk if you're with me and I want him to talk. He knows every fence in the area and he might be able to tell me something about the other stolen items."

He nodded. "Call me when you find out something."

Ever the gentleman, Gerard handled her rejection gracefully. She only wished he'd have done as much after their first kiss. Had he been a gentleman then and handled her rejection, she wouldn't be in this pathetic situation now.

"I'll call," she said, and made her escape.

Of course the wedding set wasn't Gerard's grandmother's—a solid lead right now when Harley needed one would have been too convenient, of course. The Gooch hadn't come across Stuart's Rolex, either. But he had looked at the list of stolen items and agreed to help her out. He knew all the fences in town and might hear of one running through the expensive but not easily traced jewelry items.

Harley would have called Gerard to break the bad news, but before she drove away from the pawnshop, her contact with the telephone company called with information about the fax number that changed the whole course of her day.

15

SMILING, MAC GLANCED through the bedroom window to Harley's cottage. He'd noticed his SUV parked up the street and assumed she was inside with the workmen, hopefully finding the extermination progressing satisfactorily. He made a mental note to ask her later.

He'd stopped home to activate the surveillance equipment before Nice and Neat's arrival. The armored pinhole cameras they'd placed in the vents would record for up to forty-four hours, but several of the other devices, including the remote receiver video and the audio recorders, had less duration.

Skimming his gaze over the dresser, he took in the colored pen camera he'd placed near the jewelry box. The cloisonné bracelet sat inside with the diamond chain of the nipple clamps dangling outside as if the piece had been carelessly tossed in.

When Mac heard the key in the door, he glanced at his watch, which confirmed the cleaning service wasn't scheduled for another two hours yet.

"You up there, Gerard?" Harley asked. "I saw your car."

"In the bedroom." A place he would have enjoyed meeting up with her if not for their impending visit from Nice and Neat.

He heard her footsteps on the stairs and then she appeared in the doorway, looking delectable in fitted black slacks, a cream shell and black blazer.

Her expression was a different matter altogether. She glowered, jaw set, nostrils flaring, blue eyes blazing. She locked her arms across her chest defensively—a mannerism he'd learned usually meant she was itching to draw her gun.

"Any trouble down at your place?"

"You paid for the exterminator, didn't you?" Her voice was sharp like broken ice. "You faxed me bullshit paperwork so I'd think that there was some no-interest, no-payment special, and then you paid the exterminator to do the work."

Okay. This wasn't what he'd wanted to tackle today. "What makes you think that?"

"There's only one man I know who would ever take it upon himself to pay that bill, Gerard. But it so happens that he hocked his ass to the bank to buy a new building. He couldn't afford to front me the parts for my transmission let alone pay *ten thousand dollars* to some exterminator."

"So you think I did?"

She spit out a sound of frustrated rage and bore down on him. Suddenly she was jabbing her finger into his chest. "Who else do I know who throws around that kind of money?"

A rhetorical question, undoubtedly, so Mac just admired the way anger fueled her cheeks with a flush that made her deep blue eyes seem bluer, her mouth lusher, more kissable.

"Who else do I know who's arrogant enough to charge in like he's some sort of freaking Prince Charming?"

"I wanted to help."

"As usual it's about what *you* want. I don't care what *you* want. I didn't ask for your help."

No, she hadn't asked and he hadn't cared about that at

the time, a very sobering reminder that he was guilty as charged no matter how noble his intentions.

Unfortunately, his intentions hadn't been all that noble.

When he'd first discovered she had termite troubles, he'd assumed from her conversation with Anthony that coming up with the money was a problem, so he'd made some routine inquiries into her finances to learn she was deeply in debt.

He had wanted to help. Not only because Harley clearly cared about her home, but he'd wanted to help her clear her plate so she could focus on other things—like *him.* If helping her out happened to give him an edge over Anthony down the road…better still.

His reasoning had seemed pretty straightforward at the time. But looking back, Mac knew he'd been in over his head with his feelings for her even then.

He had wanted to play Prince Charming.

"You needed the money, Harley. I knew you wouldn't take it if I offered."

"Of course I wouldn't have taken it. I can't pay you back."

"I didn't ask you to."

"Argh!" She thumped her hand against his chest hard enough to make him brace himself. Clearly that wasn't the answer she'd been looking for.

"Listen," he said, catching her hand and hanging on so she couldn't get away. "You're right. I did act presumptuously, without thinking about anyone but myself. I'm sorry."

Her eyes widened, and he might have laughed at her reaction—she obviously hadn't expected him to own up to his mistake—but he heard a noise downstairs.

The sound seemed to be coming from outside the front

door. They both spun toward the landing and, sure enough, a key rattled in the lock, before the door creaked open.

Harley recovered first. She bolted to the window to peer out at the street. "Nice and Neat."

They couldn't be caught inside the house. They'd made it clear that no one would be home during the day, hoping to generate a false sense of security with the cleaning service. If they were caught home on the first visit, they'd set their work back by weeks, possibly more.

"In the closet." Mac eased the door of the long wall closet open, slipped into the clothes at the back, just as Harley landed against him. She closed the door and arranged several of his suits in front of them, so they wouldn't be easily seen if the cleaning person opened the door.

Adrenaline had his heart pounding and his breaths coming hard, but he wouldn't miss an opportunity to pull Harley into his arms. His arms around her, he forced her to lean back against him for balance. He buried his face in her hair and took total advantage of her inability to stop him.

Self-serving was self-serving, and sometimes he just couldn't fight his basic nature. The last time they'd been sandwiched inside a closet together had been during the teamwork training session when he'd realized that standing so close to her threw his hormones into overdrive.

His hormones were in overdrive now. The scent of her hair snared his senses, ignited memories of the previous night with her warm and willing beneath him, her soft sighs in the dark.

And Harley noticed. Suddenly she was wiggling her bottom back against him. She wasn't as self-serving as he was, but she was vengeful, which meant she wanted to torment him.

"Control yourself," she hissed.

"Oh, I am," he breathed into her ear, gratified when she shivered. "Trust me."

She elbowed him hard enough to make her point—no small feat given the way they were wedged together, his suits and her leather crowding them. A shoe rack prevented him from spreading his legs to secure his position, and despite the distraction of her nearness, their quarters soon grew stifling.

Mac considered why the cleaning person had shown up so early. A cancellation in the schedule, perhaps. He had no idea how long it would take to clean the house, but time ground to a standstill as they stood there, barely daring to breathe.

Finally he heard someone dragging some heavy piece of equipment up the stairs. A vacuum maybe. His oxygen-deprived senses went on red alert. Harley's, too, given the way she tensed against him.

Footsteps moved around the room. They could hear the scuff of soft soles on the tiled bathroom floor and then the sound of a cabinet opening and closing. Water running.

It wasn't until their suspect reemerged into the bedroom that they heard the electronic beep of a cell phone, a woman speaking. "Grandma, if you're there, pick up."

He recognized the voice as Caroline Thompson's and, if the way Harley froze against him was any indication, she'd recognized the woman, too.

"Oh, good, I'm glad you're home," Caroline said. "I'm in the Gerard place right now. Yeah, I'm early, but I wanted to have time to look around." She paused, inhaled breathlessly. "Grandma, I think you might be right. I wouldn't have noticed anything if you hadn't warned me, but the Gerards left some really expensive stuff lying around.

"This is the first time I'm cleaning here, so they're either careless or setting us up. Do you think I should tell Mom that I want to service this account? At least until we figure out what thefts these people are trying to frame us for. I don't want to put any of our employees in a dicey position."

Harley tilted her head back enough to meet his gaze, and there was no missing the accusation in hers.

Then it hit him. There was only one way Mrs. Noralee could have known Nice and Neat was under suspicion of theft—if his grandfather, Miss Q and their friends had told her.

By THE TIME Caroline Thompson had completed her work and left the house, the forced confinement had given Harley too much time to analyze this unexpected turn of events and her anger rose with each possible explanation.

Even though Gerard claimed he had no idea what was going on and seemed genuinely annoyed himself, she didn't believe him. *Wouldn't* believe him. She'd married this man, damn it, had gotten her feelings all tied up in knots over him. *Someone* had to be responsible for this stunt and it needed to be him.

Only knowing that he was responsible, that he'd purposely and selfishly manipulated her, would help her rein in all these stupid emotions she didn't want to feel for him. Would make her stop melting inside every time she thought about him paying off the exterminator because he knew she wouldn't accept his help.

Yes, he'd been presumptuous and self-serving. Yes, he'd been outrageous and excessive.

But no man would invest this much time and energy and *money* into her without caring. No man would look at her with *that* sort of expression unless he cared.

And Gerard couldn't care about her. One of them with runaway emotions was bad enough, but two... Her chest suddenly felt tight, as if someone was sitting on it. She couldn't breathe.

"Harley, it's all right," he said, his expression going all soft around the edges, one of *those* expressions that Josh reserved for Lennon. That their groom friend had reserved for his giddy bride.

Only Harley couldn't let his expression make a difference.

"We'll go talk to my grandfather and find out what's going on." Gerard knew she was losing it, knew she was struggling not to get sucked further into his web.

She *couldn't* believe him.

"Why did you make me marry you?" She fought hard to keep from turning away, the impulse to run so strong she could barely meet his gaze.

"I told you. I wanted a chance to seduce you."

She laughed, a hysterical, broken sound. "The money, Gerard. There's nothing I do that's worth ten thousand dollars."

His expression grew more gentle still and he reached out to stroke her cheek. "Everything you do is priceless."

She pulled away from him so fast that she stumbled. He caught her arm, pulled her toward him, looked down into her face with translucent eyes so honest her heart seemed to stall in mid beat. "I don't know what my grandfather's doing, but we'll find out. I'm not real thrilled myself right now. I was starting to make headway with you and now you're angry with me again."

That was enough to bring Harley to her senses. She broke away and squared off with the bed between them. She wanted to scream. "You said you wanted a fling. I slept with you. That's it, we're through. I'll figure out some way to pay you back.''

"You're my wife, Harley. Everything I have is yours."

"Why are you doing this?" she demanded, knowing the instant the question was out of her mouth she wouldn't like his answer.

"I'm in love with you. I'm surprised you haven't figured that out yet."

Harley did scream then, loudly.

AFTER SWINGING BY his family's house, Mac learned that his grandfather wasn't at home but at the Eastman Gallery for a meeting of the Second Story Society. He'd never heard of this particular organization or his grandfather's affiliation, but if the group met at the Eastman Gallery, Miss Q was somehow involved. She'd been the benefactress behind the memorial gallery inside the local art museum.

Christopher and Lennon, both longtime friends, had shared their stories about how Miss Q had involved herself in bringing about their recent marriages. Miss Q had shown up in Judge Bancroft's chambers to witness his own marriage, too. But since she'd been a victim of theft and Josh had owned the firm hired to investigate her case, Mac hadn't questioned her presence.

Now he had a really bad feeling. He needed some answers and they needed to be good enough to get him off the hook with Harley. But when he escorted her into a conference room in the art gallery and took one look at the table filled with all his grandfather's friends, Mac knew he wouldn't get them here.

Noralee Thompson sat beside his grandfather, along with Miss Q and several of their friends from their Garden District neighborhood. These were friends who'd all shared lifetimes of adventures, not unlike his own long-standing relationships with Christopher and Lennon.

One glance around that table, and Mac knew they'd been had.

"Grandfather, if you wouldn't mind, Harley and I need a private word with you."

His grandfather didn't get a chance to reply before Miss Q clapped her hands. "It's the newlyweds," she said with a smile. "Come in, dears. We were just discussing you."

The men stood to greet Harley, whose eyes were growing wider by the second. Mac slipped his arm around her shoulders, a show of support he knew wouldn't make any difference.

"Friends," Mrs. Noralee said. "Meet the new Mr. and Mrs. Mackenzie Gerard."

Miss Q and Mrs. Noralee burst into a humming rendition of "The Wedding March," reinforcing that eccentricity abounded in this room. Sitting around the table as they were, Mac's grandfather and his friends looked like a geriatric version of the Little Rascals.

"We so enjoyed watching the videotape of your wedding," Mrs. Noralee told them. "But we've decided we'd like a real wedding. You know, to firm up the deal."

"The next logical question would be to ask why Harley and I were the topic of conversation at your meeting," Mac said to segue past all talk about weddings. "But I don't think I need to. The thefts were a setup, weren't they?"

"A setup?" His grandfather frowned. "What makes you think that, Mackenzie?"

Mac looked at Mrs. Noralee. "We overheard Caroline's conversation with you."

"Oh, hang that girl." She scowled darkly. "I knew I shouldn't have picked up the phone."

"If she'd left a message, we'd have overheard anyway," Mac said.

"Now, Noralee, it's not Caroline's fault," Miss Q said. "She was just trying to save your family business, that's all."

"She really thinks Nice and Neat is under suspicion of theft, and we put her up against professionals." Christopher's grandfather, the man Mac's friend had been named for and whom he had always known as Mr. Christopher, swept his gaze over them with a respect Mac didn't feel they earned. Their closet surveillance had been nothing more than chance.

Miss Q smiled. "The acorn didn't fall far from the tree. Caroline's protective of her family. She's to be commended."

"Indeed she is," his grandfather agreed. "I'd say she has earned a medal of honor for services rendered."

Mr. Christopher made a notation in a notebook. "I'll make the arrangements with approval."

Mac watched in amazement as his grandfather tapped a wooden gavel on the table and said, "We need a motion."

"I move to recognize Noralee's granddaughter for her service to the Second Story Society," Miss Q said.

Mrs. Noralee raised her hand. "All right. I'll second the motion, but the girl is still going to get a talking-to."

The gavel banged sharply. "So moved. Christopher, you're in charge. Noralee, as recording secretary, you make sure the motion gets entered into our minutes and submitted for board approval."

Harley's mouth popped wide open and Mac's mood took a sharp decline.

"Grandfather, what's this all about?" he asked. "Exactly what is the Second Story Society?"

Miss Q reached out to pat his grandfather's hand as every face at the table turned toward them.

Before his grandfather could answer, Harley spoke up. "The name suggests you've all taken up burglary as a sideline. Except you haven't stolen anything and nothing was really stolen from you, was it? So basically the function of your Second Story Society is to plot and plan *fake* thefts."

She looked recovered, cool and distant with her shields so completely in place a nuclear blast couldn't have shaken them loose. "The real question here is: what was the point?"

Faces broke into smiles. Someone—Mac didn't catch who—began to clap and the applause increased until Harley was the recipient of very noisy acclaim.

She folded her arms across her chest and stared stoically around the table, wouldn't glance his way. The applause finally died down and his grandfather said, "Brava, Harley." He winked at Mac. "She's sharp as a tack, Mackenzie."

"The point, my dear," Miss Q added cheerily, "was to get you and Mac together, of course."

"The Second Story Society was formed to promote the happiness of our members' loved ones," Noralee explained.

Mr. Christopher nodded. "That's our mission statement."

This was the absolute last thing Mac wanted to hear, and he glanced at Harley again, who might have been standing behind an invisible brick wall for the expression on her beautiful face.

"I see," was all she said, leaving him to ask the obvious question. "Why?"

"Mackenzie, how can you ask me that?" His grandfather frowned. "After seeing you and Harley at Christopher's wedding, it was obvious you two are crazy about each other—''

''And too stubborn to admit it,'' Mr. Christopher added.

Miss Q smiled. ''We thought we'd give you a little nudge.''

''A little nudge?'' Harley asked, her voice so thin Mac was surprised it didn't crack. ''I *married* this man.''

Miss Q fixed her with that sparkling smile. ''I hope you made love with him, too, dear, so it's a *real* marriage.''

''Hear, hear.'' Mrs. Noralee chimed in. ''We wanted to keep you together long enough to come to your senses. Did we accomplish our mission objective?''

Mac winced. Harley just glared at *him* accusingly.

''You can't possibly think I was involved in this?'' he said.

''Were you?''

''No!''

''When you pass judgment on us, Harley,'' his grandfather said. ''Please bear in mind that we only wanted to make you a part of us. We take our own very seriously. Mackenzie needed help to win your heart, whether he realized it or not, and you're too special a young lady to let get away.''

Harley leveled that stoic gaze around the table and Mac honestly couldn't tell what she felt in that moment. Anger maybe, or perhaps she simply thought that all members of the Second Story Society had lost their minds. He didn't have a clue. She was closed to him in a way she hadn't been since they'd first made love and her inscrutable expression drove home the fact that this turn of events might have cost him all the headway he'd made with her.

''Harley—''

''Allow me to recap,'' she said, cutting him off. ''Just to make sure I get everything straight to report back to my boss. You decided to help Gerard *win my heart,* so you staged the thefts, hired Eastman Investigations to catch you, then watched the action over tea and crumpets.'' She tipped her head at the refreshment sideboard. ''Does that about sum things up?''

His grandfather nodded. ''I knew if I told Mac his grandmother's wedding set had been stolen, he'd be personally invested in the outcome of the case. And I figured it couldn't hurt to give him a chance to prove to you that he has what it takes to be a good investigator. He does, doesn't he, my dear?''

She gave him a tight smile. ''Yes, Stuart, he does.''

Before Mac could even absorb that admission, Harley said, ''I'm sure Josh will make contact if he has any more questions. Thank you all for answering mine. Good day.''

Then she turned and walked out the door. Mac started after her, but his grandfather said, ''Mackenzie, a moment please.''

He paused in the doorway as Harley moved down the hall, all long-legged strides and bristling pride, before he turned back around to find everyone looking worried.

''We honestly thought we'd buy you more time,'' his grandfather said. ''We didn't think you'd catch us so quickly.''

''Which is an argument against any of you going into crime as a sideline.'' He couldn't criticize these meddlers when he'd been guilty of the exact same crime—believing he'd have time before Harley discovered his arrangement with her exterminator.

Everyone had been meddling in her life, all well-intentioned actions that manipulated her mercilessly in the process. But what struck Mac was that if he hadn't acted, if none of them had acted, he would have never stood any chance at all at getting past Harley's defenses. Loving her had been a no-win situation all along, except for a few brief moments when he'd actually stood a chance.

Was that chance gone now?

"The girl is so in love, she's scared half to death." Miss Q smiled thoughtfully. "You can still win her, Mac. Trust me."

Mac wasn't so sure.

He took off without saying goodbye, but his delay had given Harley enough time to disappear. She wasn't in the lobby or at the car. So he returned to the museum and questioned the security guard to find she'd left in a cab.

So he stood on the steps of the museum, peering out into the busy French Quarter street, where strangers rushed around working, sight-seeing, partying, *living,* while he felt as if his whole life had just vanished into thin air.

He only had a chance with Harley if she wanted them to have a chance. He didn't think she did. He'd watched her retreat behind her shields, hiding behind that tough exterior she showed the world, safe from the Second Story Society and from him.

So what did he do now? Push her to choose between him and Anthony? He'd lose that contest, not because Harley didn't care about him, but because she felt safe with Anthony.

Mac wanted to know what the man had done to earn such unswerving devotion. Unfortunately, he didn't think Harley, or anyone else who knew her, would answer that question. She trusted the people in her life for a reason—they were all fiercely protective of her.

Mac needed some answers about her involvement with the DiLeo family and the only way to get them was to stick his nose in places he had no business sticking his nose. None of them had the right to interfere in her life or manipulate her—not him, not the Second Story Society. No matter how well intentioned the interference was.

But Mac couldn't get past the fact that if they hadn't acted, he'd have never gotten close enough to Harley for her to care about him at all.

And yes, Harley cared, but did she need him, or Anthony?

A question she would have to answer.

Mac stared out into the bright street, isolated from the passersby by the turmoil inside him. It went against his gut to even consider stepping aside to let Anthony DiLeo have the woman he loved, the woman he hadn't cherished enough to claim as his own a long time ago. But Mac knew in his heart that if he wasn't the man Harley needed, he would back off.

He loved her that much.

Which meant he needed to know whether to push her into making a choice. Answering that question meant digging into her past, an action that would surely cost him every shred of her trust if she ever found out. It was a huge risk. One he was willing to take.

He loved her that much.

Mac went back to his car and headed downtown to the only person who could help him—his sister Courtney.

He was lucky to catch her in the social services office so late on a Friday afternoon. Her load of casework was routinely staggering and she usually went into the field after completing her office work for the day. He stuck his head through her open door, found her sitting at her desk behind a mountain of paperwork, glued to the computer screen.

"Courtney, the receptionist said to come in."

She glanced up, gave him a fried-around-the-edges smile. "Surprise, surprise. What brings you here, little brother?"

"I need your help."

She waved him in. "Close the door."

Mac did as she asked, leaning against the side of her desk and proceeding to give her a rundown of the events that had led him to marry Harley, including a nutshell version of the Second Story Society's involvement. He gave her the unadulterated truth. Mac trusted his big sister to have his best interests at heart and to keep her mouth shut when it counted.

Courtney listened without interrupting, but she sank back in her chair to stare at him, her jaw slackening as his story progressed and, when he finally finished, she said, "Whoa."

"Yeah, whoa is right."

"And you love her?"

He nodded.

"Jeez, Mac." Thrusting fingers through her hair, she gave him a weak smile. "When you said you wanted to shake your life up... Whoever said 'Be careful what you wish for, you just might get it' knew what they were talking about, hmm?"

He gave an equally weak laugh. "At this point, the good is still outweighing the bad. I'd like to keep it that way."

"Think that's possible?"

"I don't know," he said honestly. "I have to try."

"What exactly do you want me to do?"

"I need to understand how Anthony DiLeo and his family fit into Harley's life. I need to understand why she feels so safe with them."

"Did you ask her?"

"You're kidding, right? She let me believe she'd worked as a stripper in a sex dungeon."

Courtney frowned. "This isn't sounding like a solid basis for a marriage. You do realize that, don't you?"

"That will change, *if* Harley decides to let me in. *If* I

can earn her trust. But I don't know whether to push. I don't want to hurt her, but I don't want to lose her, either. And I'm in trouble now. Our grandfather pushed me back five steps today."

Mac gave a frustrated laugh. "And I can't even blame him. If it hadn't been for him and his crazy idea, I'd have never married Harley in the first place." He exhaled heavily, met Courtney's eyes. "She deserves to be treated a lot better than the way Anthony DiLeo treats her, but he makes her feel safe. I want to know why. I know she goes way back with his family."

"My poor little brother," she said, not unkindly. "You do have it bad. But how am I supposed to help you—" Understanding dawned. "Her parents died. Was she involved with social services?"

"I need you to tell me." He detailed Harley's involvement with Judge Bancroft and the clues that had all led him to his conclusion. "I'd never ask you to jeopardize your career, Courtney, you know that, but if you could go into the archive and take a peek. See if the name DiLeo shows up anywhere."

Courtney scowled. "Don't you have friends with the D.A.'s office who can help you?"

"All my connections will go through the police and I can't risk Dominic DiLeo finding out that I'm inquiring."

Mac was gratified and grateful when she pushed her chair back to stand without further deliberation. "Only for you, little brother."

"Thanks, Courtney."

"Thank me by reassembling these files."

"You got it."

He put her files back together, wondering exactly what, if anything, she would find, and as it turned out, he didn't have to wait long. He'd no sooner closed the last folder than she reappeared carrying a file at least four inches thick.

One glimpse of Courtney's face and he knew she'd already looked inside. She reserved that expression for her tough cases, the ones that made her struggle to keep her distance.

"You aren't going to get into any trouble, are you?"

"Not if you're quick." She placed the folder in front of him. "I'll go grab coffee while you look through this."

"Stay."

Courtney shook her head and left the office without another word, pulling the door closed behind her.

Mac looked at the folder.

Case number LA743874: Harley Price.

He'd been right, and he hadn't realized until that moment how much he wished he wouldn't be. Flipping open the cover, he skimmed school records, copies of medical and police reports. He thumbed through each, noting names, dates, learning a local elementary school had filed official complaints with the state about Harley's situation as early as her second-grade year.

Mrs. Price had left home when Harley had been five, and given the police report copies in this file, her abandonment came as no great mystery. Harley's father had been an alcoholic with a tendency toward violence.

Mac had seen the M.O. often in his years with the D.A.'s office and had prosecuted his share of domestic-abuse cases. What he didn't understand was why Harley's mother would leave her five-year-old daughter at the mercy of a man out of control.

Nothing in the file explained that. Yet someone had meticulously researched Harley's life, perhaps to compile the case for Judge Bancroft, as Mac suspected he'd been the man responsible for ultimately making her a ward of the state.

Three school clinic reports of various injuries. Another reporting that Harley as a kindergartner had contracted a skin infection. She'd been sent home early from school four days running before the principal had personally delivered her home to explain the need for medical attention before she could return.

Harley had gotten medical care. She'd arrived back at school the following day with a prescription and no idea how to apply it since she hadn't learned to read yet.

Mac's chest grew tight as he scanned a guidance counselor's report from her fifth-grade year detailing a twelve-day unexcused absence where all attempts to contact her parent had failed. Harley's explanation upon her return: she'd had to cover for her father at his job because of an illness.

"She worked for him sometimes. Joe would've cut the unreliable bastard loose a long time before he died if not for Harley," Delilah had told him.

Mac forced himself to keep skimming the documents, blindly processing each bit of information, refusing to stop long enough to dwell on what he read. Not yet. Not until he could somehow reconcile the woman he loved with this neglected child and still keep himself together.

But then he came across transcripts of Judge Bancroft's first interview with Harley, which confirmed his suspicions about their connection.

"Why did you lock yourself in the closet, Harley?"

"My dad was drinking."

"From what I see in these reports, your dad has drunk before. Do you always lock yourself in the closet?"

"No."

"What was different about this time? What made you think you had to hide to protect yourself?"

"He tried to touch me."

"Touch you? Do you mean he hit you?"

"No, he didn't hit me. He touched me. I think he got me mixed up with my mom. I know he didn't mean to. He was just drunk, but I needed to hide."

"For three days, Harley? Couldn't you find a way to get out in all that time."

"He was drinking. Sometimes he got quiet and I thought he might have passed out, but I wasn't sure. My dad's sneaky like that when he drinks."

"How long did you plan to stay locked up?"

"Until Anthony came to get me."

"Anthony? Is this your neighbor, Anthony DiLeo? Why did you expect him?"

"He always checks on me to make sure I'm okay. But his grandma died so he went away to Baton Rouge with his mom and everyone. I had to wait until he came home."

Anthony DiLeo had indeed gone to check on Harley. Mac read the report summary that detailed how a thirteen-year-old Anthony had gone up against her drunk and combative father, broken his nose and knocked him out. He'd dismantled the closet door to rescue an unconscious Harley and had helped himself to his sixteen-year-old brother's car to drive her to the emergency room rather than call an ambulance and run the risk of her father regaining consciousness and confronting them.

Mac understood. This black-and-white smudged copy of a long-ago interview explained why Harley trusted Anthony—he protected her no matter what.

For Anthony's efforts that time, he'd spent the night in a juvenile detention center until Judge Bancroft had ruled his assault justifiable self-defense and lectured him on the consequences of grand theft auto and driving without a license.

Judge Bancroft had placed Harley in protective custody, which struck Mac as a little late given she'd wound up in the hospital recovering from severe dehydration.

There was also a petition from an attorney on behalf of Mrs. DiLeo, who'd tried to adopt Harley. Her petition had been denied. Then she'd applied for foster status, also to no avail. Her socioeconomic situation as a widowed mother with six children of her own to care for had rendered her ineligible.

But according to the remainder of the reports, Harley hadn't taken no for an answer. She'd repeatedly run away from each of the foster homes she'd been placed in during the next seven years.

She'd run home to the DiLeos. And the DiLeos had welcomed her every time.

"I was a juvenile delinquent, Gerard," Harley had told him.

She'd claimed to be a troublemaker, and Mac supposed in some regards that was true. Most kids would have obeyed the law. But not Harley. She'd wanted to live with people who loved her and wouldn't take no for an answer.

The pieces fit. Her devotion to Anthony and his family. Cajun Joe. Her volunteer work at the domestic-abuse shelter. She knew children in social services needed all the help they could get because she'd been a child in the system and it had failed her in every way that mattered.

Mac was standing at the window when Courtney returned. She stopped in the doorway when she saw him, that expression back on her face. She felt bad for him and he wanted to tell her that he didn't need her sympathy. He hadn't had the childhood from hell. In thirty-three years, he'd never faced anything that had even come close to what Harley had lived through.

But all he could ask was, "What do I do with *this?*"

He was so far out of his league it was a joke. He didn't know how to prove to Harley that he loved her or how to handle the ugly truth about her past.

But Courtney did. She covered the distance between them, slipped her arms around his waist and hugged him. "You just love her, little brother. You just love her."

16

"ANTHONY'S IN HIS OFFICE." The woman with the head-phone growing from her ear looked up from the service desk. "You can go back."

Mac already knew the way. What he didn't know is what sort of welcome he'd get. Nothing friendly, he assumed, and wasn't disappointed when he pushed the door open to find Anthony facing him across the desk with a scowl. "What the hell do you want?"

"Harley."

"And you expect me to whip her out from under my desk and hand her to you?"

"No. I need your help getting her to decide which one of us she wants a future with."

Anthony's laughter grated on Mac's nerves. "You can't really be that stupid?"

It was a question. One that also grated on Mac's nerves. He wanted to ask if Anthony was even on speaking terms with her yet, but he refused to be sucked into a pissing contest.

Forcing an even tone, he said, "Only if trusting you to care about what's best for her is stupid."

That stopped Anthony cold, which was some consola-tion. He glared, visibly struggling to control his temper. "I take that to mean you think *you're* best for her."

Mac nodded. "I *am* best for her. But I respect that she

has feelings for you. She might think what you offer is more comfortable than what I can offer.''

''Comfortable?''

Mac nodded. ''She knows what to expect from you and she trusts you. I've learned that trust means a lot to her. I'm new to the equation and until recently, she hasn't had much of a reason to trust me.''

''Am I supposed to be impressed,'' Anthony said, dripping a sarcasm Mac recognized as an echo of Harley's. A very humbling reminder of the long history between them. ''But what makes you trustworthy now? She's been telling me about you for months. She thinks you're an idiot.''

Mac folded his arms across his chest and swallowed his pride. ''In many regards I was. I met her after spending nearly two years deciding to rearrange my life because I wasn't happy with where I was going. I was looking for a lot of things and I found them all in her. Suffice to say, she wasn't exactly what I'd had in mind.''

''I am the dead last person you should be telling that she's not good enough for you.''

''I'm not telling you she's not good enough. I'd recently gotten out of an engagement. I was looking to enjoy myself, not get involved again—especially not with someone who consumes me the way she does.''

Anthony spread his hands magnanimously. ''Then I don't see the problem. If she's not what you want, move on.''

Mac almost smiled. In Anthony's place, he'd have probably made the same suggestion. ''She *is* what I want. It just took me a while to realize it. Harley recognized it faster than I did.''

''And she wanted no part of you. Why don't you understand that? You had to *pay* her to marry you, man. That's pathetic.''

No argument there, and Mac steeled himself, refusing to let Anthony see that he'd landed his blow. "I paid Harley to marry me to get her away from you. I knew I wouldn't get anywhere with you dropping by whenever you felt like it."

Anthony scowled. "*I'm* best for her."

"You think so? From where I'm standing, you look like you've had a decade to make a commitment. You didn't, so I assume you don't want one."

His blow landed this time. Anthony exhaled sharply, looking slightly stunned, and Mac didn't miss the opportunity to strike again while his opponent was down. "Harley and I are married. I want to stay that way."

To Anthony's credit, he recovered fast. "Your marriage doesn't mean shit. She told me about your trust fund and how you wanted to collect your money. You paid her to marry you and she did because she's broke."

Mac's turn on his knees.

Harley *hadn't* jeopardized their investigation. She'd kept up her end of the bargain, even with Anthony, who Mac now knew was a lot more to her than a sometimes boyfriend. He'd underestimated her commitment to him big time.

Sitting heavily on the arm of a chair, he absorbed the realization, the thought that he'd had more of a chance than he'd ever known, maybe enough of one to still give him a fighting chance now.

"You're all wrong about Harley and me," Anthony scoffed. "We're not about commitment. We've been committed. We just haven't settled down yet. We both have had things to accomplish and she likes her space."

"She's *comfortable* with her space. There's a big difference, Anthony."

"Okay, she's *comfortable.*" It was a concession, a small one, but a concession nevertheless.

"Looks like you're comfortable with that space, too."

Anthony shrugged. "She gets what she wants from me. I'm here for her. *Always.*"

Mac inclined his head in acknowledgment. No denying that, but... "I don't think letting Harley breeze through life, never getting close to anyone because she doesn't know how or is afraid she'll get hurt is in her best interest."

"Since when are you the authority on what's best for her?"

"I'm not, but I know how she feels about me. She's resisting because she's scared."

"She's resisting because she thinks you're an idiot."

"Sometimes she does, but she loves me anyway."

Anthony threw his head back and laughed, but this time his laugh didn't grate nearly so much. Mac had more hope than when he'd walked through this office door.

"You're dreaming, Gerard. She's said a lot of things about you, but *love* was never one of them."

"Given your reaction to our marriage, did you expect her to tell you how hard she's been fighting how she feels?"

Anthony pushed away from the desk and stood, a position that let him look down at Mac.

Mac thought it was encouraging he felt the need to.

"She's dated before, Gerard. Lots of times."

"So I've heard. From you and her."

"What makes you think you're any different?"

"She's pushing too hard to get away."

"Maybe you should take the hint."

"Yeah, that would have been easier, but she's too special to let get away." His grandfather's words, and he meant them. "Listen, Anthony. Harley might decide that feeling safe beats being in love. But I think she deserves the chance to move past feeling safe. She deserves to be loved. And not *sometimes*. She shouldn't have to be afraid. Not anymore."

"She had a lot to be afraid of growing up."

"I know."

Anthony looked surprised, but he held Mac's gaze. "How much?"

"A lot."

"She doesn't talk about her past. Not to anyone."

Mac didn't correct him. Knowing about Harley's past seemed significant and he wasn't going to lose his edge. Anthony might have experienced her youth up close, but Mac knew and respected it now. How he found out didn't matter. "She doesn't deserve to live her whole life expecting people to hurt her."

Anthony thrust his fingers through his hair, clearly troubled. "What do you want from me?"

"Harley and I reached the end of the line a few hours ago. Technically, she doesn't need to be married to me anymore. My guess is that she's going to divorce me as soon as she can get the papers drawn up."

"And you're convinced she's in love," he said with a sharp laugh.

"I'm just asking you to take a look. You know her better than anyone. If I'm wrong and she'd rather be safe with you than in love with me, then I'll sign the divorce papers and be on my way. I'll even hire on with another investigative agency, so I'm not in her face at work."

Anthony nodded. "That's fair."

"But she has to choose."

"And how do you expect to make her? The princess isn't big into being pushed, and she and I aren't even talking right now."

"I've been giving this thought," Mac said, pleased that Harley hadn't run to Anthony yet. "If she can't find me, she can't serve me divorce papers. If I'm right and she's in emotionally as deep as I think she is, that's going to make her nuts. She needs this divorce so she can get on with trying to get over me."

Anthony gave another snort of laughter.

Mac ignored him. "I think she'll do what she always does when she's in over her head—she's going to run to you. Then she's all yours. You decide whether she's in love and what to do about it."

Anthony braced both hands on the desk and leaned toward Mac, a threatening look that Mac returned with a cool stare. "And you're willing to trust me to make that call?"

Mac nodded, taking the biggest leap of faith he'd ever comprehended taking. "I believe you'll put Harley's happiness above your own. I'm willing to risk my happiness on it."

He gave a dry laugh. "You really love her."

"I do."

HARLEY PULLED INTO THE back lot of Love Cajun Style not caring that she'd parked beside Delilah's car in Joe's private spot. Joe always helped her out when she was desperate, and right now qualified.

She *desperately* needed to get a pen into Gerard's hand.

After learning about the Second Story Society, Gerard had gone on the run, dodging her every attempt to serve him with divorce papers. More than a week had passed since he'd first disappeared, a week where he hadn't shown up for work or at his new house, or his old house, or his family's house.

She'd been left to explain the whole humiliating situation to Josh, who'd only rolled his eyes and asked what she thought of relocating Eastman Investigations to the West Coast, far away from meddling family members.

Harley was all for it—the more states between her and the memory of this nightmare the better.

But she knew Josh had reconsidered inviting her to make the trek west when she'd refused to accept any money from this case—not her professional fee nor the reward that the Second Story Society had insisted on paying. As far as the crazy senior citizens were concerned, the investigators had recovered the goods. But Harley had no intention of stooping so low for money ever again.

Been there, done that, had wound up married to a man she couldn't find to divorce.

Josh had called her stubborn. In fact, he'd called everyone stubborn. Her and Gerard for refusing their fees, the Second Story Society for insisting on paying rewards in addition to their bill. Now he had all this money and no one to give it to. Well, she supposed he had a right to toss the word around.

If stubborn kept her out of situations like this one in the future, then Harley was all for that, too, damn it.

She'd hocked her wedding ring to pay a lawyer to draw up the divorce papers and then began conducting an all-out search for Gerard. How hard could it be to find the man when she'd trained him? She would eventually outthink him and to his credit, it had taken a while, but she finally got him.

He'd enlisted the help of the Second Story Society and had been taking turns hiding out in each of their family homes.

That's when she'd called Anthony.

They hadn't spoken since the night he'd learned of her marriage, but Harley knew when push came to shove he'd help her out if she was desperate.

She was. *Desperately* in need of him and his equally large and tough brothers to collect her husband and relocate him to Cajun Joe's, where she would have him restrained in the bondage room until he signed the documents to dissolve their marriage.

Harley entered through the back entrance of the club and found Delilah behind the bar, tallying what appeared to be last night's tickets. "Good morning, Delilah."

"G'morning, Cha Cha. Your boys are upstairs waiting," she said with a bright smile, as though having several men upstairs in the bondage room was an everyday occurrence. Then of course, she supposed it *was* an everyday occurrence around here. "Just let me know if you want coffee sent up."

"Thanks." She wouldn't have minded espresso right now and promised to treat herself when she could celebrate managing to hang on to her last shred of common sense. Gerard had apparently abandoned his.

She found Damon and Dominic waiting outside the bondage room like Secret Service agents. "My heroes."

Dominic gave a perfunctory knock, then kissed her cheek.

"Anthony's inside," Damon said.

With Gerard, *alone?* She wasn't sure she liked the idea of that. "Any problems?"

Both men shook their heads, and Harley supposed Gerard hadn't stood much of a chance against three DiLeos with more martial arts training than most men achieve over a lifetime. "Well, wish me luck."

Damon gave her a hug, and she said, "Thanks for the help."

Steeling her spine, she wiped her expression clean and entered the room, letting the sight of Anthony crowd out all memories of the last time she'd been here.

He stood leaning against the sideboard, arms folded

across his chest, looking as carefully neutral as she did, but there was no denying the huge sigh of relief that flowed through her, a physical sensation.

"Good morning, princess." He tossed her a key.

She caught it in midair. "Good morning, Anthony. Thanks for your help."

He inclined his head but didn't say another word, just stood there waiting...she wasn't sure for what. Maybe he wanted to watch the carnage. She didn't know. She didn't ask. Bottom line—it didn't matter. She had to face Gerard sometime. She could see him reflected in her periphery anyway.

Sliding the roll of papers from her back pocket, she turned to look at him, unwilling to avoid the moment any longer, refusing to give him that kind of power over her.

Ironically he was restrained in nearly the same position she'd been when they'd made love here. He knelt on the bed with his arms bound behind him. His clear gaze swept over her and it struck Harley how much she'd missed the way he'd looked at her. Possessively, as if he'd been waiting forever to see her. She'd managed to block that out of her mind this week. Damn good thing, too. Otherwise she might have melted beneath the heat of his gaze, and that was about the last thing she needed to do in front of Anthony.

Holding up the key and the roll of papers, she said, "You promised."

"I changed my mind."

"That was *not* part of the arrangement."

"Neither was falling in love with you, Harley. But I did. It changed everything."

She steeled herself against the look in his eyes, the honesty on his face that made her force her next words out. "Not for me, it didn't. You gave your word."

Then she waited.

With her heart pounding too hard, her pulse throbbing loudly in her ears, she just waited.

The next move was Gerard's. She wasn't releasing him until he agreed to sign, but she wished with all her heart that Anthony wasn't here to see her struggling so hard to stay composed, wished she'd never agreed to this whole stupid arrangement in the first place.

She should have let the bank foreclose on her house. She could have declared bankruptcy and started over fresh. There were worse things in life. She caught Gerard and Anthony's reflections in the mirror.

Much worse things.

Gerard finally nodded, acknowledging the papers she held. "I'll sign those papers...."

For one wild moment she felt relief so complete her knees nearly buckled.

"...*if* you tell me you don't want a future together. Just tell me you don't love me enough to stay married."

"Please." The word slipped from her lips unbidden, before she'd even had a chance to think, and she hated how one stupid word could sound so much like a plea. "Don't make this ugly."

She didn't want to do this, honestly didn't know if she could maintain control with Anthony *and* Gerard watching. A week of playing cat and mouse had her nerves on the edge. She felt as if she stood on a tightrope, poised over her whole life.

And even worse, she was scared, damn it. She didn't know what was scaring her because she'd leave Gerard here to rot until he granted her a divorce, but she hated being scared even more than she hated to cry.

Yeah, a lot more.

"Princess, just tell the guy you don't love him enough

to stay married and he'll sign the papers," Anthony said, and he sounded so strange that she looked at him. "If he doesn't, you have my word I'll take your gun and make him."

Harley opened her mouth to tell them both that she didn't love Gerard—a lie as it was, but she didn't care. Falling in love didn't count if she didn't want to be in love.

But then she met Anthony's eyes and what she saw stopped her cold.

Anthony knew she'd be lying.

He *knew*.

And Harley couldn't bring herself to lie to him, not to his face, not like this. Bending the truth to protect his feelings was one thing, but he *knew*.

She didn't know what to feel or what to say, so she just stood there staring at him, completely blindsided by the moment, by her emotions as she stared into his handsome face. If she didn't open her mouth, she was going to lose him, but she couldn't lie to him. Not Anthony. Not ever.

His expression was almost painfully composed, as if it was taking everything he had to hold it together.

Harley knew that look. She'd seen it before on the occasions when life dealt him a nasty hand. Mr. Tough Guy. And at any other time, she'd have wrapped her arms around him and held him. She'd offer him the same kind of unconditional love he offered her, a place where he'd always be welcomed, know he was accepted no matter what he did or how the cards played out.

But she didn't think he'd want her to touch him right now. And it was knowing that holding him might hurt more than help that finally did her in. She just wasn't sure what to do and not knowing overwhelmed her so much that tears sprang to her eyes.

His expression melted, and he sat down on the arm of the sofa and said, "Come here."

It was his gentle tone, that oh-so familiar softness in his voice that drew her to him without a thought. He braced his legs wide and looped his arms around her waist, forcing her close enough so they were almost nose to nose.

"Don't look so surprised, princess. If you weren't in over your head, you wouldn't have run to me to save you."

"You always save me."

"And I always will." His own gaze looked suspiciously moist. "It's the one thing I do that always makes me proud."

Her heart started crumbling right then, just breaking into pieces. "Why not now?"

"You don't need saving this time."

"You're wrong."

He shook his head. "I saw you that night at my house, princess. I stood upstairs in my old bedroom and watched you cry your heart out all over this guy." His voice broke and she knew he was losing it. "You know what I thought?"

"No." The word came out a sob.

"The princess I know and love would rather shoot someone than cry in front of him. When you didn't draw your gun, I knew I'd let you get away."

Her face hurt with the effort of not losing it right there, even though her heart was breaking. But she wouldn't, *couldn't*. If she did, Anthony would, too, and she wouldn't do that to him. Not in front of Gerard.

But a couple of stupid tears pushed their way out despite her best efforts and he reached up to thumb them away.

"It's not his fault, you know." He inclined his head toward the bed.

"It is. I told him to leave me alone."

Anthony gave a harsh laugh, suddenly more in control. "I wish he'd listened, believe me. But he did what any guy in love would do—he stacked the deck. Can't fault him for that. I wish I'd have done the same thing. But I was so sure of you…I let him steal your heart away. I'll regret that arrogance—"

"Anthony." His name came out on the edge of another sob and she knew she was going to lose it, but he pressed his finger to her lips and shot her a devilish smile, the very same smile she'd fallen in love with when she'd been six years old.

"Trust him, princess," he said gently. "He loves you and you love him. I'm not going anywhere. I'll still be here to kick his ass if he screws up."

He pressed his mouth to hers, and as quickly as the kiss started, it ended. He got up and walked to the door, leaving her standing there, all alone.

"You hear that, Gerard?" He paused in the doorway. "Don't screw up or you deal with me. You have my word."

And Harley let him go.

She just let him walk out the door, knowing Damon and Dominic would be there for him, even though she should be with them, too. She'd spent her whole life trying to be part of their family, *was* a part of them, but right now…right now she had to let them go, even though she felt so alone being left behind, just standing here. She wished the floor would open up and swallow her whole so she didn't have to feel this way, so helpless, hurting so much because she'd hurt Anthony.

Because she'd let him go.

And then suddenly strong arms slipped around her, pulling her close against a broad chest that felt so familiar, so painfully right. She wanted to push Gerard away, didn't know how he'd gotten loose, didn't want him to hold her. Not right now. Not when she was falling apart.

But she needed him to. She needed him so much that all the tears she'd been holding back burst out like the dam had broken. She wanted to blame him for making her feel this way, so helpless and needy…and so irresistibly *right* when he scooped her into his arms and brought her to the sofa.

Cradling her in his lap, he let her sob her heart out, whispering softly in her ear all the while, stroking her hair. He held her close, offering his strength when she had so little of her own, letting her hide from the world against his chest.

"I hate you," she sobbed into his wet shirt.

"I know."

Stupid man didn't seem to care. He just kept those strong arms around her, didn't seem to mind that she was trashing his custom-tailored shirt with a mixture of mascara and tears.

"I missed you," he said, making matters worse. "I had nothing to do at night but sleep. It was horrible, no one chasing me all over the bed trying to make love to me."

She gave a teary laugh, despite herself. "You wish."

He pressed a kiss to the top of her head, made the little pieces of her broken heart melt into a puddle. "Yeah, I do."

He peered down at her with that soft-edged expression he reserved only for her. "For a woman who professes to hate crying so much, you cry an awful lot. Dare I hope that you might yet do a striptease for me? One with real dancing?"

"You *really* wish."

He chuckled. "Done crying yet?"

She nodded, a few more tears squeezing out anyway.

"You're sure?"

"Yes, damn it." It came out a growl. "And I wouldn't act so put out. If it hadn't been for you—"

She broke off sharply when he captured her wrists in an iron grip and jerked them over her head so she couldn't break away. "Gerard, what the hell—"

"We've got unfinished business."

"Unfinished?" she asked incredulously. "What's unfinished? Anthony left and I stayed, didn't I?"

He gazed down at her with those smoky eyes and she knew in that glance he somehow understood how difficult Anthony's leaving had been for them both. "He did, and you did."

"You were never tied up, were you?"

He shook his head.

She stared at him, waiting, still too raw around the edges to start asking questions.

"Anthony and I talked this week," he said.

"About what?"

He gave her a quirky half grin as he maneuvered her wrists into one of his big hands so he could dig in his pocket.

The designer restraints.

She thought about resisting but found she simply didn't have it in her. She was too frayed right now, emotionally on her knees. Gerard said there could be more to their future than divorce court. He said he was trustworthy, and now seemed to be the perfect time to let him prove it.

Anthony said she could trust him, too, and even if her own judgment was rusty, she could trust Anthony not to steer her wrong. And when she got down to it, Gerard was the whole reason she felt horrible right now. Let him make her feel better.

"I did most of the talking," he said. "He listened."

Listening was a bit out of character for Anthony when he was angry and she had no doubt that he'd been angry. "What did you say that he wanted to hear?"

"Come to find out, your friend Anthony is a fairly decent guy, who's more interested in your happiness than his own. Sort of endeared him to me." He clicked the bracelets around her wrists, lowered her arms in front of her.

"I'm sure that made his day," she said dryly. "You told him that you were the only man who could make me happy, didn't you?"

"Sure did."

"Sound awfully sure of yourself."

He scooted her around on the sofa to survey his handiwork. His grin morphed into a smile as he raked a lusty gaze over her, his expression reminding her that she was sitting before him, a morsel awaiting his pleasure.

And that feeling sparked inside her, that incredible awareness they shared. An awareness she'd been resisting since the moment they'd met. An awareness that promised such pleasure if she'd only stop resisting.

He slipped off the sofa and knelt before her. Without so much as a by-your-leave, he headed for her belt.

"What are you doing?"

"Getting your undivided attention. I usually have it when you're naked."

"The restraints?"

"So you won't shoot me."

He delivered that so casually she felt a smile coming on. Okay, so he was making her feel better. A little.

"Why do you want my undivided attention?"

The button popped open beneath his fingers and his expression grew fixed as he worked her slacks down her hips, taking her panty hose with them. "I have to present rational arguments about our future. I have a case to win here."

"You sound like a lawyer."

"I am a lawyer."

He was also a man who made her skin tingle with a glance. Just the sight of him kneeling between her spread legs, his hair dark against her pale skin, his expression suggesting that he'd died and gone to heaven made her feel every inch of her bare bottom. And when he slid his strong hands up her thighs, she felt as if *she'd* died and gone to heaven.

"You don't think you've already won, Gerard?"

He lowered his face to press a kiss to her knee.

She shivered.

"Nope. I'm on a mission. First of all, I want you to admit that you love me. I know it, but I want to hear you say it." He dragged his warm mouth along the inside of her thigh.

Harley sucked in a deep breath as her insides swooped crazily.

"Then I want you to agree to stay Mrs. Gerard until we're as old and senile as the members of the Second Story Society."

"You don't want much, do you?" She sounded breathless and couldn't miss his widening smile even though his face was nearly buried between her thighs.

"Got a strong argument for that, too."

"Really?"

"Really. Think about the damage to your reputation. Josh will probably fire you and who'll hire you to investigate a case if word gets out that you let a bunch of old people snow you?"

The thought that her hard-won reputation would suffer should have bothered her, at least a little, but her thighs had started to vibrate as he swirled tiny circles with his tongue along her sensitive skin. She was having trouble concentrating.... "If you wanted my undivided attention, why are you distracting me with your mouth?"

"What I want is no question in anyone's mind that we got married for any reason other than we're in love. No question in your mind, either."

"Not everyone is going to think I fit in." She thought of Aunt Frances, but there would be others.

Gerard stopped his sexy ministrations and was on his feet so fast that she could only peer up at him, blinking. He loomed over her, every inch of his fully clothed self underscoring her nakedness. Even the gun tucked neatly against her shoulder didn't offset the awareness, didn't lend her that usual sense of confidence with her wrists restrained.

Then he sank onto the sofa beside her, long legs stretched before him. He was so in her face that she could see the subtle shades of gray that formed stars in his eyes. He didn't say another word, just trailed a hand down her stomach, not stopping when her shirt ended and bare skin began.

Cupping strong fingers around her sex, he touched her in a way that claimed he'd earned the privilege, a touch that made her heart start pounding hard in anticipation.

His gaze never left hers when he said, "We fit perfectly together, Harley, in every way. What we share is unique and special. Never doubt that."

Even if he hadn't sounded so serious, she could never have doubted his assertion when her insides melted beneath his touch.

Lowering his face, he brushed his mouth against her temple, her ear. "I don't care what anyone else thinks. I care what I think and I care what you think. That's it."

He grazed his fingers over her heat to emphasize his point, and she could only sigh, letting him know that she understood his message loud and clear.

"You enjoy the way I make you feel, and that's what I want. That's *all* I want. The thought of a whole lifetime together to explore how to bring you pleasure—'' another caress, another sigh ''—*excites* me.''

Excite was rather an understatement, because Harley wanted to kiss his mouth, touch his body, feel him inside her, warming her from the inside out.

"Then get on with it, Gerard," she said breathlessly, pressing against his fingers to feed the pleasure climbing through her. "Take off my gun and your clothes and let's make love."

He nipped her earlobe with his teeth. "I'm not done making demands yet."

"What else?"

He swirled his tongue in her ear, made her shiver. "Call me Mac. You have used my name before, in case you don't remember."

How could she possibly forget the night she lay underneath him in their bed with his big body all around her, all *in* her? "I remember."

"Good. Because I'm not going to make love to you until you call me by my name and tell me you love me enough to rip up the divorce papers."

She leaned back on the sofa and curled her legs around her, an attempt to ease the ache inside. "You're a pushy bastard, do you know that?"

"So you've told me."

"Are you sure you want to stay married?"

He went to work unbuttoning his shirt. "Not a doubt in my mind. You're the star of every one of my fantasies."

"Even after I tell you that I hocked my wedding band to pay for our divorce?" She held up her restrained hands to show him her bare ring finger.

He didn't say anything, just took his time shrugging out of his shirt. Then he whipped his undershirt off, blasting her with a view of the yummy terrain below.

The man *really* was too good-looking for his own good.

Instead of shedding his slacks, he dug into his pocket and withdrew a blue velvet jeweler's box.

"You bought it back?" She winced. "I wish you hadn't done that. The Gooch must have gouged you and I have the ticket. I was going to claim it as soon as I got—"

"I didn't buy it back," Gerard said, cutting her off. "That wasn't your real ring anyway. This is."

He flipped the box open, and Harley could only stare at the heart-shaped solitaire that rested in the middle of a simple wedding band that didn't detract from the incredible beauty of the diamond. Before she'd even recovered, he was slipping it onto her finger and assessing the effect.

"What do you think?" he asked.

"This diamond's bigger than my gun."

A dimple flashed. "Not quite."

She held up her hand, disbelieving of the diamond's size. Harley didn't think she wanted to know exactly how big.

Luckily she didn't have to say anything because Gerard lifted her hand and pressed a kiss to her palm. "I want you to have a ring that will always remind you how much I love you. This one isn't nearly big enough."

That's when it hit her. She'd seen these rings before—in a picture. "This is your grandmother's wedding set, isn't it?"

Their gazes met above their clasped hands and he nodded.

In that moment, Harley knew this man had her heart and soul and there wasn't a damned thing she could do about it. Tears were welling up again, but these were overwhelmed tears. She wanted to wrap her arms around him and not let go.

"I'm not Cinderella." She sounded watery and choked up and that damned dimple flashed for real as Gerard swooped down to claim a kiss, a big moist one that didn't hide how pleased he was with her reaction.

"Would you be for a little while?" he asked. "I never knew how much I'd enjoy playing Prince Charming."

Cinderella in black leather. Great. About the last thing on the planet she'd ever expected to be...and who'd have ever guessed how much she would enjoy role-playing.

But Harley was enjoying herself and, as she looked into his startling eyes, she saw more love than she had ever dreamed of, and gave up denying this man anything.

"I'll be Cinderella for a while." Slipping her arms around his neck, she kissed him back, feeling a little rush that she could touch him so freely.

He drank in her mouth, starting up all that hot need again as he tangled his tongue against hers, a fast, intense kiss that made her forget to breathe.

When he pulled away, he said, "We'll be good together, Harley. Trust me."

"I do."

"Then you won't be needing these." He unclasped the restraints and freed her wrists, pressing a kiss to each.

"And you won't be needing those." She reached down to tug on his waistband. "Drop your drawers. Last I heard wives had rights." With around-the-clock orgasms topping the list.

Wives had responsibilities, too, and when she thought about all the wedding gifts piled up in the storage room at Eastman Investigations, she almost groaned.

But her *husband* chose that moment to drop his drawers, distracting her with hard thighs and an impressive body part that bobbled endearingly as he tugged down his briefs and kicked off his shoes. Then he was sinking down onto the sofa beside her, all naked and hard and male.

"I love you, Harley." He dragged her against him.

"I love you, Mac."

It was funny, but Harley didn't think she'd mind writing those thank-you notes, after all.

Epilogue

MAC GAZED down at his beautiful bride, standing beside him in the reception line in an official public performance as husband and wife. She looked stunning in a beaded cream silk with a deceptively demure collar that covered skin but molded her sweet curves so closely there wasn't much left to the imagination.

He'd had a designer friend create the gown for her. The past two months of married life had taught him that he enjoyed dressing his bride almost as much as he enjoyed undressing her, and she seemed content to let him do both.

At the insistence of family and friends, they agreed to renew their vows formally. They'd honored his grandfather's request to have the wedding at the Chateau Royal, the historic hotel in the French Quarter where he'd married Mac's grandmother so many years ago. A place he deemed perfect to show society that the Gerard family proudly welcomed their newest addition. They'd enlisted Judge Bancroft to officiate again.

"How are you holding up?" Mac asked when there was a break in the line, leaning close enough to bury his face in the wild tumble of her hair.

"This is torture." Her smile didn't falter.

"Then why are you smiling?"

"I must be giddy. Can you imagine?"

Actually he could. These past two months had revealed

a side of his bride that was cautiously emerging—a relaxed, loving and, yes, *giddy* side that kept surprising them both.

And if Harley lowering her shields enough to explore life by his side wasn't a big enough surprise, his own giddiness was. Mac awakened each morning with an excitement to take on the day that he'd never experienced before. He went to sleep at night holding his beautiful bride, very grateful for the turns his life had taken.

"Giddy, hmm? I won't tell anyone. Trust me."

Her deep blue eyes sparkled and she leaned back just enough to fit neatly against him, an easy move he noticed her doing more and more often of late. "I do."

And he knew she did.

Even though she hadn't yet told him anything about her past except that it had been "rough," Mac hoped one day she'd open up and share that part of herself—not for his benefit, but for hers. He wanted her to make peace with the events that had shaped her into the woman he loved so much.

But for now, he simply smiled every time she accompanied him out into the world unarmed. He felt both proud and appreciative that he was earning her trust more with each passing day.

Mac didn't think life could get much better and he greeted the next guests with a smile that reflected his contentment at how easily he and Harley had segued into life together twenty-four/seven.

Blending their loved ones hadn't been quite as easy, but it had been entertaining. He trusted that they'd all be one big happy family someday but at the moment, the Gerards and the DiLeos kept surprising each other as they came together.

The biggest surprise so far had been when Anthony had

insisted on giving Harley away at the wedding. She'd burst into tears right in Mama DiLeo's kitchen and had felt comfortable enough not to run out the back door and hide.

Vinny DiLeo, the youngest DiLeo brother and the one the older brothers were currently financing through medical school, was studying in the same field as Mac's neurologist father.

They'd had a hit there.

Cajun Joe throwing them a sex toy shower at the club turned out to be a party to live in infamy. Harley had insisted the guest list be limited to a very select group. But his grandfather had let the cat out of the bag to Miss Q, who'd demanded invitations for all of their friends and acquaintances.

Mac would honestly never forget Cajun Joe standing behind the bar with his long hair and bandanna, Delilah by his side, describing the exclusive clientele his club catered to.

Aunt Camille had wanted a tour of the place.

Miss Q and the other Second Story Society ladies had already start matchmaking their next unsuspecting victim— Mrs. Noralee's granddaughter—so they booked a meeting room during the monthly munch, which Mac learned was an informal gathering where people of different fetishes came together to make new friends.

Lennon wanted to research a romance novel and asked Cajun Joe if she could come to the club to observe for a few nights.

Josh had told her only when he was dead and buried.

Harley had offered the name of someone who would do the deed for a reasonable price.

Aunt Frances had nearly fainted.

Overall, Mac considered the party a success.

Courtney, who'd been unhappy with her hairstylist, had booked an appointment with Mama DiLeo. A hit. Mac's father had taken one look at Anthony's classic Firebird and rediscovered a youthful hobby he'd abandoned for medical school. Another hit. Not only was Josh pleased to be training in Damon's dojo, but Ben and his young son had enrolled in father-son classes there, too. A *big* hit as far as Mac's grandfather was concerned.

"They'll spend more time together, Mackenzie, and that's what life is all about," he said as he moved through the line.

Miss Q agreed. "See, my dear, your family is a good influence." She kissed both their cheeks and wished them fun in their life together.

"You listen." His grandfather took Mac's hands and squeezed tight. "You enjoy every second you have with the woman you love. You promise me, Mackenzie, and you don't break that promise."

Mac searched his grandfather's misty eyes and knew they were both thinking about his grandmother.

"You have my word."

"Always knew you were a smart boy. You'll do fine. Especially with this one to keep you in line."

He hugged Harley before escorting Miss Q into the reception, and as they walked away, that one blew a kiss over her shoulder. "Ah, *l'amour.*"

Harley laughed, a light, happy sound that was reflected in her sparkling eyes and Mac decided to start following his grandfather's advice immediately. Glancing at the next couple, he said, "Please excuse us."

Stepping back from the line, he dragged Harley with him, wrapping his arms around her as they went. She melted against him without a word and he engaged her in a kiss that started his blood crashing south and made the nearby guests cheer.

His grandfather and Miss Q were right—life was all about living and, with the woman he loved beside him, Mac wouldn't waste a second.

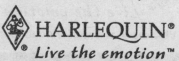

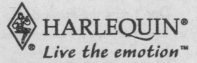

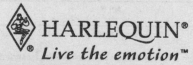

HARLEQUIN®
Temptation

THE WRONG BED

What happens when a girl finds herself in the *wrong* bed...with the *right* guy?

Find out in:

#866 NAUGHTY BY NATURE by Jule McBride
February 2002

#870 SOMETHING WILD by Toni Blake
March 2002

#874 CARRIED AWAY by Donna Kauffman
April 2002

#878 HER PERFECT STRANGER by Jill Shalvis
May 2002

#882 BARELY MISTAKEN by Jennifer LaBrecque
June 2002

#886 TWO TO TANGLE by Leslie Kelly
July 2002

Midnight mix-ups have never been so much fun!

HARLEQUIN®
Makes any time special ®

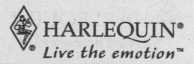

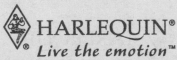